PRAISE FOR DR
AND RYAN CAR'

One of Crime Monthly's Top 5 Killer Thrillers of April 2022

'Powerful.'

Crime Monthly

'My book of the year so far.'

Lee Child, #1 *New York Times* bestselling author

'A heartfelt and eloquent exploration of the iniquities of racial bias.'

Guardian

'Dreda Say Mitchell has been flying the flag for crime writing for years.'

Bernardine Evaristo, bestselling author of *Girl, Woman, Other*

'A truly original voice.'

Peter James, #1 *Sunday Times* bestselling author

'A strong dose for readers interested in watching racial prejudices play out at every possible opportunity.'

Kirkus Reviews

Praise for Dreda Say Mitchell:

'As good as it gets.'

Lee Child

'A truly original voice.'

Peter James

'Thrilling.'

Sunday Express Books of the Year

'Awesome tale from a talented writer.'

Sun

'Fast-paced and full of twists and turns.'

Crime Scene Magazine

BELIEVE ME

Big Mo Suspense Series

Dirty Tricks
Fight Dirty
Wicked Women

ALSO BY DREDA SAY MITCHELL

Running Hot
Killer Tune

BELIEVE ME

DREDA SAY
MITCHELL
&
RYAN
CARTER

THOMAS & MERCER

Text copyright © 2023 by Dreda Say Mitchell and Ryan Carter

Published by Thomas & Mercer, Seattle

www.apub.com

Amazon, the Amazon logo, and Thomas & Mercer are trademarks of Amazon.com, Inc., or its affiliates.

ISBN-13: 9781542031356
eISBN: 9781542031349

Cover design by Andrew Davis
Cover image: ©Jose A. Bernat Bacete / Getty; ©Stephen Leonardi / 500px / Getty

Printed in the United States of America

BELIEVE ME

PROLOGUE

The child didn't know where they were going in the dark – he only knew it meant danger. Clasped tight in his mother's arms, he knew that because when she stopped for a few moments to catch her breath, he saw a sign that told him so. It nestled on the side of the sandy footpath, partly hidden by leaves. A rusty red sign lit up by the white beam of a lighthouse further down the coast. But before he could read what the danger was, his mother was off again, gasping, panting and mumbling to herself, looking over her shoulder from time to time, her eyes with a life of their own, scanning their surroundings for something that wasn't there.

The path led upwards, levelling out for a short distance before climbing again, more steeply this time, upwards towards the sky. Behind them was only darkness, and above them only the black night. Somewhere nearby was the sea. But it wasn't the sea he knew from his many visits to the beach where he'd played and paddled. The one where he'd hurried back to the sand if a gentle wave caught him by surprise. The one that had the sun shining on it. This sea was angry and violent, one more like a grown-up than a child.

He rocked backwards and forwards as his mother lost or missed her footing on the sand, stones and clods of earth that made up the path, before, finally, they tumbled into the undergrowth and were stung by nettles. His mother let go of him while she climbed to her feet and scooped him up.

'Are you all right? You're not hurt?' They were the first words she'd said to him since they'd left the house. There was no time to answer because she added, 'Don't worry, little one. We're going somewhere safe, very safe.'

When he told her about the red sign that said 'danger', she merely laughed and set off again, upwards and upwards towards the night sky, until they weren't climbing anymore and the path came to an end. A space opened up in front of them. With no trees, bushes, shrubs and undergrowth to protect them, the wind was up. A wind that seemed to be beckoning them forward. The sea was clearly in view, spread out in front. But not a blue, grey or green sea like the ones he knew so well from the daytime. This sea was black, the same colour as the night. It was hard to tell where the black night ended and the black sea began. Only a few speckled lights far in the distance showed where the horizon was.

His mother stopped for a few moments, looked anxiously around, listening for something. With a steady pace, they moved forward again before they slowed to a crawl and she took them over to the edge of a cliff. Below, the cliff fell away, far, far away, to a dark beach, which was being battered by the inky waves. He peered over with his mother.

He knew this was wrong. 'I'm cold. I want to go home. Take me home.'

She held him tighter, but she wasn't listening to him – it was something else she was listening for. Who or what was it? Her eyes darted up and down the coastline, and up and down the cliffs, over and above, looking for something. Who or what was it? She sighed and her grip seemed to loosen slightly before she stepped back from the cliff.

'I'm scared. I want to go home.'

2

She heard this time, stroked his hair and whispered something, but it was to herself, not to him. She shook her head and retraced her steps from the cliff edge back on to firmer ground. They were going home after all, away from the cliff, the dark sand, the inky waves and the empty space between them and all the darkness. Her steps seemed more secure now and whatever the hurry was on the path had come to an end. Now that they were going home, it was safe to shiver in the cold.

But a decision was made without the little boy being told. Without any warning his mother moved forward again, back towards the cliff. On the edge. With a piercing scream, and him nestled in her arms, she jumped.

CHAPTER 1

My first reaction when the police ring to tell me my father has been attacked and is lying seriously injured in hospital is to wonder why they've called me instead of my younger sister. In fact, I must have said that out loud because the police officer on the other end of the line sounds rather shocked by my attitude.

'Perhaps I didn't make myself clear,' she tells me. 'Your father has been the victim of a serious assault and is currently in a grave condition with doctors attending.'

My despairing sigh is silent this time, but I know better. This won't be a 'serious assault'. He won't be seriously injured either. He's a past master at playing the patient – he's done it to me often enough and now he'll be doing it to gullible doctors and nurses.

The policewoman begins to sound as if I'm becoming a suspect. 'Do you want to know which hospital he's in? So you can rush over there?'

The clock on my office wall says three o'clock. I've got a mass of things to get through, working as a lawyer dealing with the business and personal affairs of the sleek rich folks who live on this stretch of the coastline. Now I'll have to ask my boss if I can leave early. Again.

'OK, where is he?'

The name of the hospital makes me shudder. I know it too well for all sorts of bad reasons.

It's now only two minutes past three and even leaving at five makes the staff here look like slackers. If I decide to go over to see my father in the early evening; it won't make any difference. But the police officer has other ideas.

'If you could get over and see him as soon as possible? He's very poorly, and we understand he's a widower? I'm sure he'll need the support of his daughter at this distressing time.'

When the cop has rung off, I call my sister. It goes straight to answerphone. 'Salina, it's me. Look, Dad's in hospital and someone needs to go and see him. I can't go until this evening, so it'll have to be you. Call me when you get this message.'

I text her the same message, just to be on the safe side.

The clock winds on painfully slowly until it's half past three. There's no reply from my sister. She's got the messages of course but she's not answering. She doesn't want to go and see Dad any more than I do, probably even less.

And perhaps my father really is in trouble this time. Perhaps he's really badly injured. Perhaps he'll pass away, lonely and alone, while I hack away at my keyboard. Perhaps this evening I'll be taken to one side by a forlorn-looking doctor and told that, sadly, it's too late. My dad's an awful man and no kind of father, but nonetheless I still close down my computer, pick up my bag and jacket. This is emotional blackmail of course, and the fact that I'm doing it to myself doesn't make it any easier.

On my desk is a file with a new case that was added to my workload this morning, as if I haven't got enough to do already. It occurs to me to tuck the file under my arm to give the impression that although I'll be leaving early, it will be with a view to doing more work.

My boss looks up as I come into his office, looks at my jacket and bag, and his expression suggests he knows what's coming.

'Hi, Greg – look, my father's been taken very ill and I'm wondering if I could leave a little early to get to the hospital?' He doesn't answer immediately so I add, 'Obviously, we're very busy, but I'll make the time up.'

He looks at me with a stare that begs the questions – leaving early? Time off? He picks up some random papers from his desk and shows them to me. 'You're right, we are very busy.' He drops the papers through his fingers and turns back to his computer, shrugging his shoulders. 'But if you've got to go, you've got to go.' He notices I've got the case file under my arm but it doesn't help. 'Don't spend too long on that; it's an open-and-shut property dispute.'

He begins typing.

He should feel shame at such a callous response to an employee. But creeping out of the office, avoiding my colleagues' eyes, it's me that feels the shame both for myself and my father who's got himself attacked. Outside I find two of my co-workers smoking and going ga-ga over an Instagram beauty influencer's channel dishing out the latest make-up tips. My lips tighten as I stride past.

Fifteen minutes later, on the drive towards the hospital, my head's against the steering wheel and I'm hyperventilating in a daze. One minute I was driving and then the next trying to avoid a collision as I realise I'm about to hit another vehicle. Swerving like crazy, I managed to come to a violent stop. There's a terrible buzzing in my ears.

'What's the matter with you?' someone's shouting.

Swallowing, I raise my heavy head to see a burly, red-faced and very angry man leaning out of the driver's window of a van, which he's brought to a screeching halt in front of my car.

'Are you colour blind?' He stabs a finger towards the traffic lights a few yards down the road. 'You know what a green light means, don't you?'

There was absolutely no need to brake sharply as I approached the green light, which forced him to slam on his brakes. That meant in turn he had to veer around my car into oncoming traffic, narrowly avoiding a collision, before coming to a halt in front of me.

He mutters something else under his breath. I don't need to hear it to know it's unpleasant. Shaking his head in disgust he pulls away. He's in the right, of course. But what would he say if I told him that I couldn't avoid this? That this was always going to happen? It's my destiny? I'm doomed. That I'm going to be dead soon and there's nothing I can do about it. I can see the headlines in the local papers before my eyes. 'Lawyer, 39, killed in car crash.' Thirty-nine. Three months before I turn forty. And that's when the death bell will start ringing. Today is yet another re-run of the many accidents I've had on the road to my next birthday. Plane journeys. 'Local lawyer, 39, dies in air-crash disaster.' I rarely go swimming at the beach in the evening anymore – something that was once such a joy. 'Tragic lawyer, 39, swept away by tide.'

Behind me there's a long blow of a horn, followed by flashing headlights. I'm blocking the road.

If it was just driving, I could probably cope.

I set off again but after a hundred yards of shunting down the road at various unsuitable speeds and with my shaky steering, it's clear that enough is enough. I turn into a side road and park up, for good this time. I rest my head back and breathe. Breathe. The rhythm of my heart slowly returns to normal.

Friends have told me that there are actually people available to help when you become a danger behind the wheel. Apparently, it's not unusual to lose confidence as a driver, particularly after a minor accident or a close-run thing on the road. I even took a number for one of them. But it won't help. My fear of driving has got nothing to do with minor accidents or close-run things.

I know exactly what it is.

My mother died before she made it to middle age. It was never made clear to me exactly what it was that she died of. My sister Salina and brother Karl never knew either. The truth is I don't really want to know what it was. If I heard from a relative that it was a genetic thing and women in my family are famous for passing on young, I don't know how I'd manage. Perhaps that's why I've never married, why my relationship with Keith finished last year after three years together. With every prospective relationship, the thought's always there: will this man be able to look after my children if I die young?

There are people who can help with the syndrome where you lose confidence in your own ability to stay alive. But those people can't bring my mother back, or stop me dying in a car crash or being murdered.

I know I'm going to die young just like Mummy.

CHAPTER 2

I've been made a fool of. I know that as soon as I enter my father's hospital ward. The eyes of the nurse in charge of the ward twinkle with delight. 'You're here to see Mr Saul Lewis? You're his daughter?'

'Yes,' I answer, although a huge part of me wants to deny it.

She leads the way to his bed, smiling and chatting all the way. 'He's quite a character, your father. He's already proving to be a bit of a hit with the staff and the other patients!'

I manage to hide my disgust from her. I say, 'The police seemed to think he was quite badly injured.'

She looks grim. 'It's true, he was roughed up quite badly, a badly bruised arm and some other trauma.' Her face lifts into a reassuring smile. 'I suspect he'll be fine in a week or two.' She casts a speculative look my way. 'He'll need some looking after and TLC when he gets back home, that's all. We'll need to ensure that as part of his release package.'

I don't reply. I don't think this woman would like what I have to say. I'm left standing at the foot of his bed. He looks shrunken since the last time I saw him, which was a couple of Christmases back. The festive season is the only time I spend with him, and it's been like that since I left when I was eighteen. Saul Lewis was always such a powerful man: an inch shy of six foot, broad of shoulder with a measured slick movement of the body that drew the eye.

Now he looks like what's just happened to him, a man beaten down by the world. My father's eyes are closed with a bandage wrapped around his head, scuffs and marks on his face, his arm in a sling.

He senses my presence because a slightly puffy eye opens and he fixes me with it. 'Took you long enough.'

I catch sight of his old watch on the bedside unit. I ignore it and sit in the chair near the bed. 'Car trouble.'

His top lip hitches up and to the outsider looking at it they will take it for a smile, but I know it for what it is: a scornful sneer. 'It's always car problems with you. That's why you didn't show your face last Christmas. Why don't you get a new one?'

'I'm supposed to be buying a house.'

Saying that is a mistake, because it prompts him to say, 'You don't need a house. You've already got one. You can come back and live with me. We can look after each other.' He adds, 'I knew you would come, that's why I left you a bottle of homemade ginger beer in the fridge.'

Dad's ginger beer was a childhood favourite of mine. Intense, sweet, with a hint of vanilla. If he thinks he's now going to sway me with memories of childhood treats he's sadly mistaken. Besides, now's not the time to have the discussion about whether I'll even be staying in my home town for long. I've only been back twelve months and it's already clear that was probably a mistake.

'What happened?'

His voice is firmer now. 'Is that all you've got to say? Your own father comes close to being killed and you don't even ask me how I am?'

Another nurse appears, carrying a large box of chocolates which she places by my father's bed. 'Here you are, Saul! Your new friend two beds down thought you might like these to cheer you up. He's got plenty from his visitors.'

Dad looks at my empty hands, shakes his head slightly, before turning back to the nurse with a mischievous smile. 'Thank you, darlin'.' He shouts out across the beds in a clear voice, 'Thank you for the chocolates, Charles!'

'No problem, Saul!'

This is my father. He's only been in this hospital for a few hours and he's making friends with the other patients, flirting with the nurses and guilt-tripping his daughter. It's business as usual for him.

He finally answers my question. 'A gang of youths crowded me up on the high street and asked for a cigarette. When I told them I didn't have one, they jumped and kicked me down to the ground, rifling through my pockets. Read your Bible, girl – it's the end times when youth doesn't respect age. But some brave people came out of the shops and those boys ran away, shouting profane language as they went.'

This doesn't sound quite right. I'll say this for my father, he doesn't back out of fights. It's just as likely he threw the first punch at the youths when he was cheeked.

My father continues, 'Yes, a very nice young officer of the law was here to take a statement earlier.' Naturally, he can't resist adding, 'Much earlier.' He screws up his face. 'He's in the office at the end of the ward, writing up his notes. But they're not going to do anything, are they?' He closes his eyes again and whispers, 'All right, you've done your duty paying a visit, I can see you're in a hurry to go. I left the house unlocked when I went for my walk so you'd better go over and make sure it's all secure. While you're there you can clear out your old room for when you move in.'

I'm too shocked to fix my voice. 'Move in?'

He opens his eyes again in fury, shakes his damaged arm and snaps, 'Yes, move in. I'll need looking after when I get out of here.'

'That's out of the question. I'm under a lot of pressure at the moment. I've got too many commitments.'

He fixes his steely brown eyes on me and snarls, 'Commitments? Perhaps you can tell me what's more of a commitment than looking after your own father? Your own flesh and blood? You've always been a selfish, spoiled child – it's because the rod was spared. You're looking after me from now on! You'll do as you're told! That's final!'

He's right about one thing at least. I am in a hurry to get away. 'I'm going to check the house.'

His expression turns sour because we both know I've made no commitment to looking after him. At the end of the ward is a man who's suited and booted with a homely face, slightly on the pale side with neatly cut dark hair that's cropped close at the sides and spiky on top. He's at least a good five years or so younger than me. Thirty-five – five more years before he reaches the dreaded forty. He appears to have come out of the nurse's office.

'Ms Lewis? Saul's daughter?'

'That's right.'

'I'm Detective Craven. I'm leading the investigation into the assault on your father. You can put your mind at rest, we won't stop until we catch the man who did it.'

Frowning I say, 'You mean men.'

'I'm sorry?' He's puzzled.

'It was a gang of guys – men – who attacked Dad.'

Craven pulls out a notebook and checks his notes. 'No, it was one man. Obviously, your father is in shock and has concussion, so he's a little hazy on the details. Fortunately, security camera footage shows that it was a single perpetrator, but the footage is hazy to say the least. The two witnesses who were outside the betting shop and went to help your father corroborate that it was a lone attacker.'

He puts his notebook away and catches my eyes. Up close his face and grey eyes look anything but homely. This is a cop who likes to get the job done. 'It's a good job they chased the perp off or it might have been much worse. One witness reported that they were sure the attacker was white and very smartly dressed. Does that ring any bells about someone you or your father might know?'

'That sounds like every man in the office I work in.'

'Yes, I know, it's a very wide description. I'm still conducting door-to-door enquiries.' He gives me his card. 'If you think of anything, don't hesitate to call me. I'll be in touch.'

Alone again, I look down the ward to where my father is being fussed over by a lady with a trolley serving tea and biscuits.

He's lying again. He always lies.

CHAPTER 3

Outside my father's house, I hesitate before getting out of the car. This is the house I grew up in. The house Mummy started her death journey in. I make myself get out and stand in front of the door. I inhale deeply, because when the wind is in the right direction the smell of the nearby sea is strong. But you can't see it. My parents were housed in this Victorian cottage property when they moved to Tinfields from London. It was an odd decision on the face of it. We were the only black family for miles around. But my dad wanted to live near the sea because it reminded him of back home, which was the phrase he always used to describe the country of his birth, Trinidad. He worked on the railways, so when a job came up on the Devon coast, he took it.

Tinfields was once a fishing village; it was developed in Victorian times by an eccentric millionaire who was convinced that the local hills still had enough seams of tin left in them to make mining it viable. He built cottages for his workers and reopened the mines. Unfortunately, our millionaire soon discovered that tin mining had come to a halt centuries earlier because there was no tin left to mine. His business collapsed but the cottages survived. We grew up in one of them. When I was a child, these cottages were quaint but grindingly poor; there was unemployment and drugs.

The police decided it was the demand for drugs money that led to the one memorable, if tragic, event on our street in those days.

'Gabby?'

I turn at the sound of the excited voice. It's Jenny, Dad's next-door neighbour. She looks older but still has that bubbly and cheery quality about her. She has been a fixture in my life since I was a child, one of Mummy's closest friends, always with a sympathetic ear to lend and a cuppa to fill at her kitchen table when Mummy needed to talk about anything.

'What's brought you here then?' she asks, her eyes twinkling. 'It's not Christmas.'

Is that a faint whiff of telling me off I hear in her voice, showing she didn't approve of me not coming to visit Dad last Christmas?

'Dad's been attacked.'

She gasps, her fingers fluttering over her heart.

'He's all right, but it was nasty.'

I see the fear and strain on her face and could kick myself for not being more sensitive about how I gave her this news. Shortly before my mother's death, Jenny had an unimaginable tragedy. Since it happened she has never been the same.

'I'm sorry—'

'Nothing to be sorry about, sweetie,' she cuts over, trying to rustle her welcoming smile back. 'When you get a moment pop in. I've made some scones and homemade jam with clotted cream.'

No one makes scones like Jenny. They are one of those comforting memories I associate with my childhood – hot and delicious, floating with cinnamon and spices. As tempted as I am, the truth is I won't be here long.

I don't burst her bubble and tell her, instead I say, 'You know I wouldn't miss one of your cream teas for the world.'

When she's gone I let myself into the house. There's several days' worth of post gathered on the hall floor, many of them red letters. There are more red letters parked, unopened, on the mantelpiece in the front room. That's along with a row of half-drunk cups of tea and coffee. On the floor by his sagging armchair, several plates are piled up on top of each other. There are more of those in the kitchen sink. Scattered around are empty bottles of beer and old newspapers. They're opened at the sports pages – the football and horse racing.

Instinctively, I roll up my sleeves and begin tidying up without thinking about what I'm doing. My mother's shadow follows me around, and occasional glimpses of her in the mirror catch my eye. Before she died, it was her job to do this. She was one of those women who used a bucket and brush to clean the front doorstep. After she died it was my turn. I escaped from this workhouse when I was eighteen.

I come across Dad's homemade ginger beer in the fridge. He lied: there's two tall bottles not one. I wish I could resist but can't, and before I know it I've downed a small glassful.

The family portrait remains on the sideboard in the dining room. I almost recoil from looking at it with its protective glass long gone and never replaced. It was taken the year Mummy died. She looks tired and worn, her brown skin stretched and grey. There is fear in her face, as if she can already feel death brushing her cheek. Her arm is limply looped through my father's, who stands tall, erect and serious. In front of them, we three children stand. I'm fifteen in this photo. If you know what you're looking for, you can see the grim determination on my features. Next to me is Salina, my sister aged thirteen, already the girl most likely to be the one who stands out from the crowd. Finally, my brother Karl, eleven, forlorn, standing slightly apart from the rest of us.

My heart skips when a fleeting shadow passes the front window. I wait for someone to appear. No one does. Did I really see a shadow? Or is my exhausted mind playing tricks on me? Ever since the tragic incident on the street, despite it being all those years ago, I've always felt a dread hanging over me when I'm in this house on my own. Of course, it's not the only reason I dread these four walls.

Suddenly there's a scuffling on the step. I clench up. The lock on the front door rattles. A key turns, the front door opens. Footsteps, slow and even as if they have all the time in the world. The person walks into the room. Looks at the duster clutched in my hand like a weapon.

'Tidying up after him already, are you?' my sister Salina mocks.

'What happened to Dad?' My sister is spread out on the sofa in such a staged angle it turns the lumpy piece of furniture into a work of art.

Beautiful, stunning, out of this world are a few of the words I've heard used to describe my sister over the years. Every last one of them is correct; nevertheless there's one word that sums her up – exquisite. The gloss of her hair, the glow of her skin, the glitter of her eyes; Salina is a human jewel. I'm large compared to her dainty size. No matter where she is or what she's doing, she always wears make-up. Sometimes I wonder if she actually goes to bed decked out in designer eleganza and high heels.

'He was attacked. His version is it was a group of youths; the cop in charge's account is it was a young white man.'

Salina wrinkles her nose. 'If there's a dispute between their word and our father's, I know whose version I'm going with.'

'He's got a badly bruised arm and some bumps and scrapes. He'll be out in a few days,' I tell her.

'Thought so. I knew it'd be a false alarm.'

That's the small talk over. Now it's time for the argument, the same one that's gone on for most of our lives in one form or another. 'Why didn't you pick your phone up when the police called? Why didn't you get back to them when they left a message? Why leave it to me? You know how busy I am at the moment.'

Salina waves her hand with the air of a queen. 'I had my phone switched off at the time. I was working – I work too you know.'

Salina is married to a wealthy businessman by the name of Luke and lives in a 1920s' modernist mansion overlooking the Devon gold coast. At least he says he's a businessman. I've got my own views on what he does for a living, which is why I avoid him and don't go to their house much.

She pulls out her phone and shares an image of her work. 'I've got over a hundred thousand followers on Instagram. Big cosmetic firms are sniffing round trying to buy up the rights to the make-up I've created.' Salina is the make-up influencer my colleagues were gushing over outside the office when I left.

'One of my followers called me the Michelangelo of make-up.' She preens. 'That requires creativity, initiative and hard work. I was on a shoot for my site when you called. Professional photographers cost proper money, so my phone was off. As soon as I picked up the message, I called the hospital and discovered you'd already visited, so I came to the house instead.' Her voice slips to a sly sneer. 'I'm glad he's living like a trapped rat.'

I realise it's not a sneer in her tone but pain. We don't have the type of sister-to-sister relationship where we lay bare our wounds and talk about our pain.

My sister gets to her feet. 'Gotta run. We're entertaining guests for dinner tonight.'

'Going? You've only just got here.'

She shrugs. 'Just checking in to see the old man's not six feet under.'

Tentatively, I ask, 'Aren't you going to see him?'

'Tomorrow. Maybe.' Salina becomes vague. 'Maybe the next day, we'll have to see.' She picks up her bag and makes to leave, before stopping. 'Do you want a bit of advice, sis?'

I don't want it. I resent the way my sister reverses our roles in life. I'm the older sister, not her. I'm the successful lawyer, not her. She's the trophy wife, not me. And anyway, there's no prizes for guessing what the advice is going to be.

'You need to put your foot down, because he'll have you living here and running around after him in no time. You can start by putting a cease and desist label on the whole Mrs Mop routine.' She gestures at the duster I hold. She gives the room one final look of contempt and then is gone.

My sister blames our father for our mother's death and she's never forgiven him for it. She's never said that out loud, but I know it.

I know it because I've never forgiven him either.

CHAPTER 4

I leave Dad's and go back to my rented room in Tinfields with two things from his house: both bottles of his homemade ginger beer and Mummy's make-up bag. The old zip-up canvas bag with a slight scent of mildew brings back so many memories. It hurt me to discover it in the loft among the dumped, unwanted things of my family's life – school reports, old clothes, broken suitcase and the rest. I tip the contents out next to me on the bed. Powder compact, nail varnish, small bottle of scent and some lipstick.

The lipstick is difficult to open as it's both congealed and crumbling inside. I brush it along the back of my hand. Mahogany red with an undertone of cherry, it lies daring against my brown skin. I think Salina gave it to Mum because even back then my sister was in love with make-up. The lipstick would transform Mummy, changing her from ordinary stay-at-home mum to something more glamorous. What do you really know about your parents? From the time you can walk, they're just adults who manage your life and order you around. But who were they before that? My mum never liked to answer those kinds of questions. I push the cosmetics and my thoughts of my mum aside and reach for the other things on my bed: the file containing the paperwork about unravelling this cold case property dispute the boss gave me.

◆ ◆ ◆

There's an impressive sea view from my rented room. Unfortunately, I'm going to have to move out soon because the landlady is selling up. This run-down guest house where my landlady once scratched a living hiring rooms to holidaymakers in the hope that she'd make enough money to see her through the empty winter months is now where the real money in Tinfields lies these days. It's not the bucket and spade brigade anymore. This is the Devon gold coast where even pokey flats and tumbledown cottages sell for silly prices to those 'down from London' seeking second homes. In a few months, this building will be gutted and converted into luxury flats with commanding views over the esplanade and on to the sea.

My third-floor room itself is disintegrating. Peeling wallpaper hangs off the powdery wall, insecure stucco features on the ceiling spread white dust over everything and the window takes some proper tugging to close properly. There's very little space left with my single bed by the door pushed up against a wardrobe that looks like it was designed for a growing child rather than an adult. That in turn is pushed up against my 'desk' which is little more than a panel of wood on some insecure legs. But I've grown to like this room. I like the fact it involves no commitment on my part and I can view the sea, day or night.

I'm not sure where I'm going to move to when I leave here. '*He'll have you living here and running around after him in no time.*' My sister's warning comes back to me about ending up living with Dad again. Live back in my childhood home? That will never happen. Never.

I get straight down to business with a view to getting this property dispute done and dusted tonight with a summary on Greg's desk tomorrow morning. As I read, I realise what a tragic case it is. There's no photo of the property, which doesn't surprise me. On and off this house has been disputed for many years so a few things getting lost from the file along the way, like a photo, is common. However, from the address, I suspect that the house is on the outskirts of Tinfields. And it has a name. Ocean Haven. I process the information I read.

Ocean Haven started life in the nineteenth century, owned by a man who was a senior manager at the local tin mine.

Twenty-six years ago the ownership of the house was undisputed. It was owned by a widow called Mrs Carol Shore. Her deceased husband's family had owned the house for at least a century.

Twenty-five years ago, Mrs Shore signed the ownership of the property over to a trust. No reason is given why she did this.

The chair of the board of trustees was Mrs Lewis.

Mr Robert Delbrook is . . . I can't quite figure out what his significance is here. I check over the paperwork, which is no easy thing as the deeds of the trust run to just over one hundred pages.

Within months of the trust being created, both Mrs Lewis and Mrs Shore were dead.

Robert Delbrook disappeared. Seven years later he was declared dead.

Ocean Haven passed to the Crown.

The Crown passed it on to the local authority, who used it over the years for various purposes, including temporary housing for the homeless and the like. It is currently empty.

I come up for some much-needed air and a slug of Dad's ginger beer. This is one unlucky house. Death and disappearances.

I head back into the paperwork.

Over the last twenty-five years, through various court cases, Mrs Shore's family have contested the ownership of the house and have been trying to get it back. The family must be quite wealthy because they've hired lawyers, psychiatrists, private detectives and retired police officers to prove that Mrs Shore was not of sound mind when she agreed to the trust.

Now the family are making one last desperate attempt to get the house back because the council have put Ocean Haven up for sale.

To make matters more complicated, an anonymous letter claims there's proof Robert Delbrook is alive, so the council have no right to sell the house. The truth is, unless Delbrook puts in an appearance, the council can do what they want.

My summary will be brutally frank. The Shore family don't have a leg to stand on. I close the file, place it in my bag, and as I do so, something falls out of my bag. It's Mummy's original passport. I was wrong earlier; I took three things from Dad's house. I found her passport in the loft too. Her thin face is barely recognisable in the photo. She's so young. I glance at her maiden name: Marcia Siparia Mackenzie.

Siparia was her middle name. She was always so proud of that name because it is one of the religious festivals in her home-land of Trinidad. I've never met anyone with that name before. I frown. Siparia. The name starts nagging me. I've seen it somewhere recently. But where? Where?

My face falls as I scramble in my bag for the Ocean Haven property dispute case. My fingers flick through the pages. Stop at the page about the board members of the trust. The chair of the board.

Mrs Lewis.

But I didn't read it correctly before. It doesn't just say Mrs Lewis.

It says: Marcia Siparia Lewis.

My mother.

CHAPTER 5

TWENTY-FIVE YEARS AGO

MARCIA

Not again! Please, please not again! Marcia Lewis screamed inside her head. The pain was back, hitting her with a vengeance. It felt like her gut was being twisted and knotted by flames. For once she was thankful for her daughters squabbling loudly as they all sat at the dinner table. As usual Marcia had laid on a mouth-watering feast for the family. Rice and peas with stewed chicken, fried plantain and a choice selection of greens. Unlike other children, her kids never turned their noses up at her greens because she knew exactly how to steam them just right to bring out the sweetness.

With hurried desperation, she choked back a groan of distress. Below the table her fingers curled into her palms, the nails clawing into her flesh as she fought for control. The last thing she wanted was for her beloved daughters, Gabby and Salina, to know that the illness Marcia had struggled with for the last three months was back. She'd been to her family doctor four times – *four times!* – and he was adamant he couldn't find a thing wrong with her. Marcia wanted him to refer her to the hospital but she was too respectful to ask. Her doctor should know what he was talking about. So she did what so many of her friends did, dealt with their aches and pains as best as they could.

As a distraction from the pain, Marcia latched on to her daughters arguing. *My girls are going to be the death of me. That's if this sickness doesn't get me first.*

Gabby pointedly accused, '*Someone* went into my special drawer. It was you, wasn't it?'

Salina came back, that smart mouth of hers trying to put her older sister in her place, 'What *special* drawer? I didn't even know you had one.'

'You took my lipstick. God knows what you did with it, and then you put it back with some of the top hacked off.'

Saul, their dad, wasn't a fan of his girls having make-up but Marcia thought that Gabby, at fifteen, was old enough to have a stick or two. Her eldest was growing up fierce and fast. And Salina was obsessed with cosmetics.

Salina hissed, dissing her sister with her eyes. 'Like I'd want anything to do with your lippy. I mean, Flamenco Red doesn't even go with your brown skin tone.'

'Flamenco Red?' Gabby contemptuously kissed her teeth and went in for the kill. 'I never told you what colour it is. The only way you could've known was if you touched it.'

Her sister's face fell, realising that her words had tripped her up, creating her own trap for Gabby to yank her into. She should have known better. Gabby was a listener, a watcher, searching for any crack that helped her drag her opponent down.

Salina recovered, her expression that of the heroic wronged. 'Are you calling me a liar?'

Her girls were so different. Salina was outgoing and a talker, while Gabrielle always had her head stuck in a book and didn't seem to have much time for others. Marcia loved them both with a passion that only a mother knows.

'Mummy?' Salina ran a troubled gaze over her mother. 'Are you feeling OK?'

Of all her children it was always Salina who guessed when she was in pain and took care of her when it was really bad.

Before Marcia could answer, Saul entered the room. The atmosphere instantly changed. The girls and Marcia tensed. Her husband was a strapping man, filling the doorway with his muscle and presence. He cast his gaze around without uttering a word and then took his place at the head of the table, in front of the family portrait that rested in pride of place on the sideboard.

His gaze, sharp and lethal, settled on his daughters. 'How many times have I told you that there is to be no street talk and arguments at this table. Carry on . . .' He didn't need to say the rest.

Don't take out the watch. Not the watch. Not that, not today, Marcia silently begged. Quickly Salina and Gabby looked down at their plates. Despite the pain, Marcia dashed into the kitchen, dished her husband a plate of food and returned to the table; unlike the children's, his meat and gravy was always put into a separate bowl. A tapping in the kitchen grabbed her attention. Avoiding Saul's sour gaze, she got up again from the table and went to the kitchen. At the back door was Jenny and Fred, their neighbours, accompanied by Marcia's son Karl. Aged eleven, Karl was the baby of the family. Jenny and Fred had welcomed the Lewis family wholeheartedly to the community, as had so many. In the end, Marcia had preferred living here to London because it reminded her of the smaller rural life that she'd had growing up in the Caribbean.

Fred's hands rested affectionately on Karl's shoulders. 'He's worked hard today, making a new wooden car. Next time we'll paint it.'

Fred had taken Karl under his wing and Marcia would be forever grateful. She worried about her boy who seemed too often to be wrapped up in his own little world, sometimes quietly retreating to his room and it would be minutes before any of them figured out he was gone. Then again, maybe that was just boys for you. No, Marcia dismissed that – she couldn't shake it off, something about her son was off. Normal little boys didn't use a penknife to carve their names into things around the house.

Karl moved out of Fred's arms and shyly grinned at him. In a conspiratorial whisper, Fred reminded him, 'Don't forget not to breathe a word about our secret.'

Karl nodded and headed upstairs to wash his hands before joining the others at the dining table.

'I can never thank you enough,' Marcia told Fred. 'He's a different boy when he's with you.' She threw her arms around him and kissed him on his cheek with gratitude.

Jenny caught Marcia's eye and Fred knew that was his cue to give the women some time alone.

Jenny got straight into it. 'Did you ask that doctor to refer you to the hospital?'

Marcia was embarrassed. 'I don't want to cause any bother.'

'Bother?' Jenny's voice rose a touch. 'That's what his job is. You make sure you get yourself down that surgery tomorrow and demand he does it.' Gently she touched Marcia's arm. 'It's not natural to be in pain.'

Marcia knew her neighbour was right. She needed to get tested up at the hospital because the pain was so bad sometimes it felt like it was cutting her into small pieces. Just as Marcia closed the kitchen door behind her neighbour, she heard the commotion coming from the dining room. Saul's loud-pitched voice. Oh no! Heart banging against her ribs, she rushed into the dining room and stumbled to a halt at what she saw.

Saul had laid his watch next to him on the table. It was an old-style brass pocket watch that had long ago lost its chain. The girls looked terrified. Thank God Karl was still upstairs, although she had not been able to shield him from similar scenes in the past.

Saul's laser stare was fixed on his daughters. 'I told you to stop with your quarrelling at the table.' He picked up his watch and waited for the hand to reach the start of a new minute. The tick-tock of the watch wasn't audible but it was as if they could all hear it in the room.

Tick. Tick. Tick. Twelve.

Saul ordered his children, 'You have one minute to eat all the food on your plate. One minute.'

Marcia watched with heartbroken dismay as Salina and Gabby began to shovel as much food as possible into their mouths. Marcia's fingers dug into the door frame. She couldn't do a thing because her grandmother had taught her to always obey her husband. The food stuck around the girls' faces as they crammed more and more into their mouths.

Ten seconds.

Shovel, swallow.

Three seconds.

Shovel, swallow.

'Time,' Saul announced. He stood up and as the girls trembled he inspected their plates. They had managed to eat their food. But they knew this was far from over. 'Get more food from the kitchen,' he instructed.

'Saul,' Marcia tried to intervene but his poisonous glare stopped her.

The girls were back seconds later with filled plates. Their dad picked up the watch, waited for the new minute, then, 'Three minutes.'

They gobbled up their food until Gabby couldn't take it any-more and ran gagging out of the room to be sick upstairs, while tears ran down Salina's face. Inside Marcia was breaking apart.

Saul thundered, 'What I say goes in this house.'

He twisted to the sideboard, picked up the family portrait and violently punched a hole right through it, shattering the glass.

CHAPTER 6

'Did you know Mummy had another house?' I let out urgently as soon as my sister opens her front door.

I'm still in a daze about what I found. Initially I thought I must be wrong, that there are a million other Marcia Siparia Lewises out there, but there aren't. Only one. My mother. What unsettles me the most is that people connected to that house died. Was that why my mother died an early death?

My sister stares at me with open disapproval. 'You could have put on something a bit more snazzy.' She leans over and whispers, 'We've got guests. I told you I'm hosting a dinner party tonight.'

Of course she did.

Salina lives in the posh end of Tinfields on an incline overlooking the coast. I hear the waves breaking on the beach below.

I ignore her sniping about my clothes. 'I tried calling you and once again you weren't picking up.' Sarcastically, I add, 'On another photoshoot, were you?' I know I shouldn't snipe back but sometimes my sister brings out the worst in me.

Her bold maroon nails cling to the door. Salina doesn't want to let me in. 'Can't this wait until tomorrow?'

Luke, her husband, appears over her shoulder. 'Gabby.' He draws my name out like I've won a prize. 'Come on in.'

His arm snakes around my waist, drawing me in. His red hair is slicked back at the sides and fuller and more playful on top. An open-necked purple silk shirt and gold chain offset the green of his eyes. A pair of herringbone trousers and, to complete the look, some kind of moccasin footwear. He's very good-looking, no doubt about that. It's a pity I don't trust him. When he wants something he goes after it and there is nothing he won't do to get it. Ruthless with a smile.

'Take no notice of my darling wife,' he whispers, guiding me towards the dining room. 'You look great. You're setting a new fashion trend. Spider chic.' He pauses. 'What is it about me that you don't like?'

I'm not expecting that. 'What makes you think I don't like you?'

'Oh, I don't know. Maybe it's the way you look at me like I'm a reptile.'

Ouch! I hadn't realised I'd been wearing my dislike like a facemask.

'It's just a shame we can't get along, what with me being married to your sister. Why don't we go out together sometime, just me and you, and do some stuff? Let you get to know me? You might find I'm quite likeable after all.'

Before I can awkwardly dig myself out of this hole, we're in the dining room, which is painted white with bifold doors that open out to a stunning view of the sandy beach and sea. The lighthouse looks tall and strong, its pinprick of light shooting over the water. It is so picturesque, the scent of the salty air intense here. I missed the sea so much when I left Tinfields.

It isn't a huge crowd for dinner, about six other guests who sit around a long glass table. There are caterers serving, silent in their black uniforms. Typical of Salina, any opportunity to wave her and Luke's money in others' faces. Maybe I'm being unfair. Why shouldn't she be proud to wave the flag for girls like her who'd never even heard the phrase 'silver spoon', much less had one in their mouth when they were growing up.

Luke introduces me. 'Everyone, this is Gabrielle, Salina's big sister.'

They're all members of the wealthy gold coast elite.

'I never knew you had a sister,' says Alan, who according to Luke manages property for the local authority.

'You work with the council on their property portfolio?' I quickly ask him. 'Do you know anything about a property called Ocean Haven?'

He replies eagerly, 'Ocean—'

Luke cuts in. 'Give Alan here a break, Gabby. The last thing he wants to do tonight is talk shop.'

I catch Salina's eye as she sits down at one end of the table. Beneath that overstretched smile of hers I can see she doesn't want me here. That makes two of us. I don't want to be here either. However, I need to talk to her about Mummy. In private.

Salina addresses the group. 'Gabby's a lawyer. I keep telling her she should set up her own firm instead of being someone else's dogsbody.'

'Sadly, that can't be the lot of someone living in rented accommodation.' My sister appears alarmed, which is exactly what I want. If I keep up this show of bringing the stench of poverty into her home she'll whip me out of the room quicker than you can say eyebrow pencil.

I continue, 'I'm going to be on the street soon. Nowhere to go.'

Luke offers, 'I'm your man if you're looking for a place to put your head down.'

Alan, the property manager, shakes his head. 'It's a scandal what's happened to some parts of the town. Property is so expensive that locals and their children can't afford to buy anything; priced out of the market.'

Bless Alan! He has no idea he's helping me in my quest to get Salina alone. 'I'm probably going to have to live in a hostel. One of those ones near the seafront. I don't think they're very safe. I might end up with the community of homeless on the beach who live under the jetty—'

Salina is on her feet. 'Gabby, remember earlier when I said something slipped my mind, I recall what it is. Let me show you.' She gives everyone one of her gorgeous smiles. 'We won't be long.'

Her mouth is tight and ugly and not speaking as she takes me to a large lounge with expensive paintings on the wall. She rounds on me. 'I don't appreciate you behaving like that in front of our friends.' Her lip quivers. 'Why do you have to put me down?'

I grapple for a response, seeing how upset she is. I'd never want to really upset my sister. We've butted heads since we were kids – that's what sisters do, isn't it? – but I would never knowingly want to make her feel uncomfortable. I do resent her and have never explained why.

Salina carries on. 'I know I'm not like you, bookish and bright—'

'Stop.' My palm comes up. 'To create the make-up empire you have, of course you have to be bright. And a great businesswoman.' I see my opportunity. 'Did you know about Mum's other house?'

Salina sighs. 'What other house?'

'Didn't you listen to any of my voice messages?' Of course she didn't. 'It appears that Mum owned or was on the trust of a house in Tinfields. I haven't seen it but I think it's one of the large ones at the end of town.'

Salina looks puzzled. 'A large house? You must've got mixed up. Mum never had any spare money.' Her voice lowers. 'Did you know she never even had a bank account?'

I'm astonished. I didn't know that. Then again, back then was a world where some men were still very much in charge of the household finances, so there was no reason for their wife to have a bank account.

My sister resumes, 'If she didn't have a bank account how could she have bought a house?'

'I'm not sure she bought it. She was definitely the chair of the board of trustees.'

Salina shrugs. 'So what?'

'So what?' I answer incredulously. 'I'm sorting out a dispute on a legal case where a family are insisting that the woman who once owned the house was swindled out of it. Our mother is in the middle of all of that and all you can say is, "So what?" The owner died. Someone else connected to it disappeared.'

Salina feigns concern. 'That's right, it's all coming back to me now. Mum was well-known as "Don Marcia" in the Devon under-world, specialising in grand larceny and property fraud.'

There's no point losing my temper with Salina, she'll simply smile it away. Instead, I quietly counter, 'This is our mother. Don't you care?'

'Our mum's dead, Gabby. She died in a lot of pain. Why she died we still don't know. Pass this property dispute on to one of your colleagues and let our mother rest in peace.'

Her words leave me feeling winded and exhausted. I hate thinking of the last time we saw our mother alive.

Salina guides me to the front door and outside. When she switches on the art-deco porch light her features change as she notices something. 'What on earth is that you've got on your lips?'

'I found Mummy's old make-up case. It's Mum's lipstick. Didn't you give it to her?'

She draws closer. 'It makes you look the spitting image of Mum.'

CHAPTER 7

There's a Sunset Boulevard vibe about Ocean Haven. It's half past two in the morning and I'm wetting my lips with a small glass of Dad's ginger beer as I look at the house online. You can imagine that it was once something of a film star but is now very much a has-been that no one calls. Most strikingly of all, the house looks freezing cold, although the photos were taken on a warm summer's day. The whole place has been let go. It was clearly once quite a stately property, not quite a manor house, but not far off. Nature has had a free run of the grounds around the house.

I find all of this on the website of the estate agents who are acting on behalf of the council. There's the usual artful language that's used to sell property. Apparently, Ocean Haven could do with some 'tender loving care' from a new owner. But the need for the TLC is not reflected in the price, which still looks astronomical to me. The details reassure any potential buyer that any past legal issues have been resolved. That's not quite true of course, the legal work is still in my bag.

I know that it's a strange time to be looking online, but the truth is I couldn't sleep after leaving Salina's. Her advice was to leave well alone, which I'm not following. Mind you, I don't sleep very well and talking about how Mummy died has only worsened my insomnia. I wish we hadn't talked about Mummy's death, because it haunts me. Has always haunted me. Most nights it's the reason I can't sleep. The anxiety of it wakes me up, leaving me struggling to breathe, covered in sweat.

I haven't seen a doctor and I won't for many reasons. I'm a classic DIY medical forum junkie looking for cures from fellow sufferers. But they don't help, because the real cause of my symptoms is the fear that death has slid into bed with me and entwined its icy arms around my body.

So I use the time in these early hours to try to find any online info on the people connected to Ocean Haven. Mrs Carol Shore, Robert Delbrook and the house itself. I make a note of the details and the estate agent.

Carol Shore seems to have come and gone without a trace. It's true that twenty-five years ago, people's lives weren't plastered online as they are today. But even so, she's not there. I can't find much in the local papers that might be connected either, although they too were less internet-friendly then. Apart, that is, from one curious incident. Cliffs rise high along the coast road from Ocean Haven and there are a number of stories about campaigners who were demanding guard rails along the path that runs along these heights. Several of the stories mention the loss of a woman who fell from a particular spot called Cliff Heights on to the beach below. This, protestors felt, was all the evidence needed to prove a fence was required. No names are mentioned or the circumstances.

Still no mention of Robert Delbrook. I check out the firm of solicitors who created the trust and discover a fact that makes me sit back with interest. The solicitor who did the work was a senior partner who was prosecuted for fraud fifteen years ago, ending his career. Unfortunately, he's dead so not available to tell me how Mummy was involved with this house.

A potentially dodgy solicitor? It makes me think that there's something fishy about this trust, the one Mummy was the chair of. I'm going to have to read the legal documents with a fine-tooth comb to find it because at over a hundred pages it won't be easy. I add contacting this firm of solicitors to my 'to do' list.

Next up is my mother. A secret agent would have more of a digital footprint than my mother. I'm not surprised that I find no mention of her. She was one of those ordinary women who worked hard and took care of her family, the backbone of our country. The women who get left out of history, their lives and achievements never recorded on the internet. She dreamed of me becoming a teacher; that was the pinnacle of social mobility for her. She would have been double proud that I became a lawyer.

I soon give up looking for Mummy online. By way of compensation, I turn to her make-up bag again. I take out her lipstick and head for the bathroom and stand in front of the mirror. After leaving Salina's I'd rubbed the lipstick off in embarrassment when Salina noticed I was wearing it. I take my time, slowly spreading the deep red across the bumps and ridges of my lips. The yellow strip lighting over the basin gives my face a slightly sinister tinge against the white wall in the background. I inhale sharply when Mummy appears at the corner of my shoulder in the reflection. She's wearing the lipstick too but it looks like a strip of red tape gluing her mouth together, preventing her from speaking.

I hear my myself whisper against the silence, 'Who are you, Mum?'

When I get no answer, I add, 'And what were you doing at Ocean Haven?'

CHAPTER 8

I wake up the next morning stuck to the bed in unbearable pain. I don't understand what's going on. Where has this pain come from? It's as if my body belongs to someone else. I'm scared, terrified, have no idea what's going on. My mouth hangs half open trying to suck in spurts of air, the sound of my breathing horrible and choking, wheezing and rushing around me in jagged waves. Light-headed, dizzy, vision blurry. The white of the walls moves in a sickening river of motion. My knees, elbows, ankles, the place that connects my hips to my back are a mass of agony. My head hurts so bad, so very bad. But the worst, the absolute worst, are the soles of my feet, which feel like the top layer of the skin is being ripped, inch by slow inch, away. The pain is indescribable, the worst I have ever experienced in my life. Instinctively, I roll to the side and tuck my body into a protective ball like some magic trick that will abracadabra the pain away. It doesn't, instead it intensifies. My body's on fire. I muffle my lips against the bed sheet and let out a silent scream that rocks me from the top of my head to the tips of my unnaturally stretched toes. *Someone help me! Mummy, please help me!*

Then I hear another scream; unlike mine this one is audible and piercing and coming from down the landing. It's Mummy, all those years ago, she's in pain. My eyes squeeze tight, dragging me back to being a terror-stricken teenage girl clutching the door frame of my parents' bedroom door, helplessly watching Mummy on the bed, pain suffocating her, body arching up, her head rolling from side to side. Daddy is nowhere in sight. He never is. Only Salina is in the room. She's bathing Mummy's forehead with a cool cloth, soothing her by humming the latest Mariah Carey beneath her breath. Salina is always there taking care of Mummy during these terrible times. I want to be like my baby sister, brave enough to go in the room, but I can't. I can't look in my mother's pain-filled face knowing there's nothing I can do to help her. If the doctor says he can't stop her suffering, then how can I?

Mummy's screaming dies away and I come back to my own agony. I have no idea how long I lie there; an hour, two, five minutes? But the pain finally disappears. Face soaked in sweat, I turn on to my back and simply breathe. Breathe. Then my trembling hand shoots out, scrambling to locate the half-filled glass of ginger beer beside the bed. I find it, the cold of the glass mercifully shooting through me, cooling my body. Awkwardly I sit and slide my legs over the side and head towards the bathroom.

I run my eyes over my reflection in the mirror, shivering involuntarily. What I see makes me wince. I look exhausted and battered by life. And sad, my face full of such utter sadness that my stomach muscles cramp and clench with an unbearable tightness. One of the things I've been such an expert at is going through life with my real face, my real me, hidden from everyone else. Blank was how one of my exes put it the day he dumped me.

On unsteady feet, I head down the stairs towards the communal kitchen, the coolness of the boarding house clinging, almost digging into me as far as my bones, and finally reach the kitchen. I settle at the table with a way-too-potent cup of coffee. 'How did you cope with the pain? The constant trauma of dying?' I ask in the silent room. But I know I'm not alone. I know she's there. Mummy. My head lifts and there she is at the kitchen counter vigorously

41

grating a cocoa ball, the ritual of making her beloved cocoa-tea. The room fills with the smell of the pot of milk she has put on to boil, a cinnamon stick and grated nutmeg in the milk perfuming the room. The steam from the boiling pot partially frosts against the windows.

Mummy doesn't look at me, her hand never missing a beat as it moves up and down against the grater. 'It's the house.'

'Ocean Haven?' I shuffle to the edge of my seat, trying to get closer to her but knowing that she will always be out of my reach.

'This house is the real killer. From the floor to the roof, to the back door to the front, it's possessed by something that God had no intention of ever letting live on this earth.'

'Possessed?'

Her hand abruptly stops its work. Her gaze catches mine, the colour of her eyes those of a black river that has no bottom. 'Are you going to let that house murder you?'

I've dealt with Mr Hall, the estate agent that's selling Ocean Haven. He's helped me look for a house for myself, although that search has been half-hearted while deciding whether to stay in Tinfields. The trouble with my previous visits is that he'll have access to information that shows Ocean Haven is way out of my price range. He's given me to understand that my budget is a little low for his establishment, although he's perfectly polite about it. The window displays all the properties he has available but there's no sign of the one I'm interested in. But that's not going to stop me.

But as I go through the door, I'm brought to a halt by a phone call.

'Ms Lewis? It's Detective Craven. I just wanted to give you a quick update on the enquiry into the attack on your father. We're looking through all the security camera and CCTV footage and we've picked up another image – it's not brilliant, I'm afraid. It's out of focus and only shows the rear of the attacker as he flees down the street. He's also wearing a hoodie, which is unfortunate because it's going to take much longer to identify him.'

'I thought you said he was smartly dressed.'

'That's the problem with witness statements sometimes, they can contradict what the actual physical evidence shows. Although he is wearing very smart distinctive trousers of the herringbone cloth variety. Let me text you a photo of the image.' When it reaches me he asks, 'Does that ring any bells?'

Intently, I study the photo. Herringbone trousers? Hoodie? 'No, I'm sorry, Detective.'

'I'll keep looking and be in touch.'

I walk into the estate agent and greet Mr Hall.

'Ms Lewis again? How can I help you?' The agent doesn't hesitate before adding, 'I'm afraid we don't have much in the way of things for you to view at the moment but rest assured if anything crops up, we'll be in touch.'

I decide a little white lie is justified here. And after all, I am a lawyer. 'I'm not enquiring for myself this time; I'm here on behalf of one of my clients, a developer. He's asked me to view a property he's interested in.'

'A developer? And you're acting as his agent?'

'Agent is probably a rather grand way of putting it, but he doesn't have time to go himself so he's asked me to look at it instead. It's called Ocean Haven.'

Mr Hall obviously knows all the properties on his books. He shakes his head. 'I'm terribly sorry, Ms Lewis, but I'm afraid that property is already under offer to a charming young couple from London who are moving to the area. Of course, we'd prefer to sell to local people but that's the nature of the beast, I'm afraid.'

'But it's only under offer? That means there's still wriggle room for negotiation?'

Mr Hall sweeps me with a very disapproving look. 'We couldn't countenance that kind of sharp practice. Of course, nothing is settled until something is signed but we operate on good faith in this part of the world.'

Now I've added 'not from these parts' to that of low-rent, dishonest buyer. 'I'm sure the vendor will be happy to consider a higher offer.'

'They might be, but we're not. Now, if you'll excuse me.'

I see Mum's name signed on that document. I'm not giving up. I remember Alan, who I met last night at Salina's and Luke's and who works in the property management department for the council. 'It might interest you to know that I'm familiar with the vendor. He handles property sales for the local authority and he's a friend of my brother-in-law.'

Mentally I beat myself up for missing the opportunity to talk with him more. Maybe I'm being too harsh on myself because I did try but Luke intervened.

For a few seconds Mr Hall assesses me and then reaches for his appointments diary. 'Well, I'm afraid we're very booked up for viewings at the moment. It would have to be an evening viewing. And I'm afraid the property is very isolated and the lighting is very poor so you won't be able to get a good look.'

'That's OK.'

Mr Hall keeps trying to put me off. His devotion to the interests of the charming couple from London is quite touching. But the charming couple can have it after I've had a good look around. When he asks me if my client is familiar with the fact Ocean Haven has been the subject of a protracted legal dispute, I nod. As a final gambit he warns that the cost involved in restoring the house will be extremely high.

'It's my client's money. If he wants to spend it, I say let him splash the cash.'

Mr Hall snatches a card from a pile and writes.

Eight p.m. appointment for me to view Ocean Haven.

I'm in.

CHAPTER 9

TWENTY-FIVE YEARS AGO

MARCIA

I'm dying. That was the devastating conclusion Marcia came to as she sat opposite the consultant in his office in the hospital. His face was the dead giveaway that there was something badly wrong with her. His gaze was grave and unblinking, the corners of his mouth pinched and his jaw moving ever so slowly like he was rehearsing what he was about to reveal. Marcia knew what a face filled with bad news looked like – she'd seen way too many in her life. What unnerved Marcia the most were his hands. They rested on top of the table, fingers pale and interlocking with the tightness of coffins packed together in a deadly row. There was another man in the room, much younger than the consultant. Marcia didn't know who he was because the consultant had not introduced him.

Desperately, her teeth worried her lip, which was covered in the lipstick Salina had carefully applied this morning. Her daughter helping with her make-up was her way of trying to cheer Marcia up. Marcia tried to control her breathing, but it was quick and shallow, a gathering storm of turbulent emotions in her chest. The faces of her three children came to her. Gabby, her serious face stuck in a book, Salina's face happy and bright. And the sullen, shut-down face of Karl, her baby boy, who she didn't think she really knew at all. How was she going to tell them that she would be leaving them? How does a mother tell her children that she's dying? Tears overwhelmed and clogged her throat. Bravely Marcia swallowed them back. She braced herself for the bad news.

'As you know, the hospital has carried out extensive tests on you. Blood tests, urine samples, scans. And I'm able to tell you . . .'

Marcia held her breath.

'All the tests came back negative. We could find nothing wrong with you.'

'Wh . . . What?' She drew in a harsh punch of air. 'I don't understand. What's causing the pain?'

The consultant ignored her and addressed a younger man who was in the room. 'This concept of phantom pain is often a natural part of women reaching this age. It's their ovaries, in my opinion. Women like her have reached a point where the body will change, and, frankly, her ovaries are in turmoil.'

Marcia hung her head low, embarrassment and shame washing over her. He was talking about personal and private parts of her body as if she wasn't there. Ovaries. How could he mention a word that she had never allowed herself to say aloud. Women didn't dare discuss such private matters in public. It was shameful. Marcia didn't know where to put her eyes. Mind you, there was that time she happened to come across that late-night show on the telly. It was a group of women talking freely about how a vagina was really called a vulva. Marcia's jaw had dropped in astonishment. She should have turned the telly off right then but she hadn't. Instead she'd lowered the volume and dragged the armchair closer to the screen so only she could hear. Vulva. She hadn't been able to get the word out of her head.

47

The doctor continued, 'The pain is not real, it is in her head, often created by ovaries that no longer work. Delusional. Sadly, this state of make-believe is the natural outcome of being a woman.'

Stop, that's when Marcia wanted to call out to him, tell him to stop talking about her as if she and her body weren't there. But she didn't because she had respect for him as a doctor; he knew what he was talking about, didn't he? Still, her pain wasn't made up. It was real. There was something badly wrong inside her. The first time the pain had come was just over three months ago after that massive argument with Saul. She'd tried to reason with him about his controlling behaviour, but Saul being Saul he wouldn't listen to her. It had all felt too much for her so she'd threatened to leave, taking the kids with her. Saul had reared over her, the threat of the rage coming off his big body shoving her into the wall.

'Pack your crap and leave – but know this,' – his mouth had breathed fire into her face – 'you won't be taking my children anywhere.'

Marcia was immediately mortified. She would never leave her children behind, never. That very week the pains had come.

The consultant turned back to her. 'The treatment I recommend for you is this.' He wrote her a prescription: antidepressants. He ended with, 'Rest. Relaxation. And plenty of fresh air.'

Was this doctor laughing at her? There was something badly wrong with her and he was suggesting she go off and have fun and games. Women from her background had been taught that you just sucked up the problems of life, put your best foot forward and carry on. Well, stuff that! With fortitude and determination Marcia rose strongly to her feet. She pulled the strap of her bag securely over her shoulder. 'I thank you, Doctor, for *your* time but if you're not prepared to help, I'm wasting *my* time.'

It was the younger doctor who stood. He spoke to her for the first time. 'If you need to speak to us again don't hesitate to contact us.'

Marcia scoffed. 'What? So we can go pick daisies in the fresh air? Go off and play bingo?'

Marcia knew she was being rude but it was crushing disappointment provoking her to behave in such an uncharacteristic manner. Marcia didn't remember leaving. Remember how she took the stairs instead of the lift. Remember striding with angry purpose towards the exit. She came back to awareness when the stiff, cold air outside tightened its grip about her poor body. What was she going to do? If the hospital wasn't going to help her who was there left to go to? A private doctor was out of the question; they cost an arm and a leg. Saul's wages would never stretch to paying for one. Even if they could afford it, Marcia couldn't see her husband putting his hand in his pocket.

The tears she had suppressed coated her eyes. Marcia wasn't one for crying, but just this once, she wanted to find a quiet corner, crawl into a ball and let the hurt, the pain, the agony flow out of her. Believe me! Why won't the doctor believe me?

Marcia was so caught up by her inner turmoil that she never saw the figure walking towards her in the car park outside. Her lower body collided with them. Startled, Marcia stumbled back and looked down. It was a child, a boy of about nine, with tidy, smooth brown hair and winter-coloured eyes. Flat, staring eyes set in a chalk-white face. He looked ill. Something about him reminded Marcia of Karl.

'I'm sorry.' Frowning, she added, 'Are you OK? Who's with you?' She glanced around, trying to locate an adult, maybe a mum or a dad, but there was no one else nearby.

He didn't answer, instead turned and walked away. Something fluttered from his hand to the ground. Marcia quickly picked it up. It was a leaflet.

Waving it she stood back up and called, 'You've lost your . . .' Her words faded to nothing because the boy was nowhere to be seen. Urgently stepping forward, Marcia checked out the car park. The child was gone. How odd. Then again maybe not – he'd probably wandered off and gone back to whoever he was with. Well, that's at least what Marcia hoped, because he'd looked so ill. Marcia turned her attention to the leaflet she held. It was an advertisement for somewhere called Ocean Haven near Cliff Heights. One line held her spellbound:

'To heal the body, you need to heal the mind. Call Dr Vincent at Ocean Haven on this number . . .'

CHAPTER 10

From the pathway, the house looks drunk. Everything about Ocean Haven is tilted, out of alignment, wrongly angled or broken. The windows are crooked and the once grand front door is warped. The chimneys tilt and no amount of ivy can hide the cracks in the stone work. Its grounds resemble a moth-eaten coat. And it looks dark. The sun's just about still out but the place holds darkness close to it like a curse.

Mr Hall is beside me as we inspect the front of the house. 'You can see the weather your client would have to put up with on an exposed stretch of the coast like this. I don't think he's going to be very happy about that.'

Poor Mr Hall has been trying to curb my interest in Ocean Haven from the moment I arrived. But he's right about one thing, it is pretty bleak and isolated up here. It must be a couple of miles since I drove past another inhabited home. He's right about the weather too. It's been sunshine and showers all day with a lively wind blowing off the sea. You can clearly hear the waves as they crash below. We're in a brief interval of evening sunshine but there's no warmth in it. There seems to be no warmth up here at all.

While Mr Hall makes a couple of last efforts to put me off, I stand and admire Ocean Haven from what was once a gate but is now empty space between two posts. Resting on an incline which overlooks the sea, even in its current sorry condition you can see it was once an imposing building. Three floors, it nestles between two enormous chimney stacks, its walls overgrown with ivy, which might look quaintly rustic if it was trimmed back. Solidly built from local stone, two columns mark the front door and it has traditional sash windows. It once must have had 'grounds' but they're overgrown. There's a hedge hiding the wall which surrounds Ocean Haven, along with haphazard tree stumps. Heather from the surrounding hills is taking over what might once have been a lawn. You can imagine it as a vicarage or the home of one of those country squires who doesn't know which century he's living in.

But Mr Hall is right. It's not a desirable residence in its current state.

He sighs. 'Shall we go in then, Ms Lewis?' He walks up what's left of the gravel path to the front door. Halfway up, he turns back. 'Are you coming?'

'One moment.'

I'm inspecting something curious by one of the gateposts. A bunch of flowers rests there and they're quite a display. Attached is a handwritten card:

'To Mum. Always in my thoughts.'

But there's no name added underneath or any indication who the mum was. The flowers have been tossed about a little in the weather and have lost a few petals but they can only be a few days old. They're lilies, the flowers of death. As respectfully as possible, I lay them back against the post and walk up to join Mr Hall.

My viewing is brisk, which is not what I'm looking for. But what exactly is it that I am looking for? What is going to be here that can be connected with whatever happened in this house a generation ago? That involved my mother while I was at school and she was slowly dying?

Mr Hall escorts me around the rooms like a prison officer showing a newly arrived inmate her wing. Inside, the place looks like a recently vacated squat. The pattern of decay outside is repeated within. The walls flake, the randomly arranged furniture is stained and burned with cigarettes. Just about every floorboard groans and creaks under my feet as if their sleep has been disturbed. Ocean Haven has plenty of original features, but they're all falling apart. If the young couple from London have some money to invest, this place will be a grand, if somewhat lonely, family home again one day. But they're going to need a heck of a lot of money. I'm so disappointed because any apparent connection between this house and my mother has vanished.

Mr Hall shows me a large room at the front of the house with a commanding view over the sea. 'This would have been the morning room back in the day.' A fake smile plays on his lips. He's about to make a joke. 'Although now perhaps mourning room would be more suitable. You can imagine a coffin laid on a trestle table in here with the family gathered around.'

The awful thing is it does indeed look like a mourning room. The once expensive scarlet wallpaper has turned nearly black and becomes darker the closer it gets to the ceiling where it begins to peel away from the wall. I imagine that darkening was caused by smoke from the large ornate fireplace that still has debris in it. The material is a mixture of brick, mortar and soot that has probably fallen from the chimney stacks. The fireplace itself is discoloured, bent and twisted. Everything in this house is twisted. Lumps of coving have fallen from the ceiling, leaving grey dust scattered over the room like nuclear fallout.

There are gaps in the window frames where the wood is rotted by sea salt and they're wide enough for the breeze to blow through. The wooden door is clinging on to its hinges for dear life and one good slam would probably be enough to bring it down. The only vaguely comforting feature is a deep-pile sofa bed that seems to have avoided contamination by the rest of the room and looks as if it could still be slept on. It's grey with a red rose pattern that hasn't faded. It faces the window with its back to the rest of the room. Probably whoever slept on it last couldn't bear looking at the blackening walls and pushed this makeshift bed round for a sea view instead. I brush some of the coving dust off it. The covering is soft and dry.

Perhaps Mr Hall fears I'm going to take a seat. 'We are in rather a hurry, Ms Lewis.'

The rest of the rooms on the ground floor have the same collection of tarnished features but without the sofa bed to relieve the gloom. We mount the stairs, which might trap an unwary guest if their foot goes through one. On the next two floors, the house has given up any pretence that it might be habitable. It's an unremitting trail of damaged walls, ceilings and floors. It doesn't need Mr Hall to point any of this out, so he remains contentedly silent and lets the gloom speak for itself.

Of any connection to my mum, there isn't even a hint up here. On the third-floor landing though, a thought occurs to me. At home, everything the family no longer needs ends up under the roof.

'Can I go up into the attic?'

My voice is hesitant as I look around because it isn't obvious where the entrance to the loft is here. We're standing on the floor beneath what should be a loft but I've had a look in all the rooms up here and can't see another door – all I see is the wood-panelled walls.

I look over at Mr Hall. 'The house does have a loft?'

The estate agent reacts to my question as if I've asked to have a peep at his underwear. 'I wouldn't have thought it was necessary to look up there; you must have got a general idea of what sort of property this is?'

He's already briskly walking towards the stairs before I can find out more. I look up there, at the ceiling that guards the attic, and remember what long-forgotten treasures are hidden up there in our house. I need to come back here on my own but I'm not sure how to arrange that.

'Can I see out the back?' I ask as I follow the estate agent down. 'If you must.'

He opens the back door with a key, although I think he could probably manage it with a good shove of the shoulder. It's quite a shock outside. The wind has brought storm clouds overhead while we were inside and dusk has fallen fast. I notice a cluster of trees where about seven ravens sit. They are silent, barely moving. Odd. Mr Hall manages to find a rear lamp that should light up the back of the grounds but of course it doesn't work. All I can see is a ragged and uneven stretch of land that leads to another hedge and probably the wall again. Behind that is a hill that leads upwards to join the clouds above. The end of the day has made the heather that covers it purplish black. There's a sort of outbuilding-shed structure that carries on the drunken style of the house.

'Have you seen everything you need, Ms Lewis?'

Mr Hall is barely visible a few paces away now the light has gone.

'Yes, thank you.'

But I haven't. I haven't seen anything at all.

CHAPTER 11

'Do you know who that is?'

I've dropped by to see my father in his hospital bed, but I'm having trouble keeping his attention. He's playing cards on the ward with some of his fellow patients. When he's shown the security camera photo that Detective Craven sent me of the suspect fleeing down the street, he finally casts a glance over it and then looks again at it with something like curiosity. 'Who's that supposed to be?'

'It's the guy who attacked you.'

My father bursts out laughing and sneers, 'Really? The police are working with that, are they? You can't even see his head. He's wearing a hood. That must leave half the population in the frame.' His gaze returns to his hand of cards.

'You're sure you don't know who this man is?'

He turns back. He has a sixth and sometimes feral sense of what others are thinking. He looks at me with suspicion, as if daring me to contradict him. 'From that photo?'

'No, not from that, but you were fighting with him. You must have seen his face. A white guy. Are you sure you didn't recognise him? Who was it actually and what started this fight?'

My father shakes his head. 'You should join the police, my girl. You're as confused as they are.'

'Can I ask you something else? Do the names Carol Shore, Robert Delbrook and Ocean Haven mean anything to you?'

My dad doesn't blanch or flinch or give any flicker of a sign that the names mean anything.

'Robert Delbrook sounds like a pop singer, Ocean Haven sounds like a club he would sing in and Carol Shore sounds like the club's cleaner. Does that help?'

I don't stay long because there's nothing to stay long for. He's happy now with his new social circle of fellow hospital patients. He'll only start turning the screws and begin blackmailing me back into the family home when he comes out again.

But he knows who attacked him. I keep it to myself, but I think I know who attacked him, because there's one white man I know who wears herringbone trousers.

Is Dad also lying about knowing about Mummy and the house too?

◆ ◆ ◆

Salina's not returning my calls and I need to talk to her. But as it happens, it doesn't matter because the following day as I'm walking on the esplanade after work, I see a scattered group of men eyeing something on the beach. Some of the guys are leaning on rails that overlook the sea, others are stealing glances while pretending to play football and a few of the more honest ones have parked deck-chairs where they can get a good view. As I draw closer, it becomes clear what the attraction is. A willowy black woman in a skimpy bikini is on a lounger being eagerly photographed by a hipster-type guy with a beard. From time to time the woman holds up a bag to be photographed, or she adjusts her sunglasses or she just lies there, legs sleekly stretched out. Even before I'm close enough to tell who it is, I know. It's my sister.

'Hello, Gabby. Out for a walk?' She turns to her guy. 'Got enough shots, Jez?'

Jez shows her his camera. 'Oh yeah, babe, I'll choose the best and forward them on.'

She blows him a kiss as he dismantles the lounger and heads off across the beach, carrying it under his arm. Salina pulls on a slip dress and pumps. 'Do you want anything, sis? Only Luke and I are trying a new fusion restaurant down the coast this evening.'

'You know I want something, that's why you've got those messages on your phone.'

'Have I . . . ? What do you want then? I'm here now.' She catches my eye and groans. 'Oh no, it's not this business with our mum and the house?'

I don't need to answer. She shakes her head in despair. 'You really want to make something of this? That's typical of you, Gabby, you always have to get answers to everything, no matter how pointless. It probably comes from you being overeducated.'

She picks up the bag she was showing to Jez and tucks it away in a holdall. Now she's fully dressed, her audience of men on the beach is going back to business. I watch them drift away.

'Do you really need to lie half naked on a sun lounger for seedy men to gawp at?'

She shrugs. 'It's just some photos to advertise my new product. I'm currently doing "Latte Loox", a powder and cream combo that takes a girl's complexion to a maximum ten. It'll be selling online like hot cakes, but it never hurts to advertise. And if the local guys want to catch an eyeful while the camera's rolling, I say fill your boots, boys.' She runs her hands over her hips. 'If you've got it, flaunt it. And then flaunt it again afterwards while fanning those banknotes.'

It's hard to believe sometimes that Salina is my sister, and even harder to believe she's our mother's daughter. It's only our father she sometimes reminds me of.

58

Hardly have we sat down in the coffee shop than we're interrupted. A teenage girl starts loitering near our table trying to attract my sister's attention. When Salina notices, she smiles beautifully at the teenager. 'Can I help you?'

'Yes, sort of, it's just – are you Salina?'

It seems that on the internet my sister has now done enough to be known by her first name alone. Then again, that's what her make-up line is called. 'Yes, I am!'

'Oh wow! I just wanted to say, I love your stuff!'

'That's so sweet!' Salina waves her phone at her fan. 'Pix?'

'Oh wow!' For the next minute, Salina and the girl are doing selfies with their arms draped over each other's shoulders. For a woman in a hurry to get to a fusion restaurant, Salina suddenly has a lot of time on her hands. When the fan finally goes with her phone full of photos, my sister beckons her back and looks in her holdall. She passes her the bag she was dangling for Jez. 'This is for you. It's my latest. It's not actually out yet but you can have it as my gift.' The girl is literally dumbstruck. Then my sister adds, 'And is that your boyfriend you're sitting with? If it is, dump him, you're way better than that. Never sell yourself short, girl.'

When she's finally gone, Salina gives me a pointed look. 'When was the last time one of your clients begged for a selfie and told you they loved your work?'

That whole thing with the girl was just a performance to remind me who's best. And despite that, I still have to respond. 'My clientele has too much self-respect to carry on like that.'

She sneers. 'Your clientele is made up of rich crooks and wealthy chancers, Gabby. You forget that Luke knows most of them.'

The mention of Luke gives me a chance to get into the real reason I want to talk with my sister: is her husband the man who attacked Dad? Although, I need to tread very carefully.

'I get why you decided not to go to see Dad, what with you being busy with Latte Loox and everything. But why didn't Luke go? You could have asked him to go and check our dad was OK.'

'Why would he do that?'

I'm being careful here. 'Because it's his father-in-law?'

'I told you, Gabby, I didn't pick up any messages till later.'

I'm doing indignant. 'But surely, Luke could have gone if you'd asked him? Where was he anyway when Dad was attacked?' I quickly add, 'Or on that day?'

She squints at me, her false lashes sweeping up and down. 'How do I know? I'm not my husband's keeper and he's not mine. And talking of the old man, have you seen him?'

'Yesterday. He's getting better.'

Salina's eyes flash with hate. 'I'll bet he is. He'll be using this attack as a lever to get you back in the house as his housemaid and carer. Then you'll have to give up your job and go work for him full-time. I wouldn't be surprised if he didn't organise this assault so he could snare you again. Then he'll work you to death like he did our mum. You made a terrible mistake coming back to this town – you're falling right into his spider's web. Have you got any plans to leave again before the trap closes?'

I'm not comfortable talking about this because I know she's right. 'I haven't made my mind up. I like my job but I've got to leave my rented room shortly and I haven't found anywhere else, so everything is in play.'

She tilts her head back and rolls her eyes. 'No, you're the one in play. By him.'

'I went to the house last night.'

'What house?'

'Ocean Haven, the house our mum was involved with.'

A muscle ticks beneath her heavily made-up cheek. 'Why can't you let Mum rest?'

'I have to find out what happened.'

'Why?' Salina is clearly upset. 'I was the one who was close to her. She loved me more than you.'

Her words are a gut punch that leave me winded – and wounded – gasping for air. How could she say that to me? *You know why. Because it's the truth.* That's what leaves me devastated: the truth. Whoever said that the truth would set you free was full of rubbish. There's no freedom here, instead I'm caught in the coiled, nasty barbed wire of the past. What I can never understand is why I have Mum's face, while Salina took after Dad's side of the family. It feels like some kind of twisted joke. She has a right to Mum's face. Have I been wearing the wrong face my whole life?

I feel her fine fingers on my arm. 'Sorry. That came out all wrong.'

I move out of the past and tell her, 'There was a bunch of flowers at the gatepost with a message written on it, saying someone always had their mum in their thoughts.'

Salina sighs. 'Well, it wasn't me laying flowers and I suppose it wasn't you, and I'm guessing our brother Karl hasn't appeared out of the ether to do it. So, I'm guessing that's got nothing to do with our mum? Let me give you one bit of sisterly advice. You need to quit town before the old man gets his claws back into you. You want to worry about our mum? Think about what happened to her.'

CHAPTER 12

CERTIFIED COPY OF ENTRY: DEATH

Name: Carol Elizabeth Shore

Age: 30

Cause of death: Trauma to the body. Significant
trauma to the head caused by a fall

At my desk I read a copy of Carol Shore's death certificate. It hits
me how young she was, so young. Mum was only ten years older
than her, dying at forty. Am I next? Shaking off the morbid thought
I look at the cause of death. Where did she fall? Was it inside Ocean
Haven? How did she fall? Did someone push her?

I reach for my phone to contact the firm of solicitors that
drew up the trust, who I'm sure will have more information on
how Carol Shore died. But I never get the chance. My boss, Greg,
appears.

He's not a happy bunny. 'Have you got the Ocean Haven property dispute file, Gabby? I want to send it back to the client with a
"get lost" note on it, so we can clear the decks and get on with some
real work.' When he gets no answer, he looks appalled. 'Please don't

tell me you haven't finished with it yet? That was a five-minute job at most. Why isn't it finished? What have you been doing in here? You know the pressure we're under.'

He's not having it back yet. I need it. 'It's more complicated than I thought. There's a deed to be gone through and it's a hundred pages long. You know me, I don't cut corners.'

'But the client as good as admitted it's a no-hoper. All the client wants is a quick scan in case something was missed. Are you saying there is something in there after all?'

There's something in there all right. 'I'm studying it to see.'

His voice is flinty. 'Get it done.'

Now I've got Greg's permission to 'get it done', I ring the law firm that drew up the trust for the house. It's a long-established and highly respectable outfit in the Midlands, apart from, obviously, the original and now deceased solicitor who put the trust together, and had a question mark over his head concerning fraud.

When I get to speak to somebody, I expect I'll have to explain in detail what the case is about, but the solicitor cuts me short. 'This isn't the Shore family and that house down the road from Tinfields in Devon, is it?'

'Yes, it is.'

He sighs. 'Oh dear, you must be the nth firm that's had to deal with this. It's been the bane of our lives here. Let me give you a potted history and if you've got any questions, I'll answer them. We're very careful about who we employ here but we all make mistakes. Back in the 1990s it was subsequently discovered that one of the senior partners had an off-the-books sideline doing dubious legal documents for crooks and fraudsters. Of course, as soon he was found out, his position here was terminated. It was him who drew up the deed for the house on behalf of the mysterious Robert Delbrook—'

Excitedly I cut in, 'Robert Delbrook was the person who initiated the trust?'

He becomes more guarded, choosing his words incredibly carefully. 'Mr Delbrook was not an official client of the firm. What I will say is that he's someone we probably would not have dealt with—'

'Because he was a criminal?'

'My dear Miss Lewis, as a lawyer you should know we would never call someone a criminal without hard evidence or a verdict of guilty handed down by a court of law. What I will say is this: from what I understand, he was a very elusive man who was very private.'

Which explains why I found no evidence of him on the internet.

'Do you know anything about Delbrook's disappearance?'

'Over the years there have been stories of him in America, others of him in Brazil. Nevertheless, it's what the law says that matters, and after the required period, it declared that he was dead.'

If Robert Delbrook is really dead that will mean three deaths connected to Ocean Haven.

'I've read Carol Shore's death certificate. How exactly did she die?'

'The inquest returned a verdict of misadventure. She fell from Cliff Heights, which I believe is near Ocean Haven. But that was probably the coroner sparing the family's feelings, because it was most likely suicide. She went over the cliffs with her son—'

'Her son?' I can't hold back a sharp intake of breath. 'How did her son manage to fall as well?'

In my mind's eye I see her holding his hand, she loses her footing and they both go over. But if it was suicide, what if she deliberately pulled him to his death as well. Could a mother really do that to the child she'd nurtured and loved in her body for nine months?

'Very tragic,' is all he says in response.

He's saved me a lot of trouble. 'Thank you for your time.'

He sounds grim. 'That's all right, I'm an expert on this case now.'

Slowly I put the phone down. Carol Shore's son is another death connected to the house. A child. I'm glad to be distracted by a text from Craven. It's an update on his enquiry. Well, it's hardly any update at all, really the detective letting me know that he's still pursuing leads. I'll give Craven this, he's a cop who won't give up. I have this internal battle of whether I should contact him about my suspicions that Luke attacked Dad. It's no easy thing to contact the police to hand over a relative. And what would Salina say? It would damage our already fragile relationship.

I make a decision: I'll go over to Salina and Luke's home, sit them down and get the truth of what went on. Maybe, as a family, we can sort this out without police involvement.

I carry on working until six o'clock to prove to Greg I'm not slacking, but as soon as he leaves, so do I a few minutes later. Outside I notice a well-built man sitting on the bonnet of an upmarket German saloon, looking suspicious in a pair of sunglasses. Only when I take a second look do I realise it's actually Luke. He must be waiting for me. He walks towards me and we meet halfway.

'Hello. What are . . . ?'

I finish on a squeak when he grabs my wrist, pulling me firmly to his car.

'What on earth do you think you're doing, Luke? Get your hands off me at once.'

He doesn't answer. I struggle, but this has no effect as he continues to pull me down the street towards his car. He bundles me through the passenger door, then walks around and gets into the driver seat and starts the ignition. Once inside I notice his herring-bone trousers. Dad's attacker wore the same type of trousers. I was right, it was Luke who savagely beat Dad in the street. Is he going to do the same to me?

The door is unlocked, I could open it and run, but I'm frozen stiff. It's all I can do to stutter, 'Nothing bad has happened yet and there's still time for us to call a halt and talk about this.'

Before he can answer, my hands suddenly burst into life and I make a grab for the door handle.

He's too quick for me and takes both my wrists this time and leans into my face, his features contorted with fury. 'We're just going to go somewhere and have a little chat, that's all. I'm your sister's husband, what do you think I'm going to do to you?' He throws my hands back at me and locks the doors, before accelerating the car down the street, wheels squealing.

I could grab the wheel and pull us into parked cars. Or lean over and grab the car keys. Or start punching and kicking him, which is what I really want to do. But he's ready for me, I know he is. His eyes keep more of a watch on me than they do on the road, where he runs red lights and mounts the kerb. Fear's making my heart thump so hard, it's almost visible in my veins. It's not just what he's doing, although that's bad enough, it's the blank expression on his face, which suggests he doesn't know or care what he's doing. The face of a guy high on drugs or with murder on his mind.

With escape out of the question my only option is to negotiate and try and talk him down. 'Listen, Luke, I don't know what's going on here or why you're so upset, but if you pull the car over we can try and work it out together. Perhaps you were right, what you said at the dinner party. Perhaps we've never taken the time to get to know each other. Is that a plan?'

His face breaks into a smile, but there's no warmth in his face. 'Is this you trying to negotiate with me? Remind me never to ask you to do any negotiating on my behalf.'

We're leaving the streets of Tinfields behind and heading out on to the coast road. The houses and cottages are starting to thin out and so are the pedestrians. I'm screwed. But even as Luke drives us deeper into the country, and although I'm scared, deep down inside there's a little corner of me that feels a certain insane sense of satisfaction.

I've always known this is what Luke is really like. And now he's proved it.

CHAPTER 13

The car veers violently across the road into a layby which offers a view over the sea. Luke turns off the engine and stares impassively at the waves in the early evening sun for a few seconds, before turning to me. 'What do you think you're playing at?'

'I don't know what you're talking about.'

My answer fuels his anger. 'Accusing me of beating up your father.'

Salina must have tumbled my innocent line of questioning in the coffee shop after all. 'What on earth are you talking about?'

'Questioning Salina about my whereabouts when your dad got thumped. She told me about it this afternoon, she seemed to think it was hilarious. But she's on her own there. What kind of an animal do you think I am? I know you don't like me, Gabby, but that's too much. What possible reason could you have for thinking that?'

My heart's still thumping, my hands are still cold, but that might be because my fear is now mixed with shame. He's so angry, he must be innocent; guilty people don't get this vexed. 'I just thought it was a possibility, that's all. My father knows who attacked him and it must be a young or youngish guy. You're the only young or youngish white guy he knows. It all added up.'

Luke performs a sarcastic handclap. 'That's it, is it? I'm in the right age band? White? Good grief.'

I don't mention the fact that the attacker was in herringbone trousers and I've noticed Luke likes to wear those. I'm too embarrassed. 'I just thought it was a possibility. I'm sorry.' But then it occurs to me what's just happened. 'But if there are apologies going around, you owe me one. Kidnapping me off the streets like that. You're lucky the police aren't after you.'

He becomes sheepish. 'Yeah, you're right, that shouldn't have happened. But you can see why it did. And you know what really upsets me? I've spent this morning trying to help you out.'

'What do you mean, help me out?'

No answer. Luke turns the ignition again and pulls out on to the coast road.

'Where are we going, Luke?'

'You'll see.'

Luke drives, far more calmly this time, a few miles up the road and pulls over again. I can't believe where he's taken me. Ocean Haven.

I stammer, 'How did you know about this house?'

'My dear wife has been moaning about your interest in it. Something to do with your mum?'

I leave his question hanging and get out of the car. He waits a few moments while I inspect what looks like a new bunch of flowers. Lilies with the same message as before, freshly laid, for someone's mother. Whoever is doing this is paying regular visits to this house.

The two of us walk up to Ocean Haven where we stand by the front door. 'And how is it you can help me, Luke?'

He smiles and pulls out a set of keys like a magician conjuring something from behind someone's ear. 'You've met my friend Alan who manages the property? I asked if I could borrow the keys. Now you can have a look around if you think that'll help. You should have spoken to me in the first place.' Luke opens the door. 'Take your time.'

This is all too surprising for me to say thank you and there's still the little matter of being kidnapped to get over, but it's too good a chance to miss. I examine everything more closely this time, but of course nothing's happened here since my last visit with Mr Hall, the estate agent. Only on the top floor, does it occur to me that my brother-in-law might be able to help me get into the attic.

Eyeing the wood-panelled walls I ask, 'Do you know where the entrance to the attic is?'

I receive one of Luke's cheeky grins. 'One of the things I love about these old-style houses is that their bricks and mortar hold so many secrets.'

My heart quickens. 'What do you mean?'

'I mean this.' Luke walks over to a wooden panel and presses a palm flat against it and then moves the wood with his hand. It's a sliding door. Stepping back, he looks at me with an expression of wonder. 'Pure genius.'

The sliding door reveals a very narrow staircase with stone steps. Age has blackened parts of the stone and chipped away its edges.

Luke tells me, 'I reckon that was the staircase to the servants' quarters. Do you want me to come with you?'

'I'll be fine. See you downstairs.'

After Luke leaves me I head towards the door and look up. The staircase isn't long, reminding me of the steps walked by the condemned to the gallows. The paint has long left the walls, exposing the brick. With my first step a gush of air sucks me with the pull of being dragged into a freezer. There's no hand rail so I'm forced to use my hand against the rough brick wall to steady my journey up. The closer I get to the door at the top the harder my heartbeat bangs against my chest. At the top is a small landing with two doors. The first room is empty, very small and contains the rusty

70

metal frame and springs of an old-fashioned single bed. It must be a relic from the servant days. There's nothing else in here that can help me so I turn my attention to the other room.

The door to it takes a fair amount of shoving to get open and I'm showered with dust and crumbled material when it finally gives. This room is bigger and littered with a jumble of objects that remind me of the loft in my childhood home.

I find blackboards with faded chalk on them, which seem to have been rotas. Across the top are the days of the week, down the side are lists of flowers and fruits. But the flowers and fruits seem to be the names of people. On Mondays Buttercup does the break-fast, Fuchsia does lunch and Apple does dinner. Marigold does the washing, while it's Raspberry's job to give VF a massage.

A large box is stuffed full of material. Orange material. My hand dives in and I pull it out, and that's when I discover that it's not a single piece of cloth but bundles of dresses. I hold one out to inspect it. It's simple, probably cotton, and neck-to-toe long with a tie-back in the middle. Who would have worn these gowns? And why so many in the same colour? I continue to search, finding diagrams of what look like yoga positions or perhaps stress ones. And thick bottles with various labels peeling off. There's all sorts of paperwork, much of it cut up or done in script that makes no sense.

If you had to make a guess, you might suspect this is the debris left by a commune of some kind. What there isn't, and I look hard, is any sign of Robert Delbrook, my mother or Carol Shore. But there must be something in here, I'm sure of it.

I leave the old servants' quarters behind and make my way down the creaking and creepy stairs. Leaving the attic door open, I find Luke in the reception area downstairs.

'Anything taking your fancy?' His gaze is slightly narrowed, searching my face.

'Not sure. These keys, could you borrow them again?'

Luke is pleased with himself. 'The place is under offer but I'm sure I can sort something out with Alan until contracts are exchanged. If you need more time, I could always ask him to find a reason to delay that. I'll need to take them back and ask.'

While he opens the back door that leads on to the land outside, I slip into the pantry and push the warped window slightly ajar, so I'm not reliant on needing keys to gain access to Ocean Haven again.

When I join him outside, darkness is beginning to fall, as it did on my last visit. But there's enough light for me to see the uneven earth and the incline covered in heather and bracken. And something else. A battered wooden sign that points towards a public footpath that leads up to 'Cliff Heights'. The place where Carol Shore fell with her son.

'Are we done?' Luke asks.

'Not quite. Why don't you wait in the car for me? I just want a quick ramble out the rear here. There's something I want to see.'

He sounds suspicious. 'Are you sure? It's getting dark.'

'Five minutes.'

He watches as I climb over a stile that marks the boundary of Ocean Haven and set off up the path. In a cluster of trees are the ravens I saw before, all seven of them sit and stare and don't move. Shivering, I look away. It gets steep quickly and in the fading light it's easy to lose my footing as I brush against tall bracken and nettles that are trying to block my way. It's clear not many people use this path. Looking back, Ocean Haven soon becomes lost amongst the leaves and branches with only its chimney stacks poking over the top. It gets steeper and I struggle for breath. Signs appear – 'Danger: Cliffs'. Almost without warning I'm out of the undergrowth with a clear view of the purple sea below that's stroked with silver lines. The protestors must have won the day, because the cliff edge is now guarded by wooden rails, but they don't look very secure. Gingerly resting my arms on them, I peer straight ahead to the lighthouse and then look down at the beach below. The drop is sheer. It must be several hundred feet. On the sand, a lonely matchstick figure is walking a dog in the dusk. It's a woman; I can hear her voice but not what she's saying to her pet.

Where Carol Shore and her son fell to their deaths is not far from Ocean Haven. Did she fall or was she pushed?

Behind me, in the dense undergrowth, bracken breaks. I turn and listen. Is someone behind me? Who would be coming up here anyway? Then there's silence again, except for the woman below who I can now hear calling. 'Come on, Eddie! Time for bed!' Perhaps the wind has changed. No! There's the sound again, the crunch of bracken being broken underfoot. A quiet yelp. My eyes hurriedly scan over the way I've come. No one there. Perhaps it was a mistake to make Luke wait in the car. But then it's quiet, apart from the breeze, which is picking up. In an epic and dramatic setting like this, in the fading light, where a terrible death happened, it's easy to become nervy.

I'm taking one last view over the cliffs before returning to Ocean Haven when a shadow on my left lurches towards me. Instinctively recoiling, I hit the wooden railing. It vibrates and bends, catching my belly. The top half of my body flops over, twisting and bending over the rail. My heart shudders at the empty space between me and the beach hundreds of yards below. Am I going to fall?

A grip tightens on my wrist. 'What on earth are you doing up here, Gabby? You look like you're about to jump off.'

It's only Luke, looking concerned and worried.

CHAPTER 14

TWENTY-FIVE YEARS AGO

MARCIA

Ocean Haven took Marcia's breath away. Whatever she'd been expecting it hadn't been this. It was a large house, Victorian gothic, majestically sitting on a hill with the regality of a queen looking down at her kingdom of the sea below. Its grey stone should have made it appear hard-looking, casting the surrounding area in a dark light, but instead its walls appeared smooth, hugging and highlighting the sunshine above. In the front was a beautifully manicured garden. So pretty. Marcia's steps crunched through the gravel on the large winding driveway towards the massive front door, which was framed by an arch with two columns.

Marcia pulled out the leaflet the boy had dropped in the hospital car park and read it for what felt like the thousandth time. After her disastrous hospital visit, that night Marcia had waited until the kids were tucked up in bed and Saul engrossed by the footie on the telly before reading the leaflet again at the kitchen table. Ocean Haven was offering what it called a 'comprehensive, overarching, integrated' approach to curing sickness. Marcia didn't understand exactly what that all meant but it certainly sounded impressive.

'*To heal the body, you need to heal the mind. Call Dr Vincent on this number.*'

Could Dr Vincent heal her? Find out what the hospital couldn't? On Saturday the pain had been so bad she hadn't been able to get out of bed. As Salina had fed her soup and helped her, Marcia had noticed how upset her daughter was. Maybe it was Salina's anguished face that had made her finally contact the number on the leaflet.

Something caught her side-eye, distracting her from the grandeur of the entrance. It was some type of outbuilding – well, more like a shack really. It was set on the far side of the property, on the edge behind where the vegetation was bare bracken. It looked out of place with its weather-beaten walls made with mismatched wooden planks and a roof that sagged. There was no window, at least not on the side Marcia could see. The door was shut tight by a large, rusty padlock. Suddenly it occurred to Marcia how quiet it was. Shouldn't it be more noisy, be more active, considering what the leaflet said it was? Shouldn't there be the sound of people somewhere in this house?

Marcia put the leaflet away and turned her attention back to the door. Her fingertips nervously rubbed around the outline of her mouth just in case any lipstick had strayed on to her skin. Salina had carefully applied the lipstick on her – doing Marcia's face was her youngest daughter's way of trying to make her mum better. If only it were as simple as a child's love to make the pain disappear for good. Marcia pressed the ancient doorbell. A man, who she assumed was Dr Vincent, opened the door. He was aged somewhere between forty and fifty and wore jeans, and a baggy white shirt beneath a colourful waistcoat. And a green bow tie. His wavy chestnut hair touched his shoulders framing a face that was long with lines fanning from his grey eyes. He looked pretty well put-together, his sun-kissed skin finishing off his look.

'Marcia Lewis, come on in. I'm Vincent Fortune but everyone calls me Dr Vincent.' With a big smile he ushered her inside.

Trying to smile back, but nerves getting the better of her, Marcia tentatively stepped inside. The interior of the house was something out of *Beautiful Homes*. Marcia had never seen the like in her life. Sweeping staircase, polished floors, bright walls . . . There was too much for her to take it all in.

'I can see you like what you see.' Vincent's statement drew Marcia back to him. His voice lowered. 'The most beautiful things often aren't what we can *see*, they are what are *inside* of us.'

That got Marcia's approval. Although she was surprised there was no sign of a desk in Dr Vincent's office.

'There are no desks in here.' Marcia started at his comment. How had he known what she was thinking? He answered her confusion with, 'Desks are barriers. Here we have no lines between us. The practice of Ocean Haven is built on one simple principle: our hearts, our minds, our bodies are open.'

He guided Marcia through a room with large-leaved plants and soft furnishings. Bright light spilled through the giant ceiling-to-floor window. One wall was covered with framed certificates of his qualifications, of which there were many. Hesitantly, Marcia sat on a large armchair. Its softness wrapped around her. She had to almost stop herself sighing with pleasure because the comfort was luring her in. It wasn't just the chair, but the peace of this house. The quiet was in such strong contrast to her own home where the noise was far too frequently the sound of Saul smashing things.

Dr Vincent didn't take a chair; instead, he neatly folded himself into a crossed-legged position on the floor opposite her. 'Marcia, I'm so pleased that you made the decision to come to Ocean Haven. That's the biggest step, making that first enormous leap forward.'

'I'm in such pain,' she told him. 'Most days, some worse than others. My family doctor and the consultant at the hospital don't believe me.'

His expression remained kind and open. 'This is the promise I make to you, Marcia. I believe you. I will always believe you. I will never doubt you. Here I will provide you with a haven of healing.'

Marcia felt overwhelmed by his conviction and belief in her. It seemed like forever since anyone had not just said they believed her, but that they believed *in* her.

Vincent quietly encouraged, 'Tell me your story.'

And that's what Marcia did for the next hour, spilled her heart and soul to a man she had just met. Dr Vincent never once interrupted her, instead he listened and his silent nods of encouragement gave her the strength and determination to carry on. Marcia felt so comfortable with him, as if she had known him for a lifetime.

At the end, he gently smiled. 'Thank you for speaking your truth. I know how hard that can be. Your voice was filled with such bravery, such conviction and fight. You are a woman of power.'

His words left her speechless. A woman of power? Her? Stay-at-home mum Marcia? In that moment Marcia realised something important. She wasn't just a mother and a wife, she was also a person in her own right. Someone who had her own wants and needs, her own ambitions and dreams.

Dr Vincent resumed, 'I am going to work with your mind, your anxieties, to help lift some of the pain. I will be able to find the exact location of what is causing all your discomfort.'

Slowly, he eased to his feet and walked to another part of the room where he retrieved a small pamphlet, which he passed to her. Marcia felt a crushing disappointment when she read the fees for treatments. 'I can't afford this. I don't have this kind of money.'

Gently, he tugged the pricing list from her hands, placed it inside his pocket and then took her hands in his, easing her up. His touch, gentle voice and glowing eyes radiated confidence, wisdom and serenity. 'I have already made a commitment to help you. I won't allow the love of money to get in the way.'

'But how am I going to pay?'

His hand waved in the air as if dismissing her words. 'Don't worry about any of that. We'll come to some other type of arrangement.'

Marcia wasn't someone who liked being indebted to others . . . still, she couldn't let her principles stand in the way of getting treatment. Already she was starting to feel better. After he organised her first session and he walked with her back to the main door, Marcia queried, 'I thought there would be more people here.' *And the boy in the hospital car park, where was the boy?*

'You will meet the other women in time.'

Women? Did Ocean Haven only cater to women?

◆ ◆ ◆

Only when the door opened did Marcia realise that the darkening evening light was drawing in. The beam of light from the lighthouse passed over her. She needed to get home quickly before Saul did. Marcia was so busy listening to Dr Vincent's soothing voice as he accompanied her towards the pathway that led to the road that she took little notice of them passing the shack-like outbuilding and walking on to a grassy area filled with large trees. The remnants of any daylight faded, cocooning her and the doctor in a grey dark. A strange prickling sensation crawled along Marcia's spine one vertebra at a time. Something was here, Marcia sensed it. Her eyes darted about, she found nothing. But she could feel them, the heat of eyes. Watching her.

She let out a shriek when something fell from one of the trees. Marcia's scared gaze flew upwards. She stumbled closer to

Dr Vincent, covering her mouth in shock at what she saw. In the trees sat a group of seven women. They sat on separate branches, all wearing the same type of long, orange-coloured gowns. All the women's gazes were fixed on her. Marcia was incapable of speech.

Dr Vincent clucked his tongue when he picked up what had fallen in Marcia's path. It was a small purse.

One of the women called out, 'Terribly sorry, Dr Vincent. I hope it didn't hit your visitor.'

Looking up, he pressed his finger to his lips. 'Shush, Buttercup. Fruit doesn't talk, now, does it?'

Buttercup's face fell. 'But I thought you said it did.'

Vincent nodded. 'It does, but not with words. Fruit doesn't use words.'

Buttercup nodded vigorously. 'Of course.'

He knew what Marcia was thinking and sought to reassure her. 'Let me explain. We humans are part of nature. That's why here at Ocean Haven we use natural names – Buttercup, Fuchsia, Raspberry, Fig and so on – rather than the given names we were lumbered with as children. Also it provides each woman with much-needed anonymity. Nature bears fruit, so we bear fruit here too. The medical profession prefers to ignore nature while we at Ocean Haven embrace it. We don't heal with poisonous drugs here. We heal with trust.'

After Dr Vincent had waved her off. Marcia took the path back to the road. A few minutes later she stopped, turned and took one last lingering look up at the trees.

CHAPTER 15

I feel slightly off-kilter as I walk into work, like a drunk instead of someone whose only liquid pleasure is homemade ginger beer. And very tired too. It's my tummy that's been playing up all night, so much so I hardly slept. I've put on my lipstick, Mummy's lipstick, way too thickly, making it over bright to deflect how crap the rest of my face looks.

'Gabrielle.'

As soon as I hear Greg call my name I know I'm in trouble. Trouble has become my middle name since I found out about my mother's name on the documents for Ocean Haven. I fill my lungs with air and paste on a congealed smile, before turning to face him. Greg peers down at me from his lofty height, beneath those too bushy eyebrows of his.

'I need to speak with you. Let's go to my office.'

So this is what the condemned felt like walking to the firing line. Inside his office he gets into it straight away, not even bothering to take a chair. 'Can you explain why you've been searching the land registry on the computer system?'

The blood drains from my face, leaving my skin cold. I scrabble around to find an answer. 'I needed to find out more about Ocean Haven, the house at the centre of the property dispute.'

Annoyance puffs his cheeks in and out, like a pair of angry bellows. 'Your instructions were to give me a summary of the dispute, so that this firm can, one way or the other, wash its hands of the thing.' He pulls in his chest. 'I made it clear that there's a limited window for you to work in. There are a million and one other projects I need you to be working on.'

'I'm sorry.' What else can I say to the guy? Plus, I need to keep him sweet so that I can continue to investigate.

'And that's why,' he continues as if I haven't apologised, 'I am issuing you with a warning—'

'What?' I'm stunned. Breathless with it.

He leans towards me. 'Do you know how many lawyers are out of work at present due to cutbacks in legal aid funding, which means there's a queue of them wanting jobs. *Your* job.'

That is my cue to leave and I take it, although I hesitate for a few seconds near the open door. Maybe if I tell him what I'm doing he'll be sympathetic and give me the time to do what I need. I see the reflection of the expression on his face, the set of his body in the window that leads to the main office. This is not a man who does sympathy. I'm going to need to be more careful. I pull out the folder for Ocean Haven. Take out the estate agent photo of it and look at it.

I run my fingertips over it as I whisper, 'Mummy, what were you doing there?'

My phone rings. It's Craven. He tells me, 'I've identified who assaulted your father.'

◆ ◆ ◆

Craven is waiting for me in the same swanky coffee shop that I met Salina in. He looks out of place, thoroughly uncomfortable in the trendy white minimalism and industrial pipework that is the decor of this place. I suspect he's a more greasy-spoon-cafe type.

I take a seat opposite him. 'Who is it?' I'm eager to know who could have done this to my dad, but there's also the fact that I left the office under the pretext of fetching colleagues' to-go coffees.

He peers at me. 'Are you feeling OK?'

'I'm fine.' Tersely, I brush off his concern. I feel better but I'd give my next month's wages to be able to put my head down.

'Are you—?'

'Tell me who attacked my father.'

He's wearing one of those laser-like stares that the cop training academy must teach as one of the tricks of the trade to solicit a confession. Thankfully he leaves my personal life alone and states, 'For the record, let's be clear that the only reason I'm speaking to you is because your father's in hospital—'

'Yeah, I get it.' This police officer, I was finding out, is a real stickler for playing it by the book.

'We got lucky when another security camera in the vicinity of your father's attack gave us another angle on the attacker. We tracked his phone from the scene of the attack to the station and then back to London. Our suspect is a stockjobber—'

'A what?'

'It's a bit like a stockbroker—'

'Why didn't you say that?' Eyeroll.

He compresses his lips. 'If you'd given me a chance, I'd have told you.'

What was it with me and Craven? We always seem to get on the wrong side of each other, but not in a bad way, more the way of two best friends who have the occasional clash of swords, as besties do. I dismiss my silly thought; there's no way in hell me and this guy would ever be buddies.

We both take a breath before he starts up again. 'He's a very wealthy man who lives in London. Can you think of a connection your father would have with someone like that?'

Scowling, I think and come up blank. 'I haven't exactly been in my dad's life recently, nevertheless, I can say with my hand on my heart that his friends would not include a rich city man from London.'

'Maybe your father had made investments and this man did them on his behalf.'

'Investments? Dad? I can't see that somehow.'

'Maybe something to do with Ocean Haven.'

That throws me. I stare at him deeply. 'Ocean Haven? How do you know about that?'

He sighs. 'I'm a cop. My job is to detect, and part of this investigation threw up that you've been asking plenty of questions about Ocean Haven. It's my job to look at all angles.'

It suddenly occurs to me that I have access to a police officer who might be able to help me.

'What can you tell me about Ocean Haven? Some type of tragedy happened there, years ago. Do you know anything about it?'

Craven raises his cup and drains the dregs of his coffee. 'It sounds like whatever it was happened long before my time joining the force. And I can't say that I've heard any rumours about it at the station.'

'Would you tell me if you had?'

He lifts his lips in a lopsided smile. 'Probably not.' He pulls out a photo and places it in front of me. 'Have you ever seen this man before?'

'Is this the man who assaulted Dad?'

After his nod I peer at the photo carefully. The man's black, young and very attractive, sporting a fashionable hair style: shaved on the sides with a pop of a ponytail of small dreads in the middle of his head. There's something about him that seems familiar . . . I can't think what it is. Why would I know this person?

'I thought you said the attacker was white,' I say with an accusatory tone he won't understand. Because of what he previously assured me, I'd assumed the attacker was Luke. What an idiot I am!

Craven answers, 'That's what we'd originally assumed from the witness statement. But the other image showed that he wasn't. When we tracked him to Paddington Station he'd taken his cap off and gave us a clear view of his face.' The cop looks at me speculatively. 'You look like you recognise him.'

I push the photo back across the table as I straighten up. 'No. Can't say I've ever seen him before.' I'm not sure why I'm hiding the truth from Craven. Maybe I want to give myself time to delve deep, to see if I can figure out where I know him from before telling the cop.

Craven holds my gaze. 'He was connected to a murder years ago.'

Shock clouds my face. 'This man's a murderer?'

'I didn't say that. At one time in his past he was questioned about a murder. The information that was passed on to me didn't say what the murder case was.'

I dislike my dad with a passion, however, the thought that he was beaten down in the street by someone connected to a murder leaves me feeling so cold.

Something occurs to me. 'Why haven't you mentioned what his name is?'

'At this stage of the investigation that's confidential information.' As if to underscore his decision he places the photo back in his pocket. 'I need to interview him and it may well prove that we have the wrong man, so giving out his personal details would go against regulations.'

This leaves me frustrated, but I don't have time to feel defeated. I need to think of a way through this. For the first time I admit something that's been gnawing away in my brain. What if there's a connection between Dad's attack and Mummy's name on the paperwork for Ocean Haven?

◆ ◆ ◆

Urgently, I pull out my phone as soon as Craven leaves. I only have a small window of time to do what I'm going to do next.

The line connects. 'Tinfields Police Station,' says a polite voice. 'How may I assist you?'

'It's Detective Inspector Morse here from Hampstead division in London,' I lie. I hate lying but what other choice do I have? 'May I speak with Detective Craven?'

'I'll put you through to the admin team for his section.'

Click. Click. Then a super-efficient male says, 'Detective Inspector Morse, I'm sorry but Detective Craven is currently out doing enquiries.'

Just as I knew he would be. So I need to get this done before he either connects with the police station or returns there. 'Craven's been liaising with me about an assault on a Mr Saul Lewis. I received a text message from Craven relaying that he has located a suspect who happens to live on my patch.' I harden my voice to my best cop in charge tone. 'I need the suspect's address and name.'

Silence. Holding my breath, I wait. Then, 'Who did you say you were again?'

'Is that how you address a superior officer? We're at a very difficult crossroads with our interpersonal relationships and partnership with the public and I wouldn't want to have to be the one who contacts your divisional commander to inform them about how you're answering the phone.' In a stage whisper I add, with sniffy indignation, 'Who am I indeed!'

That gets the ball rolling. 'I have the address here.' Quickly I write it down. 'And the name . . . Oh, bother.'

'Is there a problem?' I say.

'The computers have been playing up all morning and now our IT system has gone totally down. I'll leave a message for Detective Craven to give you a call when he gets in.'

'No need for that, I'll contact him directly.' I cut the call.

I might not have a name but I have an address.

CHAPTER 16

Stunning. That's my first assessment of the address I obtained under false pretences. The second is that it reeks of money. Even from where I sit, parked on the opposite side of the road, I can smell it. It looks squarely on to one of London's most well-known green spaces, Hyde Park. It reminds me of a gleaming white-iced Victorian wedding cake with floors, cake after cake stacked on top of each other. It's six storeys with a flat roof terrace that's no doubt a picture-perfect image of slick urban outdoor living. To afford an address here someone needs a heavy-duty bank account. Why would someone like this have anything to do with my father? Why is the man's face in the photo so familiar?

I get my chance to answer that question when the front door unexpectedly opens, revealing a man. With no-nonsense determination I get out of the car and briskly head over. He lifts his head as I reach him. I see his face and stumble back in shock.

'Karl,' I stammer.

My brother looks back at me without saying a word.

◆ ◆ ◆

My life is like a suitcase that has too many things packed in it and won't close. My job, my health and my housing. My mother's house. And now this. Karl, my brother, the youngest of Marcia Lewis's children. He looks so different. No wonder I had a sense of something when I examined the photo Craven showed me but nevertheless found it hard to recognise him. Gone is the chubbiness, replaced by a muscular and gym-trained body, while the boy who used to be scruffy is now a svelte, well-dressed and manicured young man about town. Even though he's wearing stonewashed jeans, a T-shirt and trainers, you feel he could walk into a black-tie event without any questions being asked. People in the family were forever gushing that he was the spitting image of one of my mum's uncles, but now he has our father's youthful good looks etched into a tight, lean face. His hair is shaved at the sides and tied in small dreads on the top.

Karl folds his arms in the doorway as if blocking my way. 'Hello there, sis. What can I do for you?'

I'm tongue-tied, not sure what to say. What do you say to a brother you haven't seen for twenty years? Karl was what the Tinfields community called a 'bad egg'. A teenager who went off the rails. I saw some of his behaviour, but not the worst of it; by then I was long gone. I was studying law at a university in the north of England and then doing my training. In her letters Salina kept me informed of his career of crime, in fact she was very careful to do so. Every visit from the police, every court case, every sentence she relayed back. I'd felt so guilty not being there to support Karl or Salina. I remember after one of her letters I bought a coach ticket, determined to go back home for a visit. However, when I saw the coach, I couldn't breathe straight; the thought of going back to that house crippled me. The last I heard, Karl was locked up in a place where they stick young bad boys. He didn't last long on the outside when he was released, soon finding himself back behind bars again. Then Salina never heard from him. I'd assumed he'd become what they called a 'repeat offender', his chosen career one of crime, a rocky road to adult prison. It looks like I was totally wrong.

'What do you want?' His question is hard.

I don't think of the words. Perhaps it's my heart saying, 'To see my brother.'

Before he can respond a door opens behind him revealing a skinny blonde with a pale complexion standing on the bottom step, which must lead to the apartment they live in above. She bounces off the step and hovers by his shoulder, wearing a dressing gown and oozing glamour. She looks me over and, with an arched brow at Karl, asks, 'Who's this?' Her question sounds like an accusation.

'My sister.' He looks at this beauty and adds by way of explanation, 'Come on, if I was fooling around, it wouldn't be with a woman like this. Be reasonable.'

He's managed to insult the pair of us, but she doesn't take offence. Perhaps she expects him to fool around. 'Your sister? I didn't know you had a sister.'

'I've got two actually: Salina and Gabby. This one's Gabby.' He adds in a desolate undertone, 'And a mother, but she's gone now.'

Our gazes catch, for an instant both of us lost in the hell of the past.

'Come in, Gabby.' The other woman's voice slices through our brother–sister connection. Karl looks away. I've lost him again. His lady friend continues to chat away. 'I'll make some coffee. I'm Jasmin.'

I follow Karl and his girlfriend into an apartment that's been stripped of its busy Victorian past and replaced with a contemporary shell of gleaming floors, white walls and hardly any furniture. They take me up to the roof terrace, where all of London appears to be laid bare in the distance. Jasmin parks me on a chair and leaves a box of delicious chocolates with me. Karl takes the chair opposite with bad grace, while Jasmin fetches coffee. The breeze up here is soft, the light almost Mediterranean. My brother is living the high life, but you wouldn't know it from his closed-off expression.

He breaks the awkward silence. 'I suppose it was that cop Craven who tipped you off where I live?'

It's almost a relief to be overcome with surprise. 'Craven's been here?'

'A few days ago.'

Really? My surprise deepens because hadn't Craven said that he was planning to see the suspect? At no stage did he mention he'd already interviewed him. Then again, maybe I'm wrong.

I ask, 'Did you attack Dad, Karl?'

He gets up, turns his back on me and moves towards the edge of the terrace, looking out at London. His T-shirt bellows with the breeze. He answers, remaining looking away from me. 'Now why would I want to lick our father down. I mean, he's been the great-est dad ever. Always there when we wanted to talk to him. Full of cuddles and hugs and love for his children.' He twists to face me and I wish he hadn't, because his expression makes me suck in my breath. He looks like someone who would prefer dying to living. His pain is unbearable.

I say, 'I know he's never going to win the father of the year award, but why would you attack him? He's an old man now.'

'I never said I attacked anyone. That's what Detective Craven tried to do, get me to confess to a crime I never committed. But, hey, that wouldn't be the first time, now, would it? A man never forgets being accused of murder when they were eleven years old.'

Now I understand why Craven said that the suspect had once been associated with a murder. I should've guessed that it was Karl he was referring to. All those years ago he had been questioned by the police about the murder on our street when we were children. Mum had defended him to the hilt and in the end the police had let it go, but it must have remained on his record, especially when he started to really get into trouble with the law.

Karl shrugs, his dreads shifting as the wind picks up speed, his features a picture of self-satisfaction. 'As long as the old man won't ID me, your cop can't do anything. And that low life won't ID me, you can be sure of that. That means I don't have to confess to anything.'

'What did Dad do? You wouldn't have attacked him for no reason.'

He turns back away from me. 'Like I said, I never did a thing. I'm just part of one big happy family.'

I get up and move to stand beside him, not too close though, careful not to invade his space.

'Did you know Mummy was chair of a trust of a big house on the coast in Tinfields shortly before she died?'

The barely suppressed violence that's hung around my brother like an aura since I arrived explodes in an orgy of hate, like blood from a wound. He faces me. 'What are you doing here, Gabby? Why are you butting into my life? Why are you trying to mind my business? I didn't ask you to come here or invite you in.' His handsome face contorts with fury into ghoulish ugliness. He carries on in that near-dead tone, 'Get out. Don't come back! Ever!'

His fury leaves me hurting, and feeling like I've been ducked in the filth of the gutter.

There's a sound of frantic running from within the apartment and Jasmin appears. 'What's going on?' Her gaze skids between me and Karl. 'Honey, what's wrong? Why are you shouting at your sister?'

I don't hear her. All I see is my baby brother. 'What have I done to deserve this hatred?'

He appears exhausted by the storm of his own outburst, his voice is quiet now, his skin almost ashen. 'It was a mistake for you to come here. Please don't do it again.'

The fear and shock on Jasmin's face suggest she's not used to this kind of behaviour. 'Karl, stop it!'

He ignores her. 'You're not welcome here.'

CHAPTER 17

TWENTY-FIVE YEARS AGO

MARCIA

Marcia heard the gut-wrenching scream while she was getting the children's lunch boxes ready for school. The terror of the sound disrupted the beauty of her day because for once Marcia wasn't feeling any pain. It'd been like this for the last week and a half, not exactly since she'd been to Ocean Haven, but more or less. She couldn't help thinking that it was ever since Vincent Fortune had 'laid' his hands on her. It reminded Marcia of all the times her grandmother would take her to church as a child and suddenly a member of the congregation would leap to their feet, eyes wild and glazed, their body gyrating in jerky movements. Her grandmother had told her it was called being 'in the spirit' – the spirit of the Lord had entered that person and was doing its work. Marcia and the whole church would go quiet as they watched as another member of the congregation held the person from behind, while the pastor laid his hands on them, feverishly praying aloud until the person collapsed. Had Dr Vincent's hands expelled the pain from her body? It was less than a week until her first treatment at Ocean Haven and she couldn't wait.

The scream was high and piercing. It sounded like it was coming from outside, so Marcia urgently peered out of the kitchen window. The terrifying sound seemed so wrong here, because this was a very quiet and friendly street where everyone knew each other, which meant that something was badly wrong. Marcia caught a movement in her next-door neighbour's house. Jenny and Fred. Urgently she left her house and banged with her fist against the door. Jenny opened it and Marcia was shocked at her neighbour. She gasped at the blood staining the front of Jenny's clothes. Her neighbour was swaying, the grip on the door appearing to be the only thing holding her up.

'Jenny, what's happened?' Marcia spoke with a calm and control she didn't feel. She was so afraid of what was going on here.

Jenny's eyes were large, staring wildly at her, her lips frantically moving, but no words coming out. She looked like she was on the point of collapse. Gently, Marcia took her by the arm and guided her back inside. Hell, Jenny was shaking so badly. Marcia didn't want to go further into the house until she understood what had happened here.

She asked, 'Are you hurt?'

Jenny rapidly shook her head. Finally, she spoke, her voice croaking and breaking with emotion. 'It's Fred.' Her trembling finger pointed to a downstairs room that her husband had turned into his work space. Fred had what Marcia called magic hands – a skilled craftsman who could make and mend so many things.

After smoothing a reassuring hand down Jenny's arm, Marcia carefully walked towards the room. Her heart was racing because she didn't know what she would find. Maybe Fred had had a heart attack. No, that wouldn't explain the blood on his wife. With two fingers Marcia inched the door open. A hand flew to her mouth to cover and swallow her gasp. Fred lay on the floor, his limbs at a strange angle, the front of his shirt covered in blood that had also leaked, sticky and rich red, on to the floor. And his eyes, which had once been so lively and happy, stared back at her, open and lifeless.

The last time she'd seen Fred, Marcia had given him a huge hug and kiss on the cheek, which was her silent way of thanking him for spending time with Karl. Fred had made her son so happy. The last time she had seen Fred with Karl, the older man had told her son to keep their secret. At the time Marcia had not paid much attention to what her neighbour and son meant by their secret. Now she worried. What secret did Fred not want Karl to tell anyone?

Marcia left to call the police.

'Oh God! Oh God!' A grief-stricken Jenny mumbled at Marcia's back door. Her face was drawn and dirty with lines of tears. 'How could someone stab my beautiful Fred?'

The children gasped as Marcia sat her neighbour down at the kitchen table and made a very strong cup of tea. It had been at least five hours since the incident, and the children were back from school. The street was still filled with police. Things like this didn't usually happen on their street, but times were changing.

Marcia hugged her neighbour tight and asked, 'What did the police say?'

'They think it was a burglary gone wrong.' Her voice was dead. 'They stole his coin collection.'

'Coin collection?' Marcia frowns.

'Fred had the most amazing coin collection. He'd been collecting since he was a child with his dad. He had some very valuable coins.' Her brows dip. 'The police said it was probably drug addicts looking to steal stuff for a quick fix. What I don't understand is how they knew it was there.'

'What do you mean?'

Jenny wiped some of her tears back with her fingertips. 'Only me and Fred knew about his collection, and a few of his friends who are collectors as well. And Karl, of course.' Marcia's gaze darted to the doorway, expecting to see her son huddled there with his sisters. She found only a bewildered Gabby and Salina.

Jenny carried on, 'Fred loved your Karl to bits. We could never have little ones of our own and I know how much my Fred longed for a son, so having Karl around was such a joy for him.' Her voice dropped. 'He showed Karl his coins and told him to keep it under his hat. It was their great secret.'

Marcia's heart dropped as a sensation of horrible foreboding seized her. She patted her grieving friend's shoulder, before standing and instructing her girls to make Jenny another cup of tea. Then a stricken Marcia went in search of her son. On the landing upstairs it wasn't her son she found but Saul. She'd last seen him in the garden, brewing and fermenting bottles of his ginger beer in his shed.

His gaze drilled hotly through her as it so often did. 'Whoever did this needs stringing up.'

For once Marcia was in agreement with her husband. 'Have you seen Karl?'

Disdain pulled down the corner of Saul's mouth at the mention of his son's name. 'That boy's been a disappointment since the day I held him in my arms after you pushed him from your womb.'

Anger rose to the surface inside Marcia. Usually she'd let Saul's nasty comments fly over her head, but not today. Today, she was going to defend her baby boy until the death. 'You should be ashamed that our son had to find a proper father next door.'

Saul moved menacingly into her space. 'You need to mind yourself about what's coming out of your mouth.'

'Or what, Saul?' she dared him. 'You going to take your watch out and time how long it takes me to wash your clothes?'

Three months into their marriage: that was when Marcia realised that she might have made a mistake in marrying Saul Lewis. She'd been bent over the bath, handwashing his work shirts and underwear, when he'd approached her with a strange look on his face.

'You've been doing that for too long.' He'd taken off his watch. Checked the time and told her, 'Three minutes for the washing to all be done.'

'What?' she'd stammered.

His voice rose. 'Three minutes, I said.'

'Never make your husband feel small inside his own home,' were the words of advice given to her by her grandmother for when she got married. And Marcia did her best to make Saul feel like he was king of the castle. Marcia hadn't understood what was happening, but she'd tried her best to get the washing done, her pulse racing like crazy. Somehow she'd done it. But he wasn't finished with her. He brought in his dirty railway worker's uniform from his work bag and dumped it in the dirty water.

'Five minutes.'

By now Marcia was so scared, she was losing her grip on the material, water splashing everywhere. Five minutes were up far too soon and she wasn't finished. Marcia had flung her arms protectively over her head. He'd ripped his jacket from her clutching fingers and slapped it violently against the bathroom tiles. Then he'd behaved like a maniac, grabbing wet clothes with violence, his breathing snorting and heavy, chucking and smacking clothes everywhere, splashing Marcia with water. By the end the bathroom looked like a tornado had been through it. Without a word Saul had left. Marcia had sunk slowly to the floor, disbelieving what had happened. Where had the wonderful man gone who would buy her those soft-centred orange chocolates she loved?

That had set up a pattern in their marriage. He'd never hit her, he didn't have to, because the terror of what he might do at the end of the countdown was enough. That first time, Marcia had been determined to leave him, all packed and ready to go, when the doctor had told her that she was two months pregnant. A woman didn't leave her husband when she was carrying his child. So Marcia had stayed, hoping that things would get better. They never did.

Marcia came back to the present. She stared her husband down and warned, 'Remember this, Saul Lewis, there aren't many women out there who will be prepared to wash your underpants.'

With that she shoved past him, looking for her son. She found him in his small room. He held his penknife, which had been a gift from Fred. Their neighbour had recognised in Marcia's son a child similar to the one he'd been. He and Karl liked to use their hands, which explained why Karl was so withdrawn and frustrated at school – his teachers didn't give him activities where he could make and construct things. Marcia should have guessed this, because Karl was forever carving his name around the house, which drove Saul mad. And that's what he was doing now, carving his name into his bedpost. With his knife.

He looked up at her, his gaze uncertain. 'Is it true? Fred's dead?'

Marcia hurt so bad for him, but she'd vowed to always tell her children the truth. 'The angels will look after him.' She sat next to him. 'Did you know about Fred's coin collection? Was that your secret?'

He didn't answer her. Marcia grabbed his chin and turned him to her. 'This is serious, Karl. Did you take Fred's coin collection?' Marcia's breath froze in her throat with fear. What would she do if her beautiful baby boy said yes?

'No.' Huge tears whelmed up in his eyes. 'I never did.'

Marcia grabbed her weeping child in her arms and held him tight. Downstairs she could hear her husband's voice all sweet and charming for their neighbour.

◆ ◆ ◆

Two days later a knock brought the police to Marcia and Saul Lewis's front door. 'We need to talk to your son about the crime that was committed next door.'

CHAPTER 18

I look up at the house. My mother's house. But this is different from the other times I've been here because I'm standing around the back. I know there's a connection between this house and Karl because he got mad, wanting me gone when I mentioned Mummy and this house. The journey back from London was a blur, the lights of the passing traffic eventually blending into one continuous stream of light that threatened to blind me. In the end I pulled over and dropped my head against the steering wheel. I nearly cried, nearly. My heart tumbles over and over from anguish that my little brother turned on me in such a fashion.

I'll admit I feel anger and resentment too. It was me who took on our mother's role when she died and became what was effectively her replacement. It was me who made sure to get Karl up and ready for school in the morning. It was me who cooked the food that lay in front of him on the table every day. It was me who had to deal with the cops when they brought him and shame to our front door. It was me, me, me! So why does he hate me so much? No, it's *they*, why do they hate me so much? Because Salina looks like she's had a belly-load of me too. I took care of them, from afar, admittedly, when I left, but I sent money, letters; they knew I cared.

Pins and needles rake over my fingers as I block out the hate and turn back to the house. Back to seeing if this building is hiding what Karl is trying to hide from me. The dark smothers it. My gaze roams around the back, trying to find anything unusual, out of place. I find nothing, so I head for the window that I know will be open because I left it open when Luke brought me here. Of course he never saw me do it. I grasp the edge and heave it up; it proves to be heavier than I thought. One leg and then the other over the windowsill and I'm in.

Inside the darkness is thick, deep, almost choking. I shiver with the freezing cold in here. The taste of the salt from the sea is strong on my tongue. I pull out my phone and shine the light and move it around. Suddenly I realise it's just me in here. Alone. Fear kicks up my heartbeat, sweat beads along my hairline. This house is vast, full of rooms, so how on earth am I going to find anything that connects to Karl here? I suspect that I'm wasting my time, nevertheless I need to at least try.

I check the time on my phone. Thirty minutes, that's how long I will give myself and then I'm gone. Start with what you know, isn't that the saying, and that's what I do: head for the attic where I found the orange clothing. The intense shining light turns the green patches of mould on the wall of the stairs into something liquid, slimy and gives it a 3D quality that makes it look like it's going to jump off the wall and wrap around my throat. The smell of damp and decay gets stronger the closer I get to the attic.

I baulk at the entrance. The door is open, just as I left it, so it should be easy to walk up, so what's holding me back? It's the feel of the house today, the way it seems so alive as if it's waiting to pounce on me, and if I go up the tight, narrow, broken stairs before me I may never come back. The strange coldness lurking on the staircase touches me from here. Gathering my courage I move forward. Climb the steps. The chill hovers over my skin and then slowly sinks into my pores to my bones. I search the room where I found the orange dresses, but it's in vain; there's nothing that connects my brother to this house.

'Mum, can you help me?' I plead loudly.

Out of the frosty dark she appears. She's wearing a peaceful smile and long orange gown.

'You were always the inquisitive one, the one with her nose stuck in a book. What are you looking for this time?'

'Karl. I'm looking for Karl.'

Mummy doesn't answer me, instead she turns her back and moves towards the stairs. I follow her like I always do, suck up every moment I can get with her. I don't have to share her with anyone. In this abandoned house, suddenly I don't feel like an outsider anymore. We roam the house together, me looking and searching while she stands back. We find nothing. Frustrated I turn to her and plead, 'Mummy, what were you doing here?'

She looks at me, her gentle smile half slipping. She inhales deeply from her nose. 'The sea reminds me of being back home in Trinidad. Running along Maracas Beach, the hot sand running through my toes. I didn't have a care in the world back then.'

My neck shifts to the side, studying her. 'Was that the problem? Life became too hard in England? With bringing up a family? Did this house somehow help you?'

My eyes hurt because I'm trying not to blink too much, because if I blink too long, when my eyes open I know she'll be gone.

She turns her face towards the large window, towards the sea. For a time she doesn't speak. Then she turns back; the starkness of her features alarms me. I stumble back. She tells me, 'I hurt bad. So bad. For a time it was only here I could breathe. They helped me find my life again.'

'They? Who do you mean?'

I blink too long. My eyes bolt open. She's gone. I don't call her because I know Mummy won't be coming back. I slump, physically and emotionally exhausted, back near the door; my fingertips run and cling to the wooden panel between the door and the wall. I feel something, the shape of something carved in the wood beneath my finger. I freeze. Then push off the wall, crouch down and shine my torch on to it. It's letters crudely carved into the wood. A name.

Karl.

CHAPTER 19

'You look bloody terrible,' my sister announces in her usual 'all's cool 'n' great on planet Salina' manner.

I'm sitting on a rock on the beach that my mother's house looks down on. It's a relief when Salina finally strides along the beach towards me. Even though she's hurried to find me, she's remembered to put on the type of footwear that will keep her feet dry. Some might put that down to one of her top ten beauty tips for a fun day at the beach, but what so many miss about my sister is that she's practical, even in an emergency. I kinda went to pieces when Mum died, but Salina was right alongside Dad, ensuring the funeral arrangements were made and all in order.

My resentment towards her flares, and, I admit, our childhood rivalry still occasionally rears its nasty head. 'So sorry we can't all look like we're gracing the cover of *Vogue* twenty-four seven.'

She doesn't blast back at me with two barrels, but does something that makes me catch my breath: she kisses my cheek and folds me in her arms. Eyes squeezing tight, I sink into her and her rich, floral perfume. It hits me that since I've come back to Tinfields I haven't had any human contact – not a touch, a caress – from anyone, including my family. Certainly not Salina. I hold on tight as if I don't want to ever let go. Since I broke up with Keith last year I've been so alone.

When Salina releases me and sets herself down on the rock, she notices something. 'Your hands are shaking.' She takes them in hers. 'And they're frozen.' Her fingertips touch my forehead. 'You're cold but you're sweating. How long have you been like this? Have you been to the doctor?'

This sickness within me comes and goes. I don't want to talk about it, especially to her; I can imagine her stupefied face if I confess my terror of dying at forty, like our mother did.

I brush her concern off with, 'I found out who attacked Dad. I saw him in London.'

'I hope you gave him a medal.'

'It was Karl.'

Her sharp intake of breath disturbs the air, but she says nothing, so I continue, 'He looks so different, so handsome. And the house he lives in blew my mind.' My voice drops low with emotion. 'I forgot to tell him how proud I am of him.'

Salina huffs. 'I should've figured out it was him who battered the old man. I'm glad to hear one of us finally had the nuts to knock him on his arse.'

Shock turns me to her. 'That's a horrible thing to say—'

'I never took you for a liar, big sis,' she blasts.

Something odd occurs to me. 'You're not surprised that I found Karl. What's going on, Salina?'

Salina takes a deep breath as she swings her leg over the rock, fully facing me. 'OK, it's confession time; there's something I should have told you. I know you think there isn't a shred of goodness in Luke's heart, that he's the prototype for capitalist man, but you're wrong.' Her finger plays with the fringe on her designer bag. 'He doesn't talk much about his background, but I know he lost his mum when he was young. So every now and again he does what he calls giving back to the community. When I first met him he was mentoring young offenders locked up for this and that. And one of them was Karl. Luke dusted him off, brushed him down and pushed him out into the wide world.'

That certainly puts a different spin on Luke, but then again, he helped me with the house by using a favour to get the keys. Strange, because I always took him as a man who would blow his own trumpet. Whatever happened with his mother must have been deeply traumatic.

'Why didn't you tell me you knew where Karl was all this time?' I'm left feeling like the outsider again, the one stuck forever looking through the window.

Salina scoffs, eyes widening. 'It's not as if you were here to tell.' Abruptly, her palm comes up. 'Let's not go down that path again. Did brother dearest tell you why he bashed Dad?'

I shake my head, adding, 'There's something going on, because as soon as I mentioned Mum's house he hit the roof. He was almost out of control, even his girlfriend was shocked.'

Salina looks up. 'Is that the house?'

Of course, she's never seen it before. She stands up to get a better look and whistles. 'That's a big piece of real estate. How on this green earth can Mum have been involved with it? Being the chair of this trust sorta meant she owned it, right?' Pensively, she gazes down at me. 'Do you think she had a rich lover?'

That had crossed my mind. 'No. That wasn't Mum's style—'

'Nor was having a secret house . . . apparently.'

I stand next to her and for a time we're lost in the facade and the growing shadows playing across Ocean Haven's brickwork. The place where parts of my family are disappearing into shade and shadows.

'I found Karl's name there,' I tell her.

I get my sister's full attention. 'What?'

'It's carved near a door.'

This is where someone would say that this could be a different Karl. However, Salina doesn't, because she remembers our childhood, remembers how Karl would carve his name into places he shouldn't.

'He carried that penknife with him everywhere,' I quietly add.

I know what she's thinking, she knows what I'm thinking; about Fred, our childhood neighbour stabbed to death and Karl being questioned by the cops.

Salina says, 'If you'll still have me, can I help you find out how Mum's connected to the house?'

My answer is a grateful embrace.

Salina whispers, 'It feels good to be walking side by side again. Just the two sisters, Gabby and Salina, together.'

My phone rings. It's a nurse from the hospital. 'It's your father . . .'

◆   ◆   ◆

Salina hovers by the edge of the bed, which Dad notices. 'It took you long enough to show your face. Been here days, I have, and not so much as a "howdy do" call on the phone from you,' he viciously snarls. His daughter looks grim, the strain on her face pulling her skin. 'Too busy mixing potions and paints for women to tart themselves up as harlots.'

He takes out his watch and Salina's breathing turns noisy and distressed. She's still affected by what he'd do to us as kids, whereas I've spent years learning to deal with combating the nasty effects of what I call his watch trick. I move swiftly and take it from him, and with the hot feel of the prints of his fingertips against the metal I shove it inside his pocket. I wish I could shove it somewhere else . . .

'Leave. Her. Alone,' I growl in his ear and then smartly step away to address the nurse. 'Can you please explain to Dad why he can't discharge himself.' That's why the hospital had contacted me, because Dad has decided he's had enough of his time here.

'We've advised that he shouldn't. We've told him that he needs a few more days of bed rest here, and then the doctor will assess whether he's fit enough to go home.'

'I'm an old man who just wants to be inside his own four walls.' He's all sugary sweetness to the nurse. Typical! 'I miss sitting in my armchair and watching the football.'

'I'll get him home.' It's Salina who makes the decision. 'I've already called Luke, who's on his way, and we'll drive Dad home.'

The nurse mulls this over, then says, 'This isn't an ideal situation, but we can't insist that a patient stay. So you'll be staying with your father—'

'No,' my sister forcefully cuts in. 'We'll see him to his door and I'll get his neighbour to look in on him.'

The nurse is very disapproving, but the only comment she makes is, 'Let me show you his medication and when he needs to take it.'

It's just me and Dad left when they go off. We eye each other. He slumps down on the edge of the bed looking like the old, weathered man he is. I almost feel sorry for him. Almost.

He casts his gaze over me. 'You were always my favourite.' I let him speak. 'So proud I was of my girl, Gabrielle, when you became a lawyer. My daughter is the fanciest thing to come out of Tinfields.'

I visualise him in the pub, bragging about me to his friends over a pint, buying them all a round to celebrate. I bet he didn't tell them how, after Mummy was gone, he made me wash clothes when I got back from school until it was night. How he'd take out that bloody watch as I was cooking the dinner; I burned myself enough times trying to beat the clock. The second boyfriend I ever had, who was a bit of a hippy, had a peace 'n' love saying for every day of the week, most of which I'd brush off, except for one that stuck: *Our biggest enemy is our past, because we allow it to keep destroying us right to the doorway of our grave.* Every time I'm with my dad I feel like I'm tottering on the edge of my resting place.

I move over to him. 'Why didn't you tell me that it was Karl who attacked you?'

'Karl?' That airy-fairy fake tone of his doesn't fool me.

'Cut it out, Dad. I saw him in the security footage.'

His head recoils slightly like a tortoise, his voice becomes furtive. 'I don't know what you're talking about.'

'Karl has changed a lot, but a father would never forget the face of his son.'

After his quick eyes scan my face to see if there's any chance that he can bully me out of the truth, he twists his mouth. 'That boy of mine is a bum. He'll pay for attacking his own father one way or another, either in this life or the next.'

'Did he beat you because of something to do with the house Mummy owned?'

Lightning rage pushes him to his feet, his eyes are smouldering. 'That bloody house you keep talking about. I've told you I know nothing about it.'

I won't leave it alone. 'Then why are you getting so upset about it?'

Suddenly a racking cough doubles his body over, his skeletal fingers digging into the blanket for dear life. The distressed calls of some of the other patients ring around us.

'You all right there, young Saul?'

'Get him a glass of water.'

'Someone get the nurse.'

The nurse beats me to it and is back with Salina following behind. She sends me a cross look, before attending to Dad.

Just then a furious Detective Craven appears on the ward. He stalks over to me. 'You either speak to me now or I take you down the station.'

I'm puzzled. 'What's the matter? This isn't exactly a convenient time.'

He pulls out his handcuffs and dangles them in the air. 'Make it convenient.'

In the corridor he enlightens me. 'Do you know what the penalty is for impersonating a police officer?'

Ah that! 'I'm sorry. The only excuse I have is that I wanted to – needed to – find out who had assaulted my father.' I pull in a steady stream of air to calm my nerves. 'It was a shock to find out it was my own brother.'

Craven brushes his fingers through his hair. 'You interfered with my investigation. I told you I needed to interview him first—'

'But that's the strangest thing,' I butt in. 'Karl said that you'd already questioned him a number of days before. Why didn't you tell me that at the time?'

He steps back slightly. 'I don't have to explain the ins and the outs of my investigation to you.'

His response makes me sad, I'm not sure why. Maybe I thought we were beginning to understand each other. There's something about Detective Craven that makes me inwardly smile.

'I hadn't seen my brother for years.' My voice is sombre.

Craven's brows come together. 'Do you know why Karl would assault his own father in public?'

'He wouldn't tell me.' Should I tell Craven about my suspicions that it probably concerns Ocean Haven? That I know Karl went there as a child?

Craven makes my decision for me when he leans closer and says, 'I'm still deciding whether to press charges against you.'

And with that he marches off, leaving me alone in the sterile corridor of the ward.

CHAPTER 20

Twenty-Five years ago

Marcia

Marcia tightened her hold on Karl's hand as Ocean Haven's door was opened by one of the women she'd seen sitting in the tree the last time she was here. She'd been the one who'd dropped the purse from the tree. The woman was chubby, in her early thirties, with a cheery disposition, and if Marcia recalled correctly, her name was Buttercup.

'Come on in.' She ushered Marcia inside.

Marcia was about to introduce herself, when the other woman raised a warning finger. 'We don't ever, ever use our real names here.' Of course, Dr Vincent had told her that he kept all the women's personal details confidential. Buttercup added, 'Ocean Haven is our world, for us women, where we can grow and find a life without pain.'

Grow and find a life without pain, the words were music to Marcia's ears. All she wanted was the suffering to disappear for good. Since Fred's death the pain had come back with a vengeance. Maybe, if she got lucky, Dr Vincent would lay his hands on her again. Buttercup was still wearing an orange gown, which made Marcia nervous. The gowns left her feeling awkward.

The other woman sensed Marcia's discomfort and sought to ease her concerns. 'This isn't a cult, if that's what you're thinking. We can leave Dr Vincent's care any time we like.' Her stare intensified. 'I come here because he is the only one who is prepared to help me get better.'

Marcia thought back to her treatment at the hospital, where the consultant had more or less told her she was nuts and given her a bottle of antidepressants as if the drug contained a magic spell that would solve all her problems.

'And who's this fine little fellow?' Buttercup peered happily down at Karl.

Marcia's expression became strained as she introduced her son. Since the police had come knocking at her door she had kept her boy close. The horror of the whole incident would remain with her for life. Despite Marcia swearing on her heart that her son knew nothing about Fred's murder, the police still insisted that they needed to speak with him. Sitting close by Karl's side, they had questioned him. She'd give the police this, they hadn't been rough and had gently questioned him about his relationship with Fred, the last time he'd seen him and the coin collection. They'd searched Karl's room and found nothing and verified that Karl's penknife did not match the murder weapon.

When they left, what had worried Marcia the most was that Karl's face had been devoid of emotion, his eyes a blank stare. Then, last week, he'd got into a fight with another boy and been suspended for three days by the school, which had a zero violence policy. The school had also accused him of picking the lock of the cupboard where all the art supplies were kept. Marcia had vehemently defended her child; her son was no thief. He seemed to have slipped back into that silent, sullen world he'd inhabited before Fred had come into his life. Marcia was worried sick about him.

Buttercup respectfully stepped aside when Dr Vincent Fortune appeared. He wore a green bow tie and an open expression that made Marcia feel like all her troubles had gone away. His arms waved wide in a welcoming gesture. 'My dear, it is good to see you back.' His stare fell on Karl. 'And this must be your son.' He cupped Karl's head, continuing, 'Your children are more than welcome here, but' – he paused meaningfully – 'some of the women are here seeking a healing environment because of unresolved issues to do with children.'

Marcia was mortified. 'I'm so sorry, I didn't realise.'

He reassured her, his palm falling from Karl's head. 'Here, you never have to apologise.' He took a step towards her. 'It is clear that you are a wonderful mother. "Mother" is our word for today.'

Her shoulders fell back with pride at his praise. That was what Marcia loved about Dr Vincent, he made her feel good about herself. Until her dying day Marcia would never forget what the consultant had said: '*This state of make-believe is the natural outcome of being a woman.*' But now, finally, Marcia had met a member of the medical profession who did not believe she was delusional.

Dr Vincent said, 'Why don't we leave Karl in the kitchen with some refreshments, while you take part in your first treatment.'

Ocean Haven didn't have a housekeeper, so Marcia settled Karl in the kitchen with a drink, biscuits and his homework. And a stern warning not to leave. Maybe he might meet the boy who had given her the leaflet about Ocean Haven in the hospital entrance. Marcia would like that, if he found a friend here for the day.

Marcia found Buttercup waiting for her outside the kitchen. Buttercup waited for Marcia outside. The other woman's face lit up as she passed Marcia her own orange gown. 'When you've finished changing we will be waiting for you in the healing room.'

Gown on, Marcia walked slowly over to the room where the others waited. She opened the door.

◆ ◆ ◆

Inside, the women wore their long orange gowns and were sitting in a semicircle facing a single bed with a simple white sheet. Dr Vincent stood a few paces away from the foot of the bed. Marcia's nerves kicked in again. She hadn't been expecting all the women to be here for her first treatment. And the bed, why was that here?

'Come, we have a seat all ready for you,' Dr Vincent told her, indicating the chair next to Buttercup. The women's smiles and nods eased her tension.

Once she was seated, Dr Vincent addressed the room. 'We have a new member today and this is her first treatment.' He glanced at the gathered women. 'Who can show our newest member what's the most important part of a woman's body?'

Marcia expected hands to be raised, but that didn't happen; instead an older woman stood and told Marcia, 'My name is Raspberry. The essence of a woman is here.' She laid her hand against her belly and sat down.

Your stomach? Marcia was thoroughly confused but took care not to show it.

Dr Vincent said, 'Yes, your womb.' Ah, thought Marcia. 'Most of you are at an age when your womb is transitioning through a different stage.' He began to pace to emphasise his words, reminding Marcia of the pastor at church. 'Your womb is the beating heartbeat of you. As long as your womb is useful, you as a woman are useful.'

There was an energy to his movements now, a sizzle of electricity. 'Someone tell me when your womb is at the pinnacle of its power?' His body lurched with each word.

One of the women shouted, with plenty of vigour, 'During the birth of a child.'

'Yes,' he called out, the sun's rays coming through the window ringing a halo of light behind him. 'When your womb is ripe and ready to go through birth and give life.'

Inhaling noisily through his nose, he swept his gaze slowly over every woman. 'Each one of you has a womb that is no longer ready, no longer ripe. The ancient Greek word for the uterus is hysteria. Your pain is a symbol of you living in a state of constant hysteria due to the fact that your wombs no longer work.' Dramatically, his fingers waved over his stomach. 'Your core is dead. Once you lose the use of your womb a woman is—'

'Nothing,' they chorused back.

Except for Marcia, who was desperately trying to understand what she was being told. She knew that her womb was important, but this important? Why hadn't anyone ever given her this information? *Because it's shameful to talk about your body*, her inner voice reminded her.

'I can see that our newest member agrees.' Marcia was whipped out of her thoughts to find Dr Vincent's penetrating stare was fixed only on her. She sat up straighter. 'Your first treatment with us today will be to wake your womb up. Remind it of its purpose. Remind you as a woman of *your* purpose.'

Marcia tensed when Buttercup's hand touched her arm. The other woman took her hand in hers. 'Don't be afraid. We are all here to help each other. And remember, whatever you do here will eventually make your pain disappear.' Giggling slightly, she clicked her fingers. 'That's how quickly your pain will go.'

'Thank you, Buttercup.' Marcia could swear she heard barely concealed disapproval in Dr Vincent's voice. She got the impression that Buttercup had her own way of doing things. Marcia started to like her.

The other woman walked her to the bed. Marcia hesitated before lying down. Her body was stiff. The light around her dimmed as all the women gathered around. Dr Vincent inched closer to the foot of the bed. 'Anytime you want us to stop just raise your hand. Remember what I told you when you first came?'

Marcia automatically answered, 'You heal with trust.'

'For the next ten minutes the women will do an ancient ritual to wake up your womb.'

For a few seconds there was a beat of silence. With no warning the women began screaming and shrieking over Marcia. She was so startled that she nearly fell off the bed. *Trust. Trust.* It was that word, which she hung on to like a good-luck charm, that kept Marcia on the bed. The noise was deafening, the wideness of their mouths grotesque and obscene. She could see their fluid tongues, the moving flap at the back of the throat. *Trust. Trust.* Marcia closed her eyes, allowing the thunderous sound to wash over her, into her, searching for her womb. The screeching stopped as abruptly as it had started. The only sound was the erratic rhythm of Marcia's rushing breathing.

'Open your eyes, look at me,' Dr Vincent coaxed. He smiled. 'I can feel the magnetic presence of your womb in the air. It is on fire, ready to prove its worth.'

He moved to stand behind her. 'Give me your hands.' It was awkward, but she managed to do it. When his warm flesh was in hers, he instructed, 'You're going to give birth. Please remind this woman of pain how to do that.'

Someone called out, 'Bear down.'

'Strain.'

'Scream.'

'Cry out the pain.'

'Curse to high heaven if you want.' That was Buttercup.

Together they chanted, 'Give life! Give life!'

Louder and louder. 'Give life! Give life!'

Higher and higher. 'Give life! Give life!'

Their voices rose, hoarse and wild over Marcia, booming off the walls, floor and ceiling. Marcia got caught up in the frenzy. She did all that they asked, remembering giving birth to Gabby, Salina and Karl. Each one of their births was different, but also the same – through pain she created life. The voices swam around her, under her, lifting her up. Her body arched. Her neck bent back, her mouth wide, she cried out. Marcia could swear she felt the sensation of something like a child slip from her body. She lost all sense of time. Suddenly she could bear it no more. Her exhausted body slumped back on to the bed. Dr Vincent's arm rested against her shoulder.

He proclaimed, 'We have come to the naming ceremony part of our celebration of birth.' He came to Marcia's side and gazed down fondly at her. 'You are now ready to receive your name. From now on you will be known as Honeysuckle, because your essence is filled with sweetness and affection.'

The room erupted into applause, which made Marcia blush. She thought over her new name. Honeysuckle. She liked it, there was indeed a sweetness that made her feel youthful again. A young mother. Less pain.

◆ ◆ ◆

'What was all that noise?'

Marcia came tumbling back down to earth when she heard her son's question and found him waiting for her outside the room. Oh Lord, not only was he in the wrong place, he'd carved his name into the wood near the door with a knife he'd found in the kitchen. After the police had questioned him, Marcia had got rid of his penknife. She grabbed his hand, drew him alongside her and positioned him outside the door to the room where she needed to get changed. She got dressed with speed.

Outside she found Dr Vincent waiting for her. His hand was resting on Karl's head. 'Such a nice boy. I hope you found your first treatment helpful, Honeysuckle.'

Beckoning her son to her, Marcia shyly answered, 'I feel full of life.' And she did. 'The pain hasn't fully gone but thank you. I enjoyed meeting the other women.'

'You're under no obligation to come back.'

'I want to. It feels right to be here.'

◆ ◆ ◆

'Why were all those women screaming like they were in a scary movie?' Karl asked when they got outside.

She swung him to face her. 'What did we agree?'

'That I won't say anything to Dad or the girls.'

Hell, if Saul knew what she was up to there would be another murder on the street.

Suddenly, a prickly sensation of unease ran through her. Slowly her head turned towards the shack that had drawn her attention on her first visit here. Standing in front of it was the young boy who had dropped the leaflet in the hospital car park. He was so still, his face so pale that he looked like someone encased in ice. Moving quickly, Marcia rushed over to him.

She crouched down beside him. 'Do you remember me? The lady from the hospital?'

No answer. His haunting gaze looked right through her. What was going on here? Why was he standing in front of the shack?

A strident female voice called out, 'So that's where you've got to.'

Marcia twisted up to her feet to find one of the older women smartly walking towards them. She took the boy's hand, and

119

without talking to Marcia led him away. Marcia watched them go until they disappeared inside the house. Weird. Then again, this was a haven to help people and obviously the child was in need of some help.

Walking away with her son, Marcia wondered what had happened to him, what type of trauma he had been through. That wasn't the only thing that preoccupied her mind. Had she really heard groaning coming from the shack? She dismissed it. It must have been the sound of the wind. She turned back one final time, not to look at the house, but at the shack.

CHAPTER 21

I'm back at my desk, back to feeling like the living dead. Maybe it's working in this place that keeps bringing on this pain in my gut and turning my feet into ones that have walked through hot coals. Hell, my stomach's on fire too. What I would give for Dad's ginger beer, which I had last night, but I'm on the second bottle, so rationing it. The phone rings and it's the solicitor who acts for the trust that administered Ocean Haven before the council took over.

'Someone has spotted Robert Delbrook in America – Utah of all places.'

'What?' I'm finding it hard to follow him because I feel so lousy. 'Have you contacted him?'

'No. This is bound to be another case of him having been seen alongside Elvis down the chip shop. I will advise if there's an update on this.' He's gone before I can formally end our conversation.

I'm missing something here, and there's obviously no point relying on this solicitor for information about Delbrook. But what am I missing? I've read and reread the paperwork for Ocean Haven over and over. But it's like one of those optical illusions at a funfair: the closer you look, the less sense it makes. At the same time, I can't focus my eyes, making everything slightly blurry. That means it's like an optical illusion in the dark, a hall of mirrors with no lights. With a rapid shake of my head, my vision comes back into focus.

I study the papers, page after page. There are references to addendums and additional paragraphs that are stored at the rear of the document among deeds and copies of alterations to the property made long ago and which are carefully but misleadingly labelled. Something has been smuggled in here, I know it has, but I'd need a bloodhound to sniff it out.

I won't give up. I keep scanning, reading, looking . . . Ah, what's that? It's a reference to a sub paragraph 7E. But a careful examination of every page in the document shows there is no 7E. Only when I turn it upside down and begin to search from back to front, does 7E appear, typed at an angle in small print on the back of a page about responsibility for the maintenance of a well shared with a neighbouring property. I frown because there is no neighbouring property. I go back to the rear of the document. On the dotted line, my mum has signed, Carol Shore has signed and so has Robert Delbrook. Only he will have known what paragraph 7E means. After a time lapse of two years, the trust will cease to exist and Delbrook becomes the sole owner of Ocean Haven. Gotcha! I knew it. Robert Delbrook was a manipulative crook. I'd jump for joy if my head wasn't banging like the Devil was inside it.

I need to get some air. Using the desk as leverage I manage to stand. Beneath my feet are a mass of pins and needles. Someone calls out to me as I make my way to the exit. I think they're asking if I'm OK. I don't answer. I need to get out of here like now. I push the door open. Step outside. A battery of cooling fresh air seizes me, then lets go. I don't remember falling into blackness.

◆ ◆ ◆

My eyes snap open. Where the hell am I? A dreadful panic grips me. I figure out that I'm in the street, because I hear the noise of car engines nearby. Then I realise I'm wrong, the sound is the noise of my panting breath. And there's someone looking down at me, a man's face. Whoever he is, he's talking to me, but all I see are the movement of his lips.

Finally, I hear what he's saying. 'Don't move, I've called an ambulance.'

Ambulance? What for? Abruptly, like a crazy-mad movie, it all rushes back to me:

Robert Delbrook is the real owner of Ocean Haven.

Feeling sick.

Delbrook somehow got Mummy to sign those documents.

Feeling sick.

Delbrook used Mummy as cover.

Feeling sick.

Carol Shore and son falling to their deaths from Cliff Heights.

Dizzy. Sick. On the street. Everything going blank and black.

I peer up at Craven. Yes, it's Detective Craven who's looking down at me. 'What are you doing here?' He was definitely not part of my recollection of the events that find me lying embarrassingly in the street. 'Are you following me?' Despite my weakened state, my accusatory tone is strong.

Ignoring my indignant question, he answers, 'The ambulance should be here soon.'

'No ambulance.' I manage to struggle to a sitting position and that's when my mortification grows, because there's a semicircle of onlookers, a few of them colleagues, staring at me as if I'm some exhibit in a museum or a defeated animal in a zoo. Thank goodness for my dark skin, so they can't detect my blush. I hate this, being the centre of attention. I've spent most of my adult life blending into the background.

Craven senses my embarrassment and puts on his best copper voice as he addresses the crowd. 'There's nothing to see here, please can you all go about your business.'

People follow his instruction, while I give my colleagues the look that tells them I'm OK. One of them calls, 'I'll tell Greg what's happened.'

'Thank you,' I mumble, trying to get to my feet. The sensation of sick rises high in my stomach. I force it down, before it can touch the back of my throat.

Craven places an arm on my shoulder. 'Moving isn't such a good idea. Stay put until the ambulance arrives.'

I shove his hand off – yes, I know, very childish of me, he's only trying to help. 'I don't need an ambulance. Call me a cab to take me to my doctor.'

'That's pure madness.'

'Please.'

The gentleness I associate with his eyes returns. With a heavy sigh he helps me to my feet. I sway for a second or two, so he tucks me into his side and manoeuvres me to his car. I'm soon settled in the passenger seat and he drives away.

He asks, 'What do you think is making you ill?'

I'm about to lie and bluff it out with, 'Y'know the usual: tiredness, stress, overwork', but instead I tell him the truth – well, the truth as far as I know it. 'It's this town, Tinfields. Coming back here, the memories, they all make me want to gag and throw up.'

'Sometimes the only way to go forward is to face the past.'

My eyebrow kicks up. 'Never took you for a philosopher, PC Plod.' Shame immediately hits at my unkind words, so before he can speak I quickly add, 'Sorry, I know you're just trying to help me, but for once in my life, for one second if nothing else, I don't want a trip down Memory Lane, trying to dodge all the landmines littered along the way.'

'Landmines' – I feel him grimly smile – 'I've got plenty of those.'

That surprises me. 'No lady or bloke waiting for you at home?'

'Home?' His voice is so quiet I wonder if I even hear it. 'I thought I knew where that was once.'

Hell, he sounds as broken as me. After that we don't speak, instead settle into our own cocoon of brooding silence. I'm feeling much better by the time we reach my doctor's surgery. The receptionist takes one look at me and fits me in to see Dr Morris ten minutes later. I'm honoured, she explains, because usually on a Wednesday afternoon he doesn't see patients, but spends time on his PhD research, but he will see me.

'I'll wait for you.' Craven starts making himself at home in a seat in the waiting room.

I'm horrified. 'There's no need for that. I have no idea how long I will be. Besides, shouldn't you be fighting crime on behalf of the citizens of Tinfields?'

It's the receptionist who makes the decision, by leaning forward and catching Craven's eye. 'If you're a policeman I want to report a crime. For the last week some idiot has been leaving the most disgusting graffiti on the shutters. As soon as we wash it off, they're back again.'

Craven mischievously catches my eye as he takes out his notebook to record the particulars. I head for Dr Morris's room.

Dr Steven Morris is a man in his late forties with a well-moisturised face, receding hair and an expression that has perfected putting his patients at ease. Except me, that is. I'm perched nervously on the edge of my seat, because I've never felt truly comfortable in the company of doctors. '*The doctor told me there's nothing wrong with me. That it's all in my head.*' My mother's desperate words have been seared in my mind with the burning power of a lifetime branding. If they treated her like that, why would they treat me any differently? And that's why this is the first time I've ever come to this surgery, ever met Dr Morris.

'Sorry about the mess.' He gestures towards the piles of files on his desk and the few that lie on the ground on his side of his desk, which I suspect is his research for his PhD.

I interject, 'It should be me who's apologising, because I've interrupted your research.'

I'm expecting him to give me one of those grave doctor looks, but he smiles. 'What's been the trouble today?'

Voice trembling, I gather my words. 'Lately I've been feeling sick, like I want to throw up. And the joints in my body . . .' The memory of the terrible pain comes back, I feel it attacking me all over again. 'At first I thought it was something I ate, but I haven't eaten anything today, but I've been dogged by this sickness all day and fainted on the street.'

'Have you fainted before?'

I shake my head. Then remember, 'Once. At the funeral of my mother when I was fifteen.'

'Would you mind me examining you or I can call one of my female colleagues to do it.'

There's something about this man that makes me feel safe. 'I'm happy for you to do it.'

Five minutes later, after I've dressed, he says, 'From my examination I can't detect anything wrong . . .'

My mouth tightens. Oh, here we go! I'm on my feet before I know it, heading towards the door.

'Miss Lewis.' His surprised voice stops me as my hand reaches for the door. 'Have I said something wrong?'

'Wrong?' I spin back to him. 'That's what's the matter with me, something's *wrong*.'

He stands and walks over to me. He's much taller and thinner than I expected him to be. 'I get the impression that you think I'm not taking you seriously.'

'They didn't take my mum's sickness seriously. One day she was there, the next she was gone.'

Somehow, he manages to get me sat down again, this time bringing his chair around the desk to sit nearer me, but always maintaining a respectable space. He speaks, each word delivered carefully. 'When I trained to be a doctor we were always taught to abide by certain rules, one of those was never make a promise to a patient. But I promise you this, I will always believe you when you say you're in pain. I will always investigate to the fullest of my medical knowledge to find a reason for that pain. If it's not immediately obvious I will refer you to the hospital and if they find nothing we'll try another hospital.'

Not until he has spoken do I realise how tense I've been. 'Thank you.'

'I think the next step should be a comprehensive set of blood tests and a urine sample.'

'What's the next step if the test results come up blank?'

'One step at a time, Miss Lewis. Let's see what the tests yield.' Standing up, he signals our appointment is at an end.

There's no sign of Craven in reception. The receptionist sees me looking for him and tells me, 'He got a call, urgent police business. An incident at a place called Ocean Haven.'

CHAPTER 22

When I get to Ocean Haven, I'm stuck to the driver's seat of my car for a few seconds by the scene unfolding in front of me. Cops everywhere. The whole property has come alive. Police cars are parked at angles on the coast road, several large white vans have pulled up, men in white forensic overalls move back and forth, and guys in uniform are consulting with plain-clothed officers. Shouts and chatter echo around. Police tape seems wrapped at random around various parts of the site. Builders' machinery is scattered and abandoned. Why is there building equipment here?

A solitary cop stands guard at the gateposts and raises a restraining hand when I approach. 'You can't go any further.'

'What's happened?'

'We are not able to divulge that information at present.'

Slowly I walk away. The place is thick with police, which can only mean one thing – there has been a very serious incident here. I can smell it in the air. Someone is dead.

I stride to the rear of the property where the main activity is. It's focused on a hole in the ground where the mysterious builders appear to have been digging. And if I recall correctly, it was the site of the small outbuilding, more like a big shed really, that the estate agent pointed out to me. Now that outbuilding appears to have been demolished by whoever owns the digger parked nearby. The forensic team are expertly sifting through and removing earth. Occasionally they stop to take crime scene photos. There's no sign of Craven anywhere, but I'm glad. If he appears he might insist I leave. I'm not sure why he'd be here anyway, he's not one of the murder boys. Craven doesn't do dead bodies.

I know from past experience that if you walk around restricted areas with confidence, people will often assume you have a right to be there and won't ask any questions. I raise the tape and stride over, trying to sound like an official. 'I've just arrived. What have we got here?'

'Builders were doing work and they dug up a corpse. The remains to be exact.'

I nod sagely as if I'm used to this kind of thing. 'Do we know who he is yet?'

'Not yet, we're still digging.'

I move nearer to where the dead body was found and look at what's been discovered. The corpse has clearly been in the ground a long time and I feel relief that it's no one I know. The flesh has gone and there are only bones remaining, although some items of clothing aren't completely decayed. Tweed material and what's left of some leather shoes are laid out on a protective sheet with the remains of a small length of green cloth that seems to have survived remarkably well. It should turn my stomach, but death seems as natural a part of this house as its drunken chimneys and ivy.

Should I tell the police that I might have an idea who this is? That it's Robert Delbrook who disappeared all those years ago.

My arm is taken firmly and gently from behind and I'm manoeuvred backwards under the police tape.

It's Craven. 'What are you doing here? You're not the dead person's lawyer are you?'

My excuse comes quickly. 'I was down on the beach. Someone said that it's likely a murder.'

'A bullet casing was found in the grave too.'

'A gun? What . . . ?'

My voice dribbles away because I'm not sure Craven's even listening to me. All his attention is focused on the makeshift grave behind the tape.

He looks back at me. 'If that body is who I think it is . . .' His words dangle in the air, the name he was going to say tantalisingly out of my reach, then he ducks under the tape to join his colleagues at the scene. He walks over to where the bones are laid out beside the hole in the ground where they were found. He stands over them like a mourner at the graveside, head bowed, hands clasped together. He looks at Ocean Haven with a wistful stare, as if it has the answer to a question he's posed, but the house doesn't want to answer. His glance passes over to the ravens who are sitting in the tree, keeping watch on proceedings.

Who does Craven think is in the grave? Is it the same person I suspect it to be? Big question: how would Craven know about this person?

We're interrupted by the squealing of wheels down on the coastal road. A SUV roars up and judders to a halt like a getaway car outside a bank. The driver emerges. It's Salina. It's not often my jaw drops south in shock. She marches up the gravel path towards us, fists clenched, face livid. Luke jumps out, closely following her, calling out, 'Calm down, Salina, calm down.'

Craven steps forward, a hand raised to stop her. 'This is a crime scene, you can't enter.'

Salina gives him a withering look. 'I can if I own the place.'

◆ ◆ ◆

I rock back, stunned by what my sister has said. I stand with her and Luke and Craven in the shade of the trees where the ravens look down on us.

Salina peers up at them with distaste. 'Do we have to do this here? What if they pluck at my hair?'

Craven's stony face makes her shut up. He addresses both her and Luke. 'Who owns this property?'

Luke answers, 'I completed the sale yesterday. So technically it's mine.' He quickly looks to his wife, 'But what's yours is mine, darling, and all that.'

She rears up. 'I should think so, considering the money I've invested in this purchase too.'

I can see that Craven is getting thoroughly fed up with the bickering, so I intervene. 'A dead body has been found on the grounds.'

Salina shudders as her husband says, 'Our builders let us know of their grisly discovery. We came as soon as possible.'

'This is a police matter,' Craven tells my sister and her husband through gritted teeth. 'Now, if you wouldn't mind.'

Salina looks him dead in the eye and lengthens her neck. 'My husband is a personal friend of the chief constable, so you want to watch your manners.' She then turns on her husband, stabbing an irate finger at him. 'I told you to tell the builders not to touch the outbuilding; I had such plans for turning it into a sauna. You want to be thankful it's not you in that hole.'

Poor Luke raises his hands. 'I was going to tell you, Salina, but I had to move fast, and once the paperwork was signed, there didn't seem much point in delaying the work I wanted to get done, so I brought some builders in.'

'Tell me!' Her fury brings her to the tip of her toes, her palms slapping against his chest with enough force to leave burn marks. 'The one thing I ask you to do and you don't remember.'

Luke takes a step back, open irritation setting off the red colour of his hair. 'You're my wife not my business manager. Instead of making a scene in front of Gabby and an officer of the law, why don't you just calm down and stop carrying on as if your fur's been stroked the wrong way.'

Cursing beneath her breath, she does an about-turn and stomps off to her car.

Her husband shouts, 'How the heck am I going to get home?'

'Walk,' she yells over her shoulder. 'You need to get some practice in, you'll be walking everywhere by the time I've finished with you in the divorce courts.' Then she gets in her powerful car and roars off.

Luke is sheepish now she's gone. 'Sorry about that, but you know what married couples are like. Silly tiffs followed by a kiss and a cuddle and everything's all right again.'

Craven says, 'My colleagues are going to need a word with you at some stage, Luke.'

He walks off, leaving me with a fizzing Luke. I ask him, 'Why did you hide it from me that you were the buyer for Ocean Haven? No wonder you interrupted your friend Alan from the council property management when I started to ask him questions.' I also realise, 'The keys you used to let me in the house during our visit didn't belong to Alan, did they? They were your set of keys all the time.'

'Hide? That's a bit strong,' he replies. 'Property is a need-to-know business. Alan gave me a tip ages ago that the place was on the market. Its complicated, disputed ownership had been causing the council a headache, so they offloaded it to the first person who had the money to take it off their hands.'

The fury rips through me. 'And you didn't think you should have told me that?'

132

I know what he's about to say, so we do in unison: 'Need-to-know.'

I use the cover of my brother-in-law, the owner, to have a legitimate reason to be there, so I follow him around as he glares at the crime scene tape and then goes inside the house to keep an eye on the police search. When he starts kicking off about them pulling up the floorboards, I sneak upstairs to one of the bedrooms. I'm halfway inside when I realise that it's already occupied. I try to sneak out, but I've been noticed.

'Stay.' Craven's voice has the force of an order. Hands resting on a windowsill, he stares out across the sea view.

I stand next to him. 'I never knew that Salina and her husband bought this house.'

'It's Robert Delbrook.'

With enough drama to secure a place at acting school, I strain an ear forward as if I'm hard of hearing. 'Robert who?'

The subtle twitch of his fingers is the only sign I get that he doesn't believe me. 'The victim in the grave. That's what our intelligence is already suggesting. Delbrook had a number of aliases.'

I drop the act and listen so I hear every word. 'What?'

Craven continues, 'He was using a particular one when someone killed him.'

'The name – tell me.'

'Delbrook was also known as Vincent Fortune.'

'How was this Vincent Fortune connected to Ocean Haven?'

Craven turns and walks away from me. A step away from the doorway, he turns back. 'Want to know more, meet me tomorrow. We need to talk.'

CHAPTER 23

TWENTY-FIVE YEARS AGO

MARCIA

'Me Buttercup, you Honeysuckle,' Buttercup announced in the parody of a deep man's voice. Then she beat her chest like she was Tarzan. Marcia roared with laughter. She sat with Buttercup and the other women, drinking chamomile tea at the long table in the kitchen. The women were all sufferers of chronic pain. Some had headaches, hair loss and mouth sores, while others crippling pain in their pelvis and sometimes pain during sex.

They had just finished a treatment session where they had sat in the trees, but in brown gowns to show that they were ripening fruit, which Dr Vincent said showed they were getting closer to healing. Marcia was the first to admit that some of the treatments they did were a bit out there, but it really seemed to help with her pain. She wasn't pain-free – yet! – but she felt it was coming, soon. So she took part in as many treatments as possible, especially anything concerning her womb. She needed to get her womb back into working order.

If Saul knew what she was doing he'd have a fit. His wife going to see a stranger, another man, and talking about their family business . . . No, Saul would never approve. And that was why Marcia had told him that she was going to the hospital, that they were still running tests. She didn't like lying to her husband, or Salina and Gabby, but she recognised that it was time for her to put herself first for once in her life.

A number of the women, including Buttercup, were living at Ocean Haven for the duration of their treatments. The residential fees were eye-watering. Marcia had bonded with Buttercup, who was slightly younger than her. She did make Marcia laugh. However, beneath all that mischief, Marcia sensed a tightness in Buttercup, as if she was one step away from exploding.

An unnatural silence suddenly fell. Marcia looked up to find the boy from the hospital standing in the doorway. There was a young woman with him. They hovered at the door, the boy almost hiding behind the woman. Marcia sucked in a horrified breath at the woman's appearance. Marcia judged her to be in her late twenties, maybe thirty, but she looked so much older, with uneven brown hair that looked like it had been hacked with a razorblade. Her clothes were dirty – a flimsy skirt and a T-shirt that clung like a second skin. She was thin, way too thin for a woman of her height. What drew Marcia's concerned attention most of all was the woman's face. Stark-white, with large hazel eyes that bulged. Those eyes were unnerving, unseeing, a mirror image of the boy half-hidden by her.

Marcia found it strange that none of the women, even Buttercup, greeted the newcomers. Well, they might not have any manners, but she had plenty to go around. She got to her feet and tentatively smiled. 'I'm Honeysuckle. Can I get you some tea?'

The woman didn't speak, instead stiffened and stared at Marcia, while the child retreated behind her. Raspberry, one of the women at the other end of the table, brightly said, 'Carol and Master Jamie, sit yourselves down and I'll get your lunch.' She addressed Marcia. 'This is Carol Shore and her son Jamie.'

It was as if Raspberry was speaking on behalf of Carol and Jamie. How odd. Couldn't they speak for themselves? Maybe that was why they were here at Ocean Haven. Confused, Marcia sat back down. The woman and child settled down at the opposite end of the table.

Marcia tried talking to the boy. 'Do you remember me? I'm Marcia.' Her name was out of her mouth before she could call it back. The sharp look from the others was a reminder that they never used their real names. Marcia continued, 'We literally bumped into each other at the hospital . . .'

Suddenly the room filled with the sound of Carol's breathing. Erratic and harsh. Her head hung low, her fingers gripped the edge of the table with such force it seemed like her knuckles were going to saw through her skin. In a gesture of protection, the boy lay his hand over his mother's, and started rocking, forward and back. Carol's breathing switched to high-pitched whining, accentuating her sunken cheeks.

Marcia was distressed. Something she had said had triggered the shocking reaction in the newcomers. She asked Buttercup, 'What's happening? What did I say?'

Raspberry placed a comforting palm on the younger woman's shoulder. 'Now, don't get yourself all in a tangle. Honeysuckle meant nothing by it.' She ruffled Jamie's hair. 'I've got one of your favourites.'

His rocking stopped when she served him two slices of pizza. Carol calmed down and smiled at her son, then beckoned for him to start eating. The food that was laid in front of Carol shocked Marcia to the core. A thick slab of bread with butter on it and a glass of water. She picked up the bread and crammed as much of it as she could into her mouth. The sound of her breathing was heavy and noisy as she chewed with the ferocity of the starving and with such violence she was in danger of biting her tongue. Greasy butter was smeared across her lips and the side of her mouth. Marcia should have been horrified but she wasn't. What she felt was pity, an intense sense of worry and concern for both Carol and her son. All of Marcia's maternal instincts kicked in. She wanted to throw her arms around the younger woman and child, enveloping them in a circle of love and never let them go. Thank heaven they were in the right place. What Marcia couldn't figure out was why Carol was eating butter and bread.

Dr Vincent strolled in with his abundance of light and energy. And stopped when he saw Marcia. 'I didn't realise you were still here.' He was speaking to her, but his gaze darted between Carol and her son, who had stopped eating and looked right back at him.

'Today's session took a lot out of me,' Marcia hesitantly explained, 'and I just needed . . .'

His hand fell on her shoulder in understanding. 'Take your time.' He leaned down and whispered, 'For my clients there are different phases of treatments where it's not advisable for them to meet other clients. Something so innocently said by one patient is a trigger for another.' Even though he was speaking to her, Marcia sensed that his gaze still remained on the woman and child.

Vincent loomed large at the table, telling Carol, 'It's time for our afternoon session.'

Whatever colour Carol had left drained from her cheeks. She stood. Jamie started rocking again, more violently this time. Vincent smiled at the boy, his eyes piercing into him like shards of glass. 'Boys do not behave like that at the table. Remember?'

Quickly Carol gave her child a stare that mothers know the world over, the one that silently said, 'Obey me', and shook her head. Jamie stopped moving and settled back in his chair. He stuck a fingertip in his pizza and ran circles in it. His mother slowly moved towards Dr Vincent. When she passed Marcia she accidentally knocked her bag from the corner of Marcia's chair, sending the contents spilling to the floor. In a rush Carol got on her knees and started picking up items and shoving them back into the bag.

'You don't need to do that,' Marcia told her. 'I'll sort it out.'

Carol stood back up and with one last look at her child she left the room with Vincent.

'Well, I best be off,' Marcia said, after sorting out her bag. A movement out of the window caught her eye. She moved closer to it. Her breath caught when she saw Dr Vincent escorting Carol into the shack, the same place from where Marcia was sure she'd heard groans on her first visit here.

'What type of treatment does he do with her in there?' she quietly asked Buttercup.

The other woman shrugged. 'I don't know. I do know that Raspberry is the only one who Dr Vincent says can talk with her.'

'Why?'

'Something to do with the type of treatment she's having.'

Marcia's searching gaze turned back to the shack. It was like she was hypnotised and couldn't look away. Around five minutes later Dr Vincent re-emerged from the building. Alone. Instinctively, Marcia stepped slightly back from the window; she didn't want him to see her snooping on him. She squinted, still watching. Where was Carol? Why hadn't she come out of the shack too? What kind of treatment could he be doing with her in there?

He turned the key in the padlock on the door. Marcia's heart raced. Why would he lock Carol inside the shack? Then again, Dr Vincent had told her that different clients had different treatment plans. Maybe the building looked rough and tumble on the outside but inside was as picture-perfect comfy and cosy as the treatment room. Hadn't Vincent been the one who had told her during one of their sessions, 'Too often we only look at the surface of a person, not the beauty within.'?

With that ringing in her head, Marcia picked her bag up and left. Only when she stood outside the front door of her house, searching for her keys did she find it. The note inside her bag. Two words written in large black capital letters:

'HELP US.'

CHAPTER 24

My eyes punch open. I have no idea if I'm asleep or awake. All around is ink-black, it's cold and smells damp and earthy. Why does my bed feel so wet? Then I realise this isn't my bed, it's the ground I'm lying on. I know where I am. In the hole where they found the remains of the body at Ocean Haven. I know this isn't real, it's in my head, but still I'm terrified. All around me is the urgent erratic noise of my own breathing. Why am I here? I look up and a face appears on the edge of the makeshift grave. It's Mummy. I cry out her name, but she doesn't hear me. There's a shovel in her hand. She lifts it and crunches it deep into the pile of earth beside her, gathering it into the shovel. Again she lifts and tips it over, raining dirt down on my face.

I cry out.

Mummy can't hear me.

Mummy lifts more dirt and throws it on to my face.

No!

I wake up violently shaking and shaking in my rented room. The sheet beneath me is soaked with my sweat. None of it is real, but that doesn't matter. What does matter is what it tells me, something that has horrified me since the remains were found. If that was the body of Robert Delbrook aka Vincent Fortune, was Mummy involved in his murder?

◆ ◆ ◆

'You show me your cards and I'll show you mine.' Craven gets right to the point later that morning.

I sit opposite him in the cafe, the trendy coffee shop near the beach. It seems to have become our go-to place to talk. *Our place*; that sounds like a song that lovers play every year on their anniversary. I banish the thought. Craven isn't my type exactly, but his spiky hair and homespun features push a few of my buttons.

'And what cards would they be exactly?' My brow arches.

He sighs, warming his hands around his cup. 'The ones marked, "How is Gabrielle Lewis connected to Ocean Haven?"'

My expression gives nothing away. 'What makes you think I'm connected to anything?'

'Because I know you've been making enquiries about Ocean Haven. And, hey presto, you turn up at the scene of a crime where the skeletal remains of a human being are found—'

'Hold it right there.' I don't like where this cop is dragging me. 'If you're suggesting I had a thing—'

'I'm not.' He sucks in an exasperated punch of air. 'What I am suggesting is that we help each other.' I don't know what to say to that, so he ploughs on. 'To show my good faith, let me show you a few of my cards. As I told you yesterday, Robert Delbrook also used the alias Vincent Fortune. His association with Ocean Haven was medical—'

That makes me sit up. 'Medical? Was he some type of doctor?'

'He was once a practicing doctor but was eventually disbarred for malpractice. Mr Delbrook resorted to using various aliases, including Dr Vincent Fortune here in Tinfields, to make a name for himself using medical tricks to con people, particularly women, promising them all manner of treatments and herbal remedies. Of course, in return for a hefty fee.'

That sends shivers through me. Is that what happened to Mummy? She came here seeking a cure and was preyed on instead? If that's the case, how did he get her to sign the house ownership documents?

Craven informs me, 'I've been looking for Delbrook for a number of years now.'

I was not expecting that and my astonishment is plain to see. 'Why have you been searching for him? Delbrook's association with Ocean Haven stretches back twenty-five years and from what I hear no one has laid eyes on him since then. If the remains that have been unearthed are indeed Delbrook's, you're too young to have been involved. Unless the local constabulary had set up a kindergarten cop academy to involve you in this case.'

His lips stretch at my humour. I'm not sure if it's a smile or a grimace. 'For argument's sake, let's say the body is that of Robert Delbrook slash Dr Vincent. Everyone assumed that he was long gone after Carol Shore and her son died either jumping or being pushed off Cliff Heights.'

The image of them tumbling over the edge, her screaming, the boy crying, falls and spirals through my already shattered mind. I rapidly blink the tragic image away. I hide behind the refuge of my cup of tea for a while to get my composure back.

Craven continues, 'Every now and again a report would surface that Delbrook was still out there, scamming one person after another. There were even recent reports that he was in America. My governor put me on the case to track him down.'

I mull over what Craven has told me. 'Then why are you so convinced that it's his remains that were found in the ground?'

'Obviously there will need to be extensive tests—'

'Skip the CSI stuff,' I interrupt, I admit, rudely. 'Why are you nearly one hundred per cent sure that it's Delbrook/Fortune?' I stumble over his twin names. What should I call him? Fraud would be a fitting surname, or Swindler. No wonder he chose the name Fortune, he was making his own at others' expense.

'Delbrook.' Craven senses my indecision. 'That's the name he was legally given, so that's what we should call him. Witnesses who knew him from his time at Ocean Haven said that he was fond of wearing bow ties. Fragments of cloth found in the grave suggest that it was a green bow tie.'

Something suddenly occurs to me. 'Have you got a photo of him?' I've never seen his face before. I found no images of Delbrook online. But then that's all part of the con: the less evidence that associates you with the crime the better.

The image Craven pulls up on his smart phone is not the type of man I expected to see. I thought he'd be the archetypal old-style family doctor: older, round-bellied with the bald head and side tufts of hair and a style of glasses people associate with clever members of the medical profession they can trust. This man is one who takes grand pride in standing out from the crowd. There's something about him that captures the eye. Expertly trimmed grey hair that surrounds a face where every line, curve of bone and bump seem to have been expertly placed. His skin has the colour of a white man who either loves a sunbed or goes abroad often to catch some rays. And if anyone could bottle and sell the confident gleam in his gaze they'd make a mint.

'He's not what I was expecting either.' Craven's voice pulls my attention back to him. 'He's got "Beware, charmer alert" written all over him. The main purpose of my investigation was to try to get some of his victims' evidence, such as tracking down any offshore accounts that may throw up hidden finances, which will help them get at least a portion of their money back. Even if those are his remains, I can still do that. Your help may be crucial to his victims, so please tell me how you're linked to Ocean Haven?'

This is where I should bolt, run away. Let's face it, that's what I do best.

He sighs heavily. 'When I came into the Force, I didn't find it easy to connect to colleagues, and as for members of the public . . .' He leaves that one in the air along with his raised brows. 'I've been a loner most of my life. I get on with others because that's the nature of my job and life, but when I close the front door of my home that's when I feel most relaxed. Can really breathe.'

That's where I should step in and tell him to mind his business, but, you know what, I can't walk away from what I've known about Craven all along – he's like me.

'What I'm trying to say, obviously very clumsily,' he goes on, 'is that I haven't always found it easy to move out from behind my personal barriers.'

I stare down at the faint scars on the table. What he described is the spitting image of personal-me. Can I trust him? *Of course you can, he's a cop.*

Slowly I raise my head and say, 'Before Luke, who you know is my brother-in-law, bought Ocean Haven, it was owned by a trust. My mother's name and signature were there as the chair of the trust. How that all happened and how she's connected to Ocean Haven I'm still trying to figure out. Mummy was an ordinary woman, so how on earth she was mixed up with a con artist like Robert Delbrook, I don't know. Unless she was one of his unsuspecting victims.'

I keep back the part about what I found in the ownership documents, that Delbrook would have eventually become the sole owner of Ocean Haven. Being a lawyer has taught me that you have to keep a card or two up your sleeve.

'I'm assuming your mother's no longer with us?'

A lump lodges in my throat. 'She was sick and died suddenly. I don't know what of.'

The corner of his mouth lifts into a one-sided smile. 'Are we working together?'

I mull it over, then stretch out my hand and we shake on it. He looks boyishly pleased.

He kick-starts our partnership by taking out some blank A4 paper and tearing it into squares. Then he spreads them out on the table. He takes out a pen. My darting gaze observes his movements. What is he up to? Is this some kind of cop magic trick?

He reveals, 'Let's run this like a proper investigation, so I want you to imagine these papers are like a board where we'll keep track of the most important information we find.'

Talking, Craven takes us through what we have so far and records each nugget on its own separate square of paper.

Robert Delbrook aka Dr Vincent murdered & buried at Ocean Haven.

Carol Shore and Marcia Lewis — at Ocean Haven.

Marcia Lewis — Key figure in Ocean Haven ownership? How?

Luke Wilson Ocean Haven's new owner.

That last one I don't like. 'Luke has got nothing to do with this.'

Head angled to the side, Craven looks at me. 'Doesn't he? Don't you think it's odd that he should now, at this particular point in time, have bought Ocean Haven?'

He creates doubt in my mind. Dredges up the past suspicions I had about Luke being involved in the attack on my father. Maybe Craven's right, maybe he isn't, but what I do know is that perhaps we should keep Luke as a puzzle piece at the heart of our investigation.

Craven indicates our makeshift evidence board. 'I want you to keep these with you at all times, plus a pen.' Then he says, 'Talk to your brother-in-law. See if you can ferret out any information from him that shows he has a hidden history with the house.'

Would Luke have an ulterior motive? He certainly knows how to operate under the radar. Why would he buy Ocean Haven?

While I'm thinking on Luke and putting our makeshift investigation board away, I notice Craven tearing another square from a new piece of paper. He writes on it and pushes it my way:

Gabby and Craven dinner Thursday night???

I hadn't seen that one coming. His face burns bright red. 'I don't mean like *that*. I meant so we can catch up. On the evidence. Where we are . . . and stuff.'

'Hey, why not,' I answer, putting him out of his misery. I keep the paper with his invitation on it as well.

My happy feeling fades later when I see the text message:

Your test results are back.

CHAPTER 25

I feel the presence of my mother suddenly appear by my side as I reach the entrance to the doctor's surgery. At least she's not shovelling suffocating, damp earth on me like this morning. My face half turns to her. Agitation pushes her chest high as she bites out, *'Don't let him touch your ovaries. Don't let him anywhere near your womb. He'll cut them out of you.'*

Her alarming plea shocks me, making me hesitate. Maybe she's right and I shouldn't go in. What if the doctor wants to administer some strange kind of treatment that feels like he's cut away half my soul? Then my rational mind kicks in: if you don't agree with what the doc says, thank him kindly and walk away. Simple. *Simple?* Nothing about this has been simple, still I'm going to follow logic this time. Deliberately, I turn my back on Mummy and head inside.

Minutes later, when I face Steven Morris, my hand clutching my bag, I tell him, 'Let's get one thing clear, if your treatment involves slicing and dicing me, I'm out of here now.' My heart's thundering. I need to pull in a lungful of air after that.

His eyebrows shoot up, a troubled expression seizing his face. 'What on earth makes you think I'd do anything like that?'

'Aren't you?'

His answer is to look at his computer screen on his desk, which is piled high with what I know is his PhD research. 'All your test results have come back negative. They can't pinpoint what the problem is.'

I bite out, 'I am not making this up. I am ill.'

He doesn't answer straight away, as if giving me time to collect myself. I'm grateful for it, because I feel like I'm falling apart. Like I'm standing at the gallows, rope around my neck not knowing the appointed hour when the trap door will go from under me.

He folds his fingers together. 'When you first came to see me I assured you that I would never dismiss your illness. And you are ill. All we need to do is get to the bottom of what is causing it.'

'I think I'm going to die like my mother.' I have no idea where it comes from, but the admission leaves my stomach muscles convulsing and twisting until I can barely catch my breath. 'What a stupid thing to say, now you really will think I'm nuts.' I can barely meet his eye with the hot shame heating my skin.

His expression is sympathetic. 'I don't think you're nuts, and can I let you into a little secret?'

'It won't be a secret if you tell me.' That makes me half smile, slightly easing the tension.

He smiles back, the same relaxed, kind smile I recall from my first time here. 'The secret is that so many people feel the way you do. It usually hits when someone is nearing the age when one or both of their parents pass away.' He slowly adds, 'It's normal.'

I'm not the only one. It's normal. The relief unknots my stomach, pushing me back into the support of the chair. Quietly I say, 'I've never told anyone this, Doctor, but before I came back to Tinfields, on my thirty-ninth birthday, I engineered an argument with my live-in boyfriend because I didn't want him to be around to see me die when I reached forty. By the end of the week he was gone. And I was alone. Just like I wanted it, because I didn't want anyone who loved me to have to fall apart the way me and my sister and brother did when Mummy was gone.'

'Was forty the age she died?'

Most people would be crying, or at least have a few tears; not me, my eyes are stone-dry. I gave all my tears to Mummy all those years ago.

I softly continue, 'Anything out of the ordinary that happened to me made me think I was going to die. Y'know, someone nudged me too close to the platform edge at the train station, I was convinced I was going to fall on to the track and be run over by a train. If something fell next to me at work, I was convinced it had just missed my head.' I have to confess to him what no one else knows. 'It got so bad last year that I didn't leave the place I lived in for two months. I couldn't go beyond the door, because I thought the ground, the sky, were going to wrap around me and crush me.' I look at him. 'Does that sound mental?'

He shakes his head. 'How did you manage to eventually leave your home?'

'I saw an advert for a job here in Tinfields, where I grew up. Suddenly I wanted to be back in a place where I could remember my mother.' I tell him the rest. 'The symptoms I have match the symptoms my mother had, which eventually killed her. The doctors didn't help her.'

'Which explains your reluctance to be treated by me. Am I the first doctor you've seen about your illness?'

'Yes. Although before I came back here it was really an anxiety brewing in me all the time. Only in the last few weeks have the symptoms become more like Mum's, more real.'

His brows lock together as he turns back to the computer and presses the keyboard. Slowly he says, 'And your symptoms are feeling tired, joint pain, headaches, foot pain? Stomach pain?' His smile back is reassuring, but I see something else there that I can't name. He explains, 'What I'm going to do is refer you to a specialist unit at the hospital for further tests.' He gives me a big smile. 'We will figure this out.'

As I head for the door, his voice stops me. 'Your last name is Lewis?'

I turn back and nod. 'Is there a problem?'

'Not at all. I just want to make sure that the reception staff have all your correct details.'

Even when I leave I get the impression that Dr Morris is still staring at my back.

CHAPTER 26

Twenty-Five Years Ago

Marcia

'HELP US.'

Marcia read the note one final time before shoving it away and getting off the bus. It had been a week since she'd found it. A week in which she'd tried to figure out what to do. There was only one person who could have left the plea for help in her bag: Carol. It was clear now that the younger woman had deliberately knocked Marcia's bag over so that she could smuggle the note inside. It tore Marcia up inside to think of that young mother and her child being in danger. But what danger could it be?

Marcia's first instinct was to call the police and tell them . . . What exactly? That she'd found a note in her bag that said 'Help us'. She could hear them now questioning her.

Did you see who put this note in your bag?

Are you sure it wasn't one of your children who put it there?

Didn't the hospital say you have stress? Maybe you put it there yourself?

OK, pushing all her doubts about the reception from the police aside, what if they did take her seriously and visited Ocean Haven to speak to Vincent. What if this brought trouble to his door? Marcia was racked with guilt. He'd been so generous and kind to her and how was she repaying him? By potentially causing him problems?

And what about Carol's behaviour? She and her son not speaking was weird. Not normal. Why were Carol and her son at the retreat? Years ago Marcia had seen a documentary about a group of children who had made a pact to stop talking. There was a special name for it . . . She wracked her brains. Ah yes, elective mutes. That's what the kids had done; made a collective decision to stop talking, and no one could understand why. Was that what was happening with Carol and her boy? But why would they do that? Gut instinct told Marcia that something was very wrong here. Badly wrong.

Her plan was simple: get to the house early for her session, search for Carol and then ask her what was going on. Of course, if Carol chose not to speak . . . Marcia would have to cross that bridge when she came to it.

The lukewarm sunshine followed her as she made her way towards the house. She tried to walk with determination, but the truth was she was scared of what she was getting into. Frightened of what waited within the four walls of Ocean Haven. At the crest of the path that overlooked the sea, Marcia stopped to take in the house, almost as if she was expecting to see something she hadn't seen before. A sign of evil. But there was nothing out of the ordinary. The house appeared the same: light and bright and welcoming. She knocked at the door. Now was the sticky part of her plan, how was she going to find Carol? She prayed she wasn't in treatment in the shack because there would be no way she could get to her then.

152

She greeted one of the women, who commented, 'You're early. You know he likes everything to be ordered and on time.'

A man who was a stickler for timekeeping? Or someone who didn't like surprises?

'The bus came early. No need to disturb Dr Vincent to tell him I've arrived.' Casually Marcia added, 'Is he with Carol?'

'She and the young one are upstairs in her room, of course.'

'Upstairs?' All the fee-paying guests had rooms downstairs. She gazed around dramatically. 'It must have been hard for her to choose a room because I imagine that they're all lovely.'

'Choose a room?' The other woman's brows pleated together in confusion. 'This is her house. Her room's on the top floor. Well, I think it's somewhere near the top floor.'

Carol's house? Marcia had assumed the property belonged to Dr Vincent. Somewhere near the top floor? What a strange way of putting it. Carol and her son either lived on the top floor or they didn't.

Marcia had never been beyond the ground floor. The first floor was a bit of a let-down; it didn't live up to the image of the grandeur of the house. There were landscape pictures on the walls and a roll of carpet along the wooden landing, but it had this empty, unlived-in feeling. Then again, that wouldn't be strange for a retreat, where the decor needed to be more impersonal and anonymous. Marcia looked upwards to the top floor and hesitated. The lighting up there appeared faded, a never-ending tunnel that sucked you in until you vanished at the end.

She tensed. She wasn't sure she wanted to go up there. Suddenly, all of this seemed like a very bad idea. Anxiety wormed its way inside her. But so did her concern for Carol and her son. If they needed her help, she couldn't turn her back on them. That wasn't in her nature.

Marcia's trembling hand gripped the stair rail. She got ready to make the first step.

'What are you doing up here?' Vincent's voice called out behind her.

◆ ◆ ◆

Marcia held still, counted to three and then turned around. She'd learned that little trick from years of living with Saul. It was her way of dealing with his oppressive timekeeping and him smashing things.

Dr Vincent did not look his calm self. He was livid, his cheeks reddening with anger. 'What are you doing up here?'

She told him the truth. Well, a partial one. 'I was looking for Carol. Well, more Jamie really. I brought him some of my son's toys. Karl doesn't play with them anymore, so I thought he might like them.'

From her bag she pulled out three small cars. She had placed them in her bag for a moment just like this. She prayed hard Vincent didn't think it was a feeble explanation.

She added, 'I'm sorry if I've—'

'It's fine,' he cut in. Although his guarded expression spelled out a different story. 'You're only trying to do a good deed. Talking of which, I'm glad you've arrived early, because there's the matter of your fee we need to discuss and the arrangement we need to come to.'

Marcia swallowed hard, for a moment forgetting about Carol. With trepidation, she followed him into the kitchen where they both sat down.

Dr Vincent settled his sombre gaze on Marcia. 'In life there comes a time when everyone has to pay their dues.' Marcia's heart dropped to her feet, convinced this was going to be bad. He continued, 'When debts have got to be paid.'

Marcia's throat dried up. Even if she'd wanted to say something she was incapable of uttering a word. She waited and waited. Finally, he continued, 'Here we don't behave like that. Here we are a family. Your debt is my debt. You came to me in the depths of distress and what kind of man would I have been if I'd refused to help you because you didn't have the necessary finance? Money's not what matters, it's what's in our hearts.'

Marcia audibly gulped in fresh air. She couldn't believe what he was telling her. That he didn't expect her to pay him anything. That his help was freely given. Guilt consumed her that she had come to this house today with doubt in her heart about him. How could she have thought such a thing when all he had ever been to her was kind and good.

'I can't thank you enough.'

He explained, 'Just so we're clear, I need you to sign a waiver that this is the agreement we have.' He left and went to his office and when he came back Marcia was more than grateful to sign the two copies of the same paper he placed in front of her. He placed her copy in an envelope and kept the other copy for himself.

'I will always be there for you, Marcia. The same way that I'm there for Carol and Jamie.'

'*Help us.*' Carol's written plea hurtled back to Marcia. After what Vincent had done for her, Marcia dismissed the idea that whatever Carol meant related to him. He was a good man.

After the end of her session, at the front door, Marcia impulsively hugged Vincent in gratitude and kissed him on the cheek. She tensed, pulling back from him, sensing eyes on her. Was someone watching her?

When he saw her troubled gaze moving about, Vincent asked, 'Is there a problem?'

Marcia hesitated, still checking, but she found no one. She shook off the feeling with a slight smile. 'Until our next session.'

Minutes later, while Marcia was on the pathway down to town she looked back up at the house. She wasn't sure why she did it, some sixth sense or the earlier sensation of someone watching her maybe having unsettled her. She stopped completely in her tracks when she saw Vincent guiding Carol towards the shed. Even from this distance Marcia could see that the younger woman was unsteady on her feet, fragile and weak-looking.

'*HELP US.*'

'*HELP US.*'

'*HELP US.*'

Over and over, the younger woman's silent cry for help echoed in Marcia's mind, each time the desperation growing. She watched as they entered the shack and waited for Vincent to come out as was his custom after about five minutes. And he then did what he always did – locked the padlock tight. Marcia waited for him to re-enter the house before she took the path back and then deviated around to avoid being spotted by anyone. She crept through the bushes towards the back of the shack. How she would get in without keys she didn't know. In the end she didn't need any, because she found a crack in the wooden slats wide enough to peep through. And what she saw horrified her. Carol was squatting down on her haunches, knees touching her chest and her arms behind her back. She was also blindfolded. Marcia had seen this position once before, in a documentary about torture.

In as low a voice of alarm as she could muster, she called through the crack, 'Oh my goodness! Carol!' Marcia couldn't disguise the horror in her voice. 'What's going on?'

'Marcia? Is that you?' For the first time Marcia heard the younger woman's voice. It was scratchy and husky and riddled with fear.

'I found your message in my bag.'

'Will you do it? Help us? You've got to help us get away from here. You're the only one who can help us.'

Marcia had never heard such despair before. It choked her up. Despite not knowing exactly what was going on, Marcia didn't hesitate. 'I'll do it. But I don't have a key to get you out.'

Carol's heavy breathing became more laboured. 'Not now. It's not safe now. On Thursday find me . . .'

CHAPTER 27

'Get lost! If you try and come in this house, I'll have the cops here in a flash.'

My sister's temper hasn't improved since she walked out on Craven, Luke and myself at Ocean Haven yesterday. I'm standing at the front door of her house ringing the bell. But she's confused me with her husband, so I'm forced to shout through the letter box. 'It's Gabby, open the door.'

'*Talk to your brother-in-law. See if you can ferret out any information from him that shows he has a hidden history with the house.*' Craven's words come back to me. The problem is that Luke obviously isn't at home. Damn!

There's a long silence on the other side, before Salina responds with sorrowful tones, 'Not now, Gabby. I'm not in the mood. Give me a bell later.'

'I need to talk to you.' I feel silly and awkward bent down like this at her door begging for entry.

Finally, the electronic bolts are dropped. There are several of them – Luke's been well and truly locked out. She opens the door slightly ajar using a chain and peers out through the gap. 'He's not with you, is he?'

'Come on.'

She doesn't quite let me in, instead coming out, eyes darting everywhere to see if her errant husband is hiding ready to pounce. Satisfied, Salina retreats inside, leaving the door open for me to follow. She's in their dining room, sat at the table with a bottle of red wine and a glass. By the look of it, the bottle has taken quite a hit already.

I sit opposite her. 'How are you managing?' I'm not here just to dig up info for my investigation with Craven, I am genuinely concerned about my sister's welfare after her bust-up with her husband about Ocean Haven.

Her eyes flash. 'Do you know what he did?'

'I've heard his version and that was bad enough, so I'm guessing yours is worse.'

Her lips purse into a cold smile. 'Oh, he's got to work on you already, has he? That's how he rolls: he admits everything to get that out of the way and then tries to play the poor orphan card.'

'I've never heard him even mention the fact he was an orphan.'

Salina's smile bursts into laughter. 'His dad wasn't around and something happened to his mum when he was a kid and he ended up living with relatives. He won't talk about his dear mum but I know he loved her like crazy.' Her voice rises. 'Concerning that flash house on the hill, I don't mind the money he bilked out of me or the fact he went behind my back. I've been made a fool of! You'd think I'd know better after being brought up by our father.'

'Why do you figure Luke bought Ocean Haven?' Her husband might not be here but Salina might know more about his motivation.

There's a cynical glimmer in her gaze. 'Stay there a minute, sis, let me show you something that tells you all you need to know about my husband.'

While she's gone, I look around the room. The sideboard is piled with samples of her latest Salina cosmetic line, including small bottles of perfume, plus a range of products for men. This is all accompanied by a new advertising slogan: 'Why wear clothes when you can wear Salina.' I have to admit that although I'm dead proud of my sister's achievements, I don't really get all this need for so much make-up. When we were growing up I thought Mummy was a good sport for allowing Salina to practise on her face. If you want a bit of colour, in my books a splash of lipstick is sufficient.

'Fancy trying some?'

I turn to find my sister wearing a faltering smile because she's not sure if I like what I see. That's the thing with my baby sister: on the surface she's all loud 'n' proud but dig deep and the vulnerable girl that she was still lurks.

She gets a big smile of reassurance from me. 'I have no idea how you come up with the ideas for the colours and styles.'

She strolls over to me, angling her head, giving me the critical once over. 'Mummy's old lippy looks good on you, but who wants to look good. You want to look mag-nif-ee-cent. I've got just the right colours for you.'

She hands me an A4 piece of paper. 'What's this?'

'Luke's personal statement, he gives it to anyone he works with. Read it.'

I do: '*Who am I? I'll tell you. I'm the son of a man who walked out on my mum before I was old enough to walk and a woman with no resources except love and determination. Determination, that's the bedrock of my success.*'

Salina interprets for me, back with a glass of red wine. 'He learned from an early age that if you want something stick at it. Keep going and you'll eventually get it. Ocean Haven represents big time money to him. Tart it up and sell it on.'

I go somewhere I'm not sure I should. 'You don't think this has anything to do with Mummy being involved in the house?'

Belligerently, Salina knocks back her wine. 'How can you still want to go anywhere near that place after a dead body was found there, for crying out loud?' Her voice softens. 'I'm worried about you being anywhere near there. What if this killer is still on the loose?'

She has a point, but if I don't carry on it feels like I will be abandoning Mummy. I switch the conversation. 'The lease has run out on my rented room so I need somewhere to lay my hat.'

Salina beams. 'Of course you're going to come here.'

I'm tempted. Perhaps the only good thing coming out of this whole business is that my sister and I are becoming sisters in the proper sense of the word. On the other hand, I need time on my own to work things out.

I shake my head. 'Thanks for the invite, but I've got another place in mind.'

'Oh la la! Gabrielle Lewis, you haven't got a boyfriend stashed away in Tinfields?'

Craven's face fills my mind. Quickly, I banish it.

As I pick up my bag and make for the door, something strange happens. Salina gets out of her chair and spreads her arms like a minister of religion. She beckons to me with her outstretched hand. She wants us to hug. My cynical, cocky, arrogant and unsentimental sister is soon hugging me. This kind of thing doesn't really happen in our family.

At the front door she gives me a present. It's a box of her latest product. It comes from a table in the hall, rather than the ones in the dining room, and it was waiting there for me, because it has a simple note attached. 'To darling Gabby. Love Salina. X'

At Ocean Haven the police have erected a large tent surrounded with police tape around the area where the murder victim, probably Robert Delbrook, was found. But there's no sign of the police. I find Luke crouched down just inside the kitchen using a screwdriver on the back door. The kitchen and the parts of the house I catch a glimpse of in the distance are a wreck. It had a disturbing charm before, but now everything has been shifted, some things slashed, floorboards removed in the police quest to find evidence to help with their murder investigation. Luke has thrown some floorboards back into position to at least ensure the pathway from the massive reception area to the kitchen is safe.

Spotting me he says, 'I suppose you spoke to your sister?' Luke looks beat in the harsh electric light. 'There's no need to worry about me and my darling wife; we'll kiss and make up, we always do.'

'Are the cops gone?'

He nods. 'For now. I don't suppose there was a lot of evidence left in the house after the council housed the homeless here years back. The coppers did that whole thing of crawling around doing the fingertip search business and they probably found some interesting things, but nothing to do with the remains of the body they found.' He stands up and turns the door handle. 'There,' he announces with a wide grin, rising to his six-foot plus height.

'What are you doing?'

'The lock on the door was broken. That should do the trick. Do you want a cup of tea? I've stolen a kettle, milk and biscuits from the builder's portacabin outside. They won't be back until I know for sure the cops are through.'

While he's rustling up a cuppa for us both I casually ask, 'Why did you buy Ocean Haven?'

With a lengthy sigh he cocks his head at me. 'Are you still giving me the third degree about this house? First, you accuse me of

162

attacking your old man. Now I've got some link to this.' His arms wave around, indicating the house.

I press on. 'It's lost its sparkle and former glory—'

'Which is where I neatly come in,' he niftily slides in, handing me my tea. 'Know what I love after my wife? Bricks and mortar, cement and tiles, hammers and screwdrivers. Houses, homes, buildings, they are the most gorgeous things on this earth. The shapes, the lines, the light.'

How my mouth doesn't fall open in shock I don't know. My brother-in-law, who I've always taken to be an uncultured braggart, sounds like a poet.

He continues, his fingers tight about his mug, 'One of the many jobs my mum had was working for a family – y'know, the type whose clothes are made of one hundred pound notes not material. She used to clean up after them like some skivvy. And every year she was allowed to bring me to see the lady of the house on Christmas Eve and Lady Muck would present me with a little gift, all nicely wrapped, and I'd have to lower my eyes while I politely thanked her.'

I'm transfixed by him and can't look away. 'The first house I ever got my hands on was hers. The old girl had fallen on hard times. When she realised who was buying her pile in the country I could see in her eyes she wanted to take it back, but I was the only one who'd offered for her property.' His chest puffs out with pride. 'And, of course, I gave her a little present. All nicely wrapped up. A key to one of my rented properties in Tinfields. I let her live there rent-free.'

'Why?'

'Because my dear mum respected her and would have wanted me to do it.' He abandons his untouched cup of tea on the counter.

His personal story leaves me shaken, I can't explain why. Maybe it's having to see Luke as a small boy. I add boy-Luke to the other children who have been shadowing me since I arrived back in Tinfields; girl-Gabby, girl-Salina and boy-Karl.

I pluck up the courage to ask him, 'I've got to move out of the room I'm renting . . . Any chance I can stay here?'

Staying here will allow me to search this place from roof to cellar, every nook and cranny, looking for anything that can reveal more about Mummy's connection here.

He bursts out laughing. 'Here? Are you insane? Look at the state of the place.' He points to the hall where the floorboards are tangled together. 'You'll break a leg going up the stairs. And do you know how lonely and isolated this place is at night? It'll be like a convention centre for serial killers.' He turns serious. 'A dead person was found here.'

I put down my cup. 'I could stay with you and Salina, but, hey, two sisters staying together can erupt into open warfare and, let's face it, you'll be the one stuck in the middle . . .'

A set of keys comes sailing towards me, which I neatly catch. Yes, I thought my last comments might sway his decision in my favour. However, he isn't finished with me. 'Any trouble, the cops come back, you get on the phone to me.'

I go over and kiss him on the cheek. 'Cheers, Luke.'

He leans into my ear and says, 'Your sister is the best thing that ever happened to me. The way her cosmetics line is going, it'll soon be me who's the trophy spouse not her. I'll die for Salina.' His tone becoming steely. 'I hope you haven't come back here to drag my wife back to a childhood that screwed her royally over. Because if you have, you'll have me to deal with.'

I watch him leave. So do the seven ravens in the trees. We watch him pass the taped-off ground of a makeshift grave of a murder victim.

CHAPTER 28

Rucksack on my back I look up at Ocean Haven from the driveway. It's the following morning and for the first time the size of the place is overwhelming. How am I going to manage to search the whole of it for clues? And I'm not too big to admit that the thought of moving in here makes my blood run cold. I work up the courage to move to the entrance, put in Luke's key and turn it. I step inside and am instantly seized by the sensation of something else being here. Despite the light, I feel shadows pressing in on me. Shadows of the people who once lived here? Mummy?

Stop it! Stop being stupid. There's no one here but you.

I enter the room I've already chosen to live in during my temporary stay here. The morning room. I chose it for two reasons. Firstly, it's at the front with a large window that has an eagle-eye view of anyone approaching the house. The other reason: if there's any trouble I'm near the front door and can make a run for it. I'm not anticipating any trouble . . . but you never know. The room doesn't look as much of a mess as when I first came here. The scarlet shows up prettily in the blackened rot of the once-stylish wallpaper and the fireplace might be falling to bits and have no mantle, but it has a striking front with a large mirror that dominates the whole wall. There are two figures carved in it that I can't make out from here. I move nearer to have a look, then stagger back. On either side is a stone creature, a cross between a gargoyle and bat, with a pointed face and sharp teeth. The big curved wings springing from their backs make them look like they're about to fly off.

My blood runs cold again. Maybe this isn't the best room after all. *Stop. It.* I dump my rucksack on to the grey, rose-patterned sofa bed, take out my last bottle of Dad's ginger beer and head towards the kitchen where I find a surprise waiting for me – a nice surprise. Luke has left me a camping-sized fridge. Aww, bless him! Shame colours my cheeks at the way I've always treated my brother-in-law; he's a good person at heart. I pop the ginger beer in the fridge and look out of the window. Using the broom I find in a corner, I sweep away the plaster that's fallen from the ceiling in my room. *My room.* I like the sound of that. Then I take a glass of cool ginger beer and wander down to the beach.

Eyes closed, arms wide, I spin in a circle on the beach below Ocean Haven. I'm barefoot, the sand gritty, soft and damp between my toes. Salty sea air shoots through my nostrils, clearing my lungs. I used to do this as a child, not with Mummy but with Daddy. His love of the sea was almost an obsession; I think because it took him back to his own youth in the Caribbean. Some days we'd come and he'd stand for a good hour on the shore, watching the rhythm of the waves on the water and the fishing folk going off to sea. That's why it's been so hard to completely hate Dad through and through, because there were times in my childhood when he did spend time with us, did try to show us love in his way. Then again, aren't I doing what most children do: trying to remain loyal to a parent they know is rotten to the core?

When I open my eyes there's a woman striding with purpose down the beach accompanied by a very lively dog on a lead. The dog's a dachshund with the most gorgeous, rust-coloured glossy coat. The woman is wearing a black beret tilted to the side and I suspect she's in her fifties. This is the woman and dog I caught a glimpse of on the beach when I stood on Cliff Heights that time Luke took me to Ocean Haven.

'Eddie The Seventh,' she cautions the dog in a controlled manner. Eddie The Seventh? Is this dog royalty? 'Remember, don't go out too far. You don't want to go home with a soggy bottom.'

Quietly I chuckle. The dog wags its tail with vigour and barks as she lets him off his lead. Eddie's off. Picking up my empty glass from the sand, I go over to her and can't help commenting, 'He's a beautiful dog.'

She grins, her chin pointing with pride. 'He's been with me for five years now. I got him from the rescue service.'

'I'm Gabby.'

Her grin widens. 'I'm Aphrodite. Never Afro or Ditty.'

I chuckle. I like this lady. 'Do you live around here?'

'Me and Tinfields are old friends.'

It occurs to me. 'Do you know anything about Ocean Haven? The grand house up there on the hill? There was a terrible tragedy there, a mother and her son fell from the cliff and died.'

She thinks awhile, fiddling with a ball that she's taken out of her pocket for the dog to play with. 'That was long ago.'

'Twenty-five years.'

She throws the ball to Eddie, who leaps and does the doggy version of cartwheels. 'I don't recall the details, but it was a very sad time.' With a respectful nod, she moves off to her dog. Then she turns back to me, scowling. 'You've got some of the events muddled.'

'What do you mean?'

'The boy didn't die.'

◆ ◆ ◆

I rush into the restaurant for my dinner 'date' with Craven, because I'm twenty minutes late. The sickness caught me just as I was about to go out the door. Oh hell, it was so bad this time I had to lie on the bed. It finally passed, but my ankles and head throb like crazy. I was reluctant to take some heavy-duty painkillers because they often make me drowsy and I want to be on full alert tonight. Craven is already waiting for me inside the only Vietnamese restaurant in Tinfields. I'm not surprised the place is packed, because word on the street is that their cold rice noodle dishes with salad is one of the best things you will ever eat.

He stands up and it's nice to see him out of his regulation suit and in black jeans and a smart T-shirt, which displays the muscles in his lower arms.

He rushes around the table to pull my seat out for me. Really? I quirk my dubious brow at him. Us modern gals can pull back chairs. Still, I say nothing, he's obviously doing his best to make me feel at home, which I am grateful for.

'I like the lipstick. Nice shade,' Craven compliments me.

'My sister, Salina, gave it to me,' I self-consciously reply. The lipstick was accompanied by foundation and face powder in the gift Salina gave me. I'm not sold on the shade of the lippy – too much earthy brown – so in truth I may go back to wearing Mummy's old one. 'She's one of these online make-up sensations.'

Then I confess, 'I don't know much about Vietnamese cuisine.'

He gazes at me with relish. 'Leave it to me. Many years ago I did a backpacking tour of Vietnam and learned all about its food. Great if you don't eat gluten because much of it is rice-based.'

There's a sparkle to Craven tonight, an ease that he never displays as a cop. Nevertheless, I need to set boundaries with him.

I say, 'I'm not doing men at the moment.'

'Who said anything about men? What about a toy boy?'

A very clever reminder that I must be at least seven or so years older than him. Cheeky! We both laugh and that breaks the ice. Or is that rice cracker? That's how good a time I start having with Craven – I'm cracking jokes. Well, I consider them to be funny. It's been a long time since I went out with a man and truly relaxed. There's none of that horrendous first-date ritual. You know, like thinking will I or won't I sleep with him. I did like my last long-term partner, Keith, it was just I couldn't see him looking after me if I got sick. I will never forget when I sometimes had period pains how he couldn't get out of our flat quick enough. And let's face it, I know I'm going to die. Soon. I'm convinced whatever test results come back from my doctor won't save me.

I ask, 'Have you got anything new to report?'

He shakes his head. 'I've been called to help out with another investigation, which I've managed to wriggle free of. What about you? Did you manage to speak with your brother-in-law?'

I cast my mind back to my discussion with Luke. His story about his childhood wasn't one I was expecting to hear. 'I found out what drives him and it has nothing directly to do with Ocean Haven.' My fork fiddles in my papaya salad. 'What you need to understand about Luke is he's after the next best thing, especially in property.' My brows dip. 'Someone told me today, a local woman, that Carol Shore's son Jamie didn't die in the tragedy at Cliff Heights twenty-five years ago.'

Craven looks bemused. 'The cliffs? What's this story?'

'I'll fill you in after we've finished our main course. Maybe you can ask around—'

'Well, look who it is,' a boisterous male voice cuts in.

Coming towards us is a man and a woman. He's all rugby-big alongside her doll-like small. His cheeks are the ruddy colour of someone who has downed a number of pints. He only has eyes for Craven.

'Hey! It's been a long time, mate,' he declares when he reaches our table. He looks happy enough to thump Craven on the back.

Craven's face is a pasty white. He's uncomfortable. 'Good to see you. Catch up another time.'

The man carries on, ignoring Craven's subtle hint to go away. 'Heard you became a copper. Good on you, after all that business.'

Business? I'm intrigued now. Craven appears upset. 'Another time.'

'Oh.' The guy looks crestfallen. Then, 'Yeah, I get it, not the type of thing to air in front of the girlfriend.'

Craven doesn't look like he's moving anymore. His face is devoid of colour.

The man moves on and then calls over his shoulder, 'I'll be seeing you, Jamie.' He rolls his eyes. 'I nearly called you Shore. Jamie Shore, but it's Craven now, isn't it? Jamie Craven.'

CHAPTER 29

I surprise myself by going into lawyer mode. 'Do your superior or your colleagues know that you are Jamie Shore? That you're personally connected to this case?'

'What?' His cry is savage. 'And explain to people that my mother jumped off a cliff holding me in her arms?' The despair in his tone leaves me aching for him. 'If that's what happened on Cliff Heights that night,' he quietly adds.

We're sitting on the beach, me crossed-legged, him with his arms locked way too tight around his raised knees. The surf is a strange midnight blue against the darkness of the sea, which laps forward and back with the sound of a surging wind.

I bite back asking him what he means, because I need him to open up about his story and I've found the best way to do that is to start at the beginning.

'Why did you conceal from me who you are?'

He looks away. 'I didn't know how you'd react. My father's family disapproved of him marrying my mother. It was a classic across-the-tracks romance: he came from money and she didn't. We were in the car one day, Dad lost control and it flipped over. He died and my mother fell to pieces. I . . .' For a moment, he tails off, deep in thought about the past.

With a shake of his head he snaps out of it and continues, 'My grandad's sister, Great Aunt Laura, who I didn't know very well, God bless her, agreed to look after me. I think I recall my mother telling one of the women at Ocean Haven how she met Dr Vincent Fortune at the coffee shop near the psychiatric unit she was in. The clinic didn't come cheap, so it was for patients with money—'

'Money. Opportunity,' I jump in, seeing exactly where Craven is going. 'That's how he will have chosen his targets. Firstly, they had to have money. And where would he find women with money, vulnerable women with money, women in pain – a private psychiatric clinic.'

In my mind's eye I see the vile Vincent Fortune loitering in the coffee shop near the health unit where Craven's mother was receiving treatment. Waiting, like a jackal ready to pounce. And Carol Shore was so young, so young, she probably never stood a chance. My stomach turns; the evilness of this man sickens me.

'I suspect he was looking for a substantial property where he could set up his so-called treatment centre,' Craven forcefully adds. 'Mum was so fragile and he was a master at pulling the strings of people in distress. I was so traumatised by my dad's death I couldn't speak for a long time. Couldn't utter a word.'

How awful. My heart hurts for him. I want to tell him to stop, but I don't, because I need to know what happened. I hate that he has to drag himself through his mother's pain so that I can find the truth about my own.

'When I came back to Ocean Haven, Mum wasn't alone – that bloody man was there too. I don't know how he then persuaded Mum to allow him to use it as a base to help heal women. *Heal women*. What a pile of putrid trash.' His voice softens. 'I wish you'd met her. She was so kind and beautiful, all a little boy could dream of in a mother. The first thing I did when I reached adulthood was

172

to change my last name to Craven. It was my mother's maiden name. It was one of the ways I tried to hang on to her memory.'

I wish I'd met her too. If she was anything like her son, I suspect I would have liked her very much indeed. '*Home? I thought I knew where that was once.*' What Craven told me as he drove me to the doctor's surgery has deep meaning now. How the home he'd once had with his mother was destroyed by Robert Delbrook.

However, I'm not letting him completely off the hook. 'When you told me that Robert Delbrook was aka Vincent Fortune were you attempting to milk me for information?'

His eyes flash. 'I'd have slammed Santa himself in a cell if he had information about what happened to my mother.'

'Why did Delbrook turn against her?'

'Simple really. Greed. He wanted the house, to own it lock, stock and barrel. Mummy wouldn't sign it over to him. He started playing mind games with her. I heard him tell her how she was the reason Dad died. Do you remember the outbuilding, the shack where the police found Delbrook's body? That's where he'd take my mother. I don't know what he was doing to my mum, but whatever it was it was awful, he was tearing her apart . . .'

His mouth keeps moving, but the horror and shock of what happened steals the words from him. His body trembles.

'Craven, breathe. Breathe. That's it.' I take his hands in mine. Goodness, the flesh of them is frozen. I move my fingers to rub some warmth back into them. My heart bleeds for this grieving man who remains shell-shocked at such a terrible loss.

He eventually speaks again. 'I didn't want to have anything to do with the house for years, because it made me sick to my stomach to think of all the messed-up stuff that had been done to my mother there. But my great aunt, she's a tough one, wouldn't give up contesting its ownership. She vehemently said it was my birthright and no one else had a right to it. In the last few years I've come to understand that she was correct and that's why I've joined her this time in our legal action.'

My mind goes back to the first time I visited Ocean Haven with the estate agent, to the gorgeous spray of flowers laid in quiet respect next to the mysterious handwritten card with the message, 'To Mum. Always in my thoughts.' I don't need to ask to know that this was Craven.

'What happened on the cliff?' With care I press him. 'You and your mum?'

He shuts his eyes for a time and inhales. He reopens them, gazing out to sea. 'All she told me was we were going away. I saw Mum secretly speaking to your mum a time or two. I knew that Marcia was getting us a ticket to London and had clothes and stuff ready for us in a suitcase she was keeping for us.'

He stares at me with a look that's uncomfortable, penetrating, as if he's seeing right into me. 'Your mum spoke to me a couple of times.'

'What did she say?' I sound desperate, child-like, back to being girl-Gabby wanting any scrap of her mum.

He smiles. 'She was lovely. Always so calm. Kind.' His smile dissolves. 'She was meant to come for us. She never turned up.'

My mouth falls open in shock. Suddenly it all makes sense. 'That must've been the evening she fell sick. She was so ill, much worse than usual. We took her to hospital. She died.'

'I think my mum saw Marcia as her last chance. She wasn't well, taking pills to calm her nerves. I don't think she could take it anymore. Cliff Heights is a blur. It was so dark. I'm not sure if she was running from someone or her desperation drove her there. Did she jump with me in her arms or was she pushed? I don't know for sure.'

Both our mothers died the same night.

Craven asks, 'Have you got our investigation board?'

Quickly I take out the squares of paper and lay them on the sand between us. What we have so far is:

Robert Delbrook aka Dr Vincent murdered & buried at Ocean Haven.

Carol Shore and Marcia Lewis – at Ocean Haven.

Marcia Lewis – Key figure in Ocean Haven ownership? How?

Luke Wilson Ocean Haven new owner.

'Let's talk through what new evidence we have,' he suggests. So I write our new information down:

Carol and Marcia both died the same night.

Carol murdered? Marcia murdered?

The implication of our last piece of evidence leaves us both reeling in a turbulent silence, with only the run and recoil of the waves heard. Did someone kill both our mothers?

He breaks the silence. 'There is maybe – *maybe* – one way we can prove or disprove whether your mother was murdered. Her medical records. But . . .'

'But?' The sceptical expression he wears does not fill me with confidence.

'Medical records are usually only kept eight years after someone dies. Still, leave it with me, my enquiries may draw something to the surface.'

And I promise, 'I'll have another blitz on the computer at work to see if my firm has access to any more goodies.'

When I get back to Ocean Haven I take our investigation board and lay each one on the sofa bed. Then I take out a blank square of paper and write the name of someone else who was at Ocean Haven:

Jamie.

CHAPTER 30

TWENTY-FIVE YEARS AGO

MARCIA

Eleven-year-old Karl's eyes shot open and wide. Someone was in his bedroom. A large shadow loomed over him in the dark as he lay in bed. A palm clamped over his mouth before he could cry for help. Fear gripped him. What was happening? Who was this? Usually the culprit would be Salina playing one of her stupid little tricks, but he knew it wasn't her; whoever stood over him was much larger.

'Karl, it's OK. It's me. Mum.'

Once the hand dropped away, a confused Karl sat up. His fingers gripped the blanket. 'Mum? What's going on?'

His mother perched on the side of the bed. 'Sweetie, I'm going to ask you a question and I need you to tell me the truth.' Karl nodded. 'The other day, when the school accused you of picking the lock of the arts cupboard . . .'

'I never did it, Mum. I cross my heart, hope to die . . .' His mother's arched brow and stern expression froze the words in his throat. Karl's face fell. 'I only wanted to get some paint to paint the wooden car I made with Fred.' He still found it hard to deal with Fred's death.

Instead of his mum's wagging-finger telling-off voice, she asked, 'Can you be really quiet for Mummy?' He nodded. 'I need you to put your clothes on and your trainers.'

Karl frowned. 'Why?'

'We're going out.'

◆ ◆ ◆

Marcia gasped at the familiar house on the hill up ahead. She had never seen it before in the dark. The inkiness around it seemed to push it even higher, making it look like it was floating in the air. Even in the dark the gloss of its white facade stood out. But now Marcia knew the truth. What really lay beneath all that blinding white was a thick infestation of rot. The house was rotten to the core. In all truth and honesty, she couldn't wait until Thursday, as agreed with Carol, to talk to her; she had to find out what was going on.

'Mum? What are we doing back at this house?'

The house had made Marcia forget that she had her youngest child with her. Ocean Haven had a kind of power over her. She didn't like it, not one bit. She looked down at her son and wondered if she was doing the right thing. It wasn't too late to turn around and go. Goodness, what was she thinking of, dragging her beloved child into this? But Marcia didn't have any choice, Karl was the only one who could help her. The only one who could help her better understand what was going on at Ocean Haven.

Karl's small hand touched her arm. 'Mummy, you're shaking.'

Marcia rustled up a forced smile of reassurance. 'I'm all good. Before we go any further, remind me what we agreed at home.'

'That I wouldn't tell a soul about coming here with you tonight.' He spoke with conviction. 'Not Daddy, Gabby or Salina.'

'Or any of your friends. If you tell any of them, one of *my* friends might get into trouble.'

Carol had no idea that Marcia would be coming here tonight. Marcia's curiosity had taken hold of her and would not let go. God forgive her if she was doing the wrong thing by involving her son.

Marcia warned him, 'We have to be quiet, because we don't want to wake up anyone in that big house. And you must do everything I tell you.' Her son was such a stubborn boy at times, only interested in following his own rules. 'Karl, you hear me? You follow my rules tonight, not your own.'

Marcia leading, they made their way cautiously and slowly down the pathway towards the house. Except they didn't head for the house, but to the shack instead. Marcia guided her boy around the back of it, the same place with the crack she'd looked through. The darkness was deep here, brooding and impenetrable. Karl suddenly let out a yelp. Marcia drew him close and held him there. Her gaze skated with fear towards the house. *Please don't let anyone have heard Karl. Please.*

'Karl, I told you we need to be quiet,' she admonished her child.

'Sorry, Mum, something ran over my leg.' He shuddered.

Marcia explained, 'We're going to head around the front of this building. When we get there, you know what you have to do.'

After Karl's nod, Marcia glanced over at the house one final time and then silently stepped around the shack, heading for the front. There was a nasty smell here she'd never noticed before, likely the stench of the shack's wood rotting more and more each time it rained. When they reached the corner of the building, Marcia gently grabbed her son's wrist, making them both hang back. Once more she checked over the house. Good, no sign of life. Just as they were about to step out a light shone bright against an upstairs window. It was Karl who jerked his mum behind the building. Mother and son stared at each other, breathing laboured and furious. In that moment of fear Marcia realised that her baby boy was growing up.

Marcia inched towards the corner again and looked up. Thank goodness, the light was gone, the house shrouded in darkness once more. There was no time to waste, they needed to be quick. Silently they moved into the darkness. In front of the shack. In front of the secured padlock.

Karl needed no urging from his mother, he got to work. From his pocket came the tools he needed to pick the lock. What else was Dr Vincent keeping in the shack? The need to find out was so powerful that Marcia had barely slept the last few nights. The major league fly in the ointment was how was she going to get inside? That's when she remembered Karl had been suspended from school for fighting and accused of getting into the locked art resources cupboard. Marcia had thought long and hard about involving Karl, especially as she might be giving him the message that picking locks was OK, which it certainly wasn't.

Sometimes you have to use a wrong to create a right. Marcia watched her son work, his fine young fingers moving carefully, twisting one tool, and then another. Click. Then off came the padlock which Karl handed to his mum. The shack door was ready to open.

Marcia turned to her son. 'What did we agree?'

'That I'd wait around the back.'

'And if anyone comes?'

'Scream the place down.'

'Good boy. I won't be long.'

Once he disappeared Marcia turned her full attention to the door. Deep breath in, she pulled it back. Exhaling, she stepped inside, dragging the door behind her. Taking out a torch she shone it carefully around. It was musty with the throat-prickling taste of mildew in the air. And dusty: so much so, Marcia quietly coughed into her cupped hand.

She did a walk around and found nothing sinister. She'd been expecting to find chains suspended from beams, whips coiled and ready for a lashing, a simple chair to tie someone up in. Then again, what Vincent Fortune was doing to Carol demonstrated that the only thing needed to torture someone was an evil mind.

The only other items were a collection of shovels of varying sizes stacked against a wall, an engine from some type of vehicle discarded on the floor, a broken table and a box. No, the box was more like a chest thrown on its side. Marcia had seen enough, her curiosity satisfied. She twisted about to leave when a creaking noise sounded behind her. She froze, her heart banging against her chest wall. There was something, *someone* behind her. She could sense them, feel their heat radiating in the room. Sweat beaded across her forehead, air shook inside her chest. Karl. Suddenly she remembered her child waiting outside. She would die before allowing anyone to hurt her son. And that's why Marcia mustered up the courage, steeled herself and slowly turned. And turned. And turned. Until she faced the wide yawning space. Her flashlight swung around. Nothing. No one was there.

Marcia could still sense them. She wanted to call out, but knew she couldn't, someone at the house was bound to hear her. Keeping the light level in front of her, she inched forward one silent step at a time. Oh hell, she could hear their breathing. Where were they? Maybe they were above and about to spring on her? Marcia crazily swung the light towards the sagging ceiling . . . No one there. Light back down, she kept moving forward. She stopped near the chest that was on its side. Suddenly the chest was flung open. Marcia hurtled back, tumbling on to her behind. The torch fell out of her hand. Grabbing it for dear life she shone it on the opened chest.

Straight into the terror-stricken eyes of Carol.

◆ ◆ ◆

The enormity of what she was seeing made Marcia stumble back. Things like this happened in horror movies not real life. Carol lay on her side, the space in the box so restricted she had no choice but to hug her knees to her chest. How could someone do this to another human being? It was wicked; the purest evil Marcia had ever borne witness to. Vincent was a monster. A monster. Marcia crawled over to Carol.

'Oh my God, Carol.' She extended a hand to pull the other woman out, but was surprised when Carol resisted her efforts, explaining, 'No. You can't. I can't.'

Marcia reared on to her knees. She was so upset. 'I can't leave you here like this.'

'You don't have a choice. If he's capable of doing this, think what he's capable of doing to Jamie.'

'I'm sorry, so sorry,' Marcia repeated over and over like she was in a nightmare. It was a nightmare. Still, she was not prepared to leave a young woman in such a dangerous situation. She put on her mother's voice. 'You're coming with me.'

If it were possible, Carol cowered deeper inside the box. 'I can't come with you.'

'Yes, you can.'

'No. I. Can't!' the younger woman cried. 'You don't under-stand. I can't leave here. Physically, I can't leave the house. If I put even a foot outside the door I start shaking. The last time I tried I collapsed.'

Marcia frowned. 'But how do you manage to leave the house and get here?'

'He has to physically lead me. Every time is like the purest agony.' *And Vincent Fortune will know that*, Marcia angrily thought.

There had been a woman on Marcia's street who'd had the same condition. She tried to remember what the condition was called. Actophobia . . . No . . . Agoraphobia, that was it. She asked Carol, 'Did you suffer with this before you met Dr Vincent?'

Carol's eyes dipped down in shame. That made Marcia mad; this beautiful, terrified girl wasn't the one who should be consumed with shame.

Carol lifted her eyes. 'I need to leave here with Jamie. I can't do this on my own. I need you to come, take my hand and lead me out of here.'

Although red raw rage roared through Marcia she knew there was nothing she could do about Carol's terrible predicament at present. If she carried out what she really wanted to do, which was to march up to the house, bang on the door and when it opened punch the living daylights out of that devil, it would leave Carol vulnerable to more hurt. And not just her, but the son she loved beyond words too.

Marcia took Carol's hand. 'I will lead you out of here. Lead Jamie from this place of wickedness.'

The relief in Carol's eyes made Marcia want to cry. The younger woman whispered, 'The best day for us to escape will be next Saturday. Dog-breath Vincent will be going to London on business for the whole day.'

Marcia's brows shot up. 'Dog-breath?'

'Yes.' Carol actually smiled. 'His breath always reeks of garlic.'

She's right, Marcia thought. They shared a laugh. Who'd have thought laughter could be found in such a horror-filled place.

Marcia said, 'I'll find you and your darling son on the top floor . . .'

Despair gleamed hot in Carol's eyes again. 'We used to live on the top floor.' Her breathing was laboured. 'He moved us to the attic. We sleep together on an old bed, sometimes with no heating.'

Marcia's mind quickly cast back to the time when she was told that Carol and Jamie lived somewhere near the top floor. The vagueness had puzzled her. Now she understood. Her tortured mind imagined Carol hugging her son close in bed, trying her best to keep him warm. Marcia was more determined than ever to help them escape.

Her voice dropped to barely a whisper. 'Next Saturday. In the meantime we need to plan . . .'

CHAPTER 31

When I walk into my office, the atmosphere changes. The receptionist avoids my eyes, my colleagues are unusually quiet, some whispering. I think they're whispering about me. Stolen glances follow me and are quickly averted. Greg is waiting for me near my workstation. I can't read his expression.

'Hello, Greg . . .' My greeting falters. 'Is there a problem?'

He appears cheery, but there's a strain about his mouth he can't hide. 'I think it's best if you join me in my office.'

After he closes the door we sit down. He steeples his fingers together as he starts. 'I want to thank you for all the work you've undertaken while you've been here.'

Something about the way he carefully chooses his words leaves me on edge. 'I enjoy working here. The Ocean Haven case has been a challenge, especially with the discovery of the remains of a body.'

Greg visibly flinches at the words 'body' and 'remains'. He says, 'I wish I could say that I was shocked that the disputed ownership of Ocean Haven has led to a dead body but I'm not. The whole thing reeks of the unpleasant.'

His last words prick my interest. 'Have you heard something new about the police investigation there? Did the police contact you?'

Picking up on the overeagerness of my words, he scowls, deeply scrutinising my expression. 'You sound as if you're personally involved. Are you?'

I switch to a more neutral tone. 'You know what it's like; once you get your teeth into a case you want to know the whole story.'

Now Greg's avoiding my eyes. 'I just want you to know that you're a highly valued member of our staff and we've never been less than happy with your work. But we think it's better for all, including yourself, if you sought pastures new.'

'Are you firing me?'

He clears his throat and begins to splutter about cutbacks, retrenchments, difficult business environments and the inevitable redundancies, but I cut him short. 'Oh, spare me, Greg. You tell me what the problem is and I'll go willingly. Otherwise, I'll still go willingly but you won't have heard the last of this.'

Greg purses his lips and leans over his desk. 'All right, this is in strictest confidence and if you breathe any of this outside this office, we'll deny everything.' If it wasn't for the circumstances, I'd actually feel embarrassed for him. He's clearly finding this very painful.

He resumes, 'A contact of mine in the police has notified me that an employee of this firm *may* have been impersonating a police officer in order to solicit confidential information. I understand that the matter is not being taken any further. Nevertheless, the police may change their mind and decide to press charges. If that happens and it turns out that the information this employee had obtained was connected to a case they were conducting on behalf of the firm we could find ourselves in all kinds of legal trouble as a consequence.'

I could sit here and argue, but what would be the point. Greg shakes my hand when we stand. 'I know you won't believe this, but I like you,' he tells me. 'You're thorough, a damn hard worker and don't give up.'

I'm dumbstruck. I can't believe my time here is over. I'm too ashamed to put my things in a box and walk out with it in the traditional style. Instead, I cram as many items as possible into my bag, leaving things that are important to me behind, although I think I'm too upset to care. When the way out involves as little interaction with my ex-colleagues as possible, I make a break for it. The receptionist calls me back. 'There was a call for you, but I could see you were occupied.' She's embarrassed. 'I took a message. A man says he's waiting for you at your new place of residence.'

Craven.

◆ ◆ ◆

But it isn't Craven I find, it's my brother. It's a bombshell to see him there, because after he'd ordered me from his house I thought our relationship was game over. I'm so glad to see him, so glad. He's sitting on the doorstep, long legs relaxed out in front of him.

'How did you know I was here?' I ask, puzzled.

'Luke told me.' Of course. I forget that Karl has a close relationship with our sister's husband. 'This place has certainly fallen on hard times.' He stands and steps back to run his gaze over the facade. 'When I came here as a boy it looked like a castle to me. I remember thinking, I wonder if King Arthur and his knights had lived here—'

'Guinevere and the Lady of the Lake too,' I playfully throw in. 'Let's not forget the women in that story.'

Karl's open acknowledgment that he has a connection to Ocean Haven blows me away. My heart's galloping with excitement at the prospect of what my brother can tell me about our mother and this house The dead body found here. I take him inside and straight to the place where his name is carved near the door.

'Mummy brought you here, didn't she?'

He nods and runs a finger over each letter in his name. 'Do you know why I carved my name everywhere? I felt left out, like I was invisible, especially in our family. It was my way of announcing to the world that I was here.' He looks up at me, expression mournful. 'Fred was the only one who got it, who understood.'

I want to fiercely hug his pain away but suspect he wouldn't appreciate that. However, I hang on to the hope that this is the first building block in a new relationship between us.

He answers my earlier question. 'After Fred's murder, I think Mum was worried about me, so she tried to keep me close to her side—'

'But what's that got to do with this place? Fill me in.'

As we talk I take him into my makeshift bedroom where we sit and delve into our mother's secret past.

Karl says, 'Honestly, I was sort of shocked when we came here. This woman called Buttercup—'

'Buttercup,' I sharply cut in. I know that name. Where did I see it? My mind goes on a mad movie rewind . . . The attic. Of course, Buttercup was one of the names on what looked like a rota on a blackboard. There were other names, all flowers or fruit.

I ask Karl, 'Who was Buttercup?'

He shrugs. 'A woman. She seemed to be a happy sort. Then there was Dr Vincent.'

'He had been a doctor once but was now practising the dark arts of conning vulnerable women.'

Karl leans forward. 'There was something magnetic about him, he had a quality that drew people to him. I only met him that one time for less than five minutes. He cupped my head and it was like Fred had come alive again.' Karl leans back. 'Do you think Mum came here looking for a cure for her pain?'

I nod. 'He exploited women like her, including, no doubt, Buttercup and the others.'

'Do you know why I beat up Dad?' The change of direction of our discussion takes me by surprise. 'For years I wondered who told the cops that I was close to Fred and knew about his coin collection. It was Dad.'

The breath leaves me. 'Even he wouldn't do that.'

'Come on, Gabby, you know him.' My brother's on his feet now, fury straining the veins in his neck. 'Me and Jasmin want to take our relationship to the next level and I can't do that if I keep allowing the past to cripple me, so I decided it was time to stare it down. I contacted a friend who managed to get me my juvenile file. It was there in black and white: the name of the scumbag who accused his own son of committing murder.'

In a daze I stand too. 'Why? Why would he do that?'

'He. Hated. Me.' Karl is yelling now. 'That's why I could never understand why you ran out on us, me and Salina. Left us at the mercy of that monster who passed for a father.'

'That's unfair.' I defend myself. 'I never ran out on you. I left at the age of eighteen to go to law school. Tinfields isn't noted for those. What were you expecting me to do? Stay here and get a job as a guide in the tin mining museum? I left, but I sent you letters and you wrote back to me. I even scraped money together from odd jobs and sent it to Jenny next door to give to you and Salina.'

'What money? What letters?'

'You must have got the letters because you wrote back to me.'

I rush over to my rucksack, and take out an envelope, which I always keep with me, from the inside pocket. I pull out one of the letters inside and pass it to my brother as if it's the most precious thing in the world.

He reads aloud: *'Hello, Gabby, it's your favourite brother and sister Salina and Karl. It's me, Salina, writing as usual. Everything is so cool here. Thanks for the money. Karl bought a new penknife and* me, well, I'm sure you don't have to guess, I got some make-up. Mascara. Please keep sending the money, it helps so much. Take care, big sis.'

Karl stares at me in disbelief. That little lost boy look is back, contorting his features. 'Dr Vincent wasn't the only one conning people.'

I feel destroyed and slump back down. Karl crouches beside me and puts an arm around my shoulder and harshly whispers, 'He was always smashing things up, I could never understand why. On the worst nights he would come to our rooms, take out his watch and give us five minutes to pack our bags.' I don't want to hear this. I want to put my hands over my ears because I know it's going to be bad. 'And if we didn't do it, he would smash up Salina's make-up and anything I built. I learned to hide my things away from him.'

Karl takes a deep breath. 'Then he'd bundle us in the car and force us to get out outside the closed council building. Tell us that he had already contacted the council to tell them we were bad children. So bad we didn't deserve a father like him. And then he'd drive off and leave us there in the night, alone. I often peed myself. Five minutes later, and I know it was five minutes because living with him I knew exactly how long five minutes was, he'd return and order us to get back in the car. Take us home. We always knew when he was going to do it – the nights he smashed our family home up.'

I hug my baby brother so tight. If I'd known what was happening . . . What? What could I have done? There's no way I could have taken my sister and brother with me.

Karl quietly says in my ear, 'When he would come back to pick us up, do you know what he would tell us? He'd say, "I will always come back, unlike Gabby who left you behind and never looked back."'

CHAPTER 32

I raise my hand to hammer on the door of my dad's neighbour Jenny, but I'm distracted by unexpected voices behind me. Children's voices. Confused, my arm falls limply to my side as I turn around. And there I see children playing and laughing in the street. Two girls and three boys. I don't recall any children when I got out of the car. Why is the colour so bright, the image so blurry? And why is the cottage on the other side of the street that burned down years back before we came to live here still there, instead of the gap where it once was? Then I realise that one of the girls is fifteen-year-old me, the other girl-Salina. And the boys are Karl, Jamie and all that red hair must belong to a young Luke. I know it's not real but I can't stop watching. We all seem so happy, the horrors of the world a lifetime away.

I reach out and the children, young-me, vanish like a spider's web between my fingers. I'm not even sure of what I'm seeing anymore. Voices and faces from the past, now even children are stalking me.

I can't keep going back like this.

'Get off my doorstep before I brain you.' The shock of Jenny's threatening words has me twisting back around. She's in the doorway in a dressing gown, visibly trembling, holding a large cast-iron frying pan primed to defend herself. I'm sorry that I've obviously woken her from a nap, however, what I need to ask her can't wait. Nevertheless, I should've remembered that since Fred's murder all those years ago she's remained edgy about opening her front door.

'Jenny, I'm sorry. It's me, Gabby. Can I come in, we need to speak?'

She lowers the pan, while her other hand self-consciously tightens on the collar of her dressing gown. 'Now's not such a great time—'

'I won't keep you long.'

Mummy's close friend and confidante finally pulls the door back and lets me in. We go to the lounge, where the wall is filled with photos of Fred, mainly on his own and sometimes with them as a couple. There's no offer of her scones and jam this time; I'm glad, this is not a social call.

'When I sent the money for Salina and Karl when they were children,' I start, 'you did give it to them?'

Putting the frying pan down she answers, 'Of course I did.'

'There's some confusion because Karl informed me that he never got any money, not a penny.'

Her gaze skids away from me. 'I did give your brother and sister the money, in a manner of speaking. Not directly, you understand, that wouldn't have been appropriate. They were children, I couldn't go against a parent's wishes.'

Karl was a troubled boy and my half fear, half hope that he misremembered is proved false. 'You gave them to my father so he could pass them on? I sent *you* the money not *him.*'

She's defensive. 'It would have been completely wrong to have passed things to Karl and Salina without their father's consent. I spoke to Saul and he understandably wasn't happy about being cut out of messages being passed amongst his children. So, yes, I gave them to him to give to the children.' She suddenly realises what I'm suggesting and is outraged. 'If you're implying that your dad was robbing his own children that's a shocking thing to say.'

'He's a shocking father.'

Jenny isn't having that. 'How dare you? Your poor dad loses his wife at a young age, struggles to bring up three children, one of whom takes the first chance she gets to bolt and only has time to stick her nose into his home for five minutes once a year at Christmas. And you come here calling him a common thief. You should be ashamed of yourself after all he did for you.'

I walk over to her, my fists clenched with righteous rage. 'Did you ever ask Salina or Karl if they got the money?'

Her mouth flaps like a fish. 'No . . . Well . . . What I mean . . .'

A noise outside the room makes her words dry up. Even before I've turned around, Jenny desperately explains, 'It's not what you think, Gabby.'

I brace myself but nothing can prepare me for the shock of seeing my father standing in his trousers and an open shirt.

'How long have you two been an item?' My question punches me in my belly and sends ripples through my body. I'm haunted by the fear of how long this secret relationship stretches back. 'Since Mummy was alive?'

Jenny loses the colour in her face. 'I'd never do that to Marcia, never. After Fred and your mum went, me and Saul were lonely—'

My raised hand stops her. I don't want to hear it. But there's a truth I can't back away from; my father probably gave Jenny his full-blast charm treatment. A lonely woman would be ripe for the picking.

Dad casually enters the room, his level gaze on me. 'You need to fix your face, girl. My private life is none of your concern. And I don't care for you coming here and upsetting my lady friend.'

I know it sounds more like a wife than a daughter, but I can't help myself. 'How long's this been going on?'

I won't be cowed by him. 'I tell you what is my business, the money I sent for your children. You stole the money I sent to Karl.'

'I told her that she was wrong,' Jenny intervenes. 'You'd never do anything like that.'

We don't hear her – our horns are locked. 'And the letters,' I crack out. 'They never wrote those letters back to me – it was you all the time. Penning your poisonous words.'

He's unruffled. 'A thankless child is like a serpent's tooth—'

'And you'd know all about snakes, wouldn't you?' I taunt. 'Slithering and sly, that's how you've been all your life.'

'Your brother and sister are a pair of evil twins. Rotten seeds. They were the death of your mother and they'll be the death of you too if you let them. But they'll never be the death of me.'

I round on his shocked lover. 'Did he tell you how he tormented his children by making them pack their belongings, throwing them out of the car outside the council building, threatening to dump them in the care system?'

Jenny is visibly shaken by this revelation. 'That's not true, is it, Saul? Is it?'

I snap, 'That's right, Jenny, you're screwing someone who embodies why we need a law to bar certain people from ever being parents. Bar them from coming within a hundred miles of a child, so they never get a chance to hold their little hearts and souls in their hand ready to crush.'

Saul ignores his lover's gasp. He jeers at me, 'I see you found your mother's lipstick. Such a distinctive colour. But let me tell you something, little missy: don't think wearing her lipstick means you can ever fill your mother's shoes. You'll never be an ounce of the woman she was.'

His hand goes into his pocket and pulls out his watch. His hot gaze catches mine. 'I want you out of here in thirty seconds. Not one second more, not one second less.'

I'm gone in ten, not because I'm scared of his beat-the-clock terror tactics but because I was so close to losing it and bellowing in his face about all the damage he's caused. Inside my car I rest my head on the steering wheel, knowing I will forever have to live with the guilt of leaving my brother and sister behind to the psycho tortures of that monster.

CHAPTER 33

The horror of Salina and Karl's childhood racks up my determination to uncover the secrets of my mother. So back at Ocean Haven I search and search. However, I can't shake the warning voice in my head that's insisting this house is a bad place for me to be right now. Dusk is ending, leaving the house standing in darkness. It's during the darkness Ocean Haven comes to life. I hear it as I move and search around the house. Rotten wooden shutters bang in the window frames and draughts come from all directions, creeping like breath across my flesh. The lamps and bulbs gutter and fail before they return again, casting different and disturbing shadows on the walls. The structure of the house creaks and warps in the darkness. There's a twist in the coastal road which means headlights are reflected on the tattered curtains as a car drives past. The lighthouse's revolving white light creeps through the windows and around the house before disappearing. A minute later it returns like an unhappy but punctual spirit.

Somewhere downstairs a door bangs. I freeze. Suddenly the pressure of the air in my chest feels too strong. Is that the kitchen door? The one that Luke fixed? Is Luke here? The stairs groan and creak as I go down. Is the green mould on the staircase wall moving? No, that's my mind doing overtime again, isn't it? I reach the kitchen where the back door blows and clatters back and forth like cardboard. A gust of cold air charges through the house. I'm frozen by the invading wind and by fear. I'm here, on my own; if anything happens who will hear me? It properly occurs to me for the first time just how vulnerable I've made myself.

I reach for the handle, intending to close the door, but instead do the opposite. I go outside. The wind whooshes loud and circles me in a strange dance. Instinctively I look up and there they are looking down on me. The ravens. Seven of them as usual, not moving, just watching. The strangest thing is that the blackness of their bodies should make them blend into the background, but they don't. They stand out, their chests plump and round with an alertness that suggests they never rest. Well, there's no sense in looking at them, they aren't holding any of my mother's or this house's secrets.

Slowly, I walk over to the grave. The place where Delbrook's remains were found. I stand outside the tape and tent the police left to protect the scene. Luke gave me strict instructions not to go anywhere near here, which I've complied with, but tonight some force compels me to come here. I imagine that it's me down there, shot and dead, the killer throwing wet soil down over my body, my face.

'Who killed you, Robert Delbrook?'

I don't say the answer I've dreaded thinking of. That it was Mummy who killed him. Did she do it to help Carol and Jamie? If she did, why did Carol take her son and jump off the cliff? Why did my mother die that night too? That's when another realisation comes to me. Was Delbrook gunned down that same night? There's a sound behind me. I twist around, think I see a shadow.

'Luke? Luke, is that you?'

No answer.

There it is again, the fleeting shadow just inside the kitchen door. I hurry over to find out what it is, who it is. Silly! I don't have anything to defend myself. But once inside I realise I don't need it.

I know who the shadow belongs to. Mummy. She's waiting for me, her back pressed against the sink. She's got face powder on today, it looks too stark on her because it hollows out her cheeks and deepens her usually pretty brown eyes into dark fathomless pools. We're wearing twin shades of lipstick. Her lipstick.

'What am I looking for, Mum?'

She doesn't answer me, instead calmly walks out into the large reception area with me following close behind.

Mummy tells me, 'You always tried to find the world in a book. The problem with that, daughter, is that you sometimes missed the world that's around you, the real one where you breath in and out air. The world right beneath your nose.'

What does she mean?

Miss the world. Beneath my nose. Suddenly the penny drops. I understand. What am I missing in this house? Where haven't I searched? Mummy has taken me to the reception area, so it must be here . . . somewhere. I keep looking. I've searched all the rooms down here. I do a circuit of the wall, looking closely. Nothing. Do it again, this time using my hand to feel . . . Stop. What was that? I feel more closely. Something hard and round. I tug it out, it's a door handle that was flush with the wall, so no wonder I couldn't see it. I pull. A door opens. Another hidden door just like the one to the old servants' quarters in the attic.

It's a staircase that leads to a cellar or basement. Or maybe a tunnel; I heard a rumour that Ocean Haven has a tunnel that leads straight to the disused tin mine. It's murky and old down here, the brickwork riddled with mildew, leaving a cat-pee stench clinging to the inside of my nose. I touch the metal rail. It shakes in my hand. The beats of my heart are like thunder in my chest. The darkness swallows me as I carefully go down. At the bottom I rest my head with silent gratitude against the wall. I notice a dirty light bulb in the low ceiling. I find a switch, never expecting that the light still works, but it does, shedding a weak yellowed light that reveals a door nearby. It groans against its hinges as I open it to reveal a long room. It's claustrophobic, unwelcoming, with a frosted air pouring through the pores in the wall. And an uneven, ice-cold natural ground. The sound of the sea is sinister down here, moaning with the anguish of the restless dead.

What grabs my attention is the bath against the far wall. A huge old-style bath, the type that a reclamation yard would kill to get its hands on. And it would need some serious TLC because it's lined with copper rust and water marks that have aged to a nasty green. Something about the bath holds me back. I sense bad things happened here. Pain, a lot of pain. I pray whatever it was didn't include Mummy.

I can't shake off the sensation that makes my stomach tighten and clench, but I can't let it hold me here, so I move forward and I'm pleased that I do because inside the bath are three boxes. I get stuck in, opening a box only to find it's filled with leaflets advertising Ocean Haven. The next box is the same. But in the third, I find something. A curious piece of evidence. A letter addressed to someone in Oxford, but with an unmarked stamp so it was never posted. There are two sets of handwriting: one belonging to the person who wrote it and another that's scrawled in red. The red writing reads: '*We guard our privacy closely at Ocean Haven. Don't let me find one of these in your room again, Buttercup!!!!*'

That's the third instance of Buttercup I've come across during my investigation. So it's safe to assume that she wrote this letter.

I turn my attention to it and read. It's a chatty letter from . . . can't find any name . . . writing to a sister. But at the bottom is a postscript: '*PS I've had to change my name! I'm now known as*

Buttercup. I miss my lovely Eddie. Give Eddie The Second a hug and oodles of kisses from me.'

Eddie The Second. Buttercup. Another link to Ocean Haven and my mother. But I might be wrong. There's only one way to find out, which involves getting to the late-night supermarket now to buy the tenderest and thickest slice of steak I can find.

CHAPTER 34

When I wake up the room is a block of cold, so much so I tunnel back into the warmth of the duvet for a time. I can't stay here all day. Nevertheless, for the next few minutes I savour the comfort and safety of the beaten-up sofa. Then it's up I get because I need to head for the beach. But when I stand, not only do I nearly knock off the empty glass that contained last night's ginger beer, but the room sways and rocks alarmingly around me and sick whelms up, heading for my throat. I just about make it to the bathroom on time, where I throw up and up, until I'm left with my head hanging, clutching the wall for support. And then comes the pain, hostile and hot with the cruelty of a firebrand deep in my belly and lower back. Every huff and puff is pure agony. I slide down the wall and hug my knees to my chest. *Go away. Go away.* I have a pray too that Dr Morris contacts me soon with the test results. Part of me can't wait to hear what he's found out, if anything, while the other half of me lives in a state of dread that he'll break the news to me that I'm dying, just like Mummy.

I stay there until the pain eases and finally dribbles away. How long I sit I don't know, but I need to shift myself if I'm going to get to the beach in time. Quickly, I slide my wide-toothed comb through my hair . . . and am stunned by the number of strands left in the comb. I do it again, more comes out. My hair's falling out.

I look in the ornate mirror and there's Mummy watching me. She says nothing, but I know she's remembering that time too, all those years ago at home:

'Where's Mum?' Salina asks me.

She sounds as worried as I feel. Mummy is usually already downstairs with our breakfast ready for us to wolf down before going to school. But there's no sign of her today, so I make some porridge. Salina pulls a face at my efforts. Typical! She's such a Mummy's girl anyway. I don't admit that I wish I were one too.

It's Karl who comes up with a sensible solution. 'I know that Daddy said never to knock on their door, but I think maybe we should do that.'

Salina adds, 'What if she's hurt?'

Karl. 'Or fallen down and hurt her head?'

They're looking at me as the eldest to make the decision. Usually Salina would have the front to go up there, but her thin face looks scared. I'm going to have to step up. Don't you just hate having the role of big sister?

As I get up, the door opens and Mummy comes into the room. It's me and Salina who suck in our breath, not our baby brother, at her appearance. What you need to know about Mummy is that she has thick curly, curly hair that is lush with incredible body. What me and my sister see is the new bald patch on the front of Mummy's head.

'Mummy?' She looks at me, she's been crying. 'Has something happened?' I want to ask about her hair, I really do, but the words won't come, they're stuck solid in my throat. I'm terrified that she's sick again and going to die.

'What do I do, Mummy?' I beg her reflection in the mirror back in the room.

She doesn't answer. She steps back further in the background, fades and disappears. I remain looking in the mirror knowing with certainty I'm going to be leaving this earth soon, like her. This sensation of tottering on the edge of a cliff gives me the strangest feeling; instead of remaining in shock at my hair falling out I'm filled with more determination to find out what happened to my and Craven's mother in the past.

I head for the mini fridge in the kitchen and take out the lump of steak. Minutes later I'm on the beach. The raw-red colour of the cliff has leaked into the sand at the water's edge today. The sea is calm and it's so peaceful. I place the steak near a rock, which I then perch on. I pray that my plan will work. I wait a good forty minutes and then I hear it, a dog barking on the beach. It's running and I know exactly where it's heading. And here he comes. Eddie The Seventh, the dog of the woman I saw on the beach. Someone who called their dog Eddie The Seventh must have had dogs in the past called Eddie The First, Eddie The Second . . . The current Eddie is on the steak like he's never eaten before in his life. The woman appears and looks justifiably annoyed. Despite not having pets, even I know that the rule is you never feed anyone else's. Pets should only ever eat at home.

'Eddie The Seventh,' she barks. 'Get away from that. You are a disgrace to your ancestors.'

A dog give up a tasty steak? No chance! The woman is large, with short grey hair that highlights her formidable cheekbones. I say, 'Let him eat, Buttercup.'

She tenses, only for a moment though, then throws back, 'What do you want?'

At least she doesn't deny it, which is a good sign that I might actually persuade her to open up. Hopping off the rock, I walk over to her. 'I think you might have known my mother—'

'Honeysuckle.' The word softly floats into the wind.

'Who?'

'Marcia,' she confirms. 'At Ocean Haven she was known as Honeysuckle.' She gives me a speculative once-over. 'You look just like her. I should've guessed who you were.'

'I have reason to believe you were with my mother at the house?' I point to the house on the hill.

She does not look. Instead she takes out a ball and throws it into the surf and the dachshund races off. She settles back on the rock, and when I join her she says, 'I'm Aphrodite, by the way. Aphrodite Jones. My parents named all their daughters after Greek goddesses. I'm the one who represents beauty and love.' There's a contemptuous roll of her eyes. 'What do you want to know about your mum and Ocean Haven?'

'I can't figure out what connection a stay-at-home, working-class mum would have with a place like Ocean Haven.' I withhold saying anything about my mum's name on the ownership documents for lots of reasons, including that I need to make sure I can trust Buttercup/Aphrodite.

'Mine and your mum's world was one that kept women in a perpetual state of shame. It was bred into us that it was shameful to talk about our bodies. Womb. Vagina. Vulva. Uterus. Fallopian tubes. Breasts.' She makes each word stand powerfully on its own. 'In my day you said those words in a hush, if at all, and never in public.

'The only person you were allowed to talk to about such things with was your family doctor. Mine was an old fart of a dinosaur who told me' – she starts imitating a posh male fuddy-duddy, in a garbled voice, smacking her lips together and making disgusting sucking sounds around each word – '"When your woman's time comes, the blood" – Suck! Suck! Suck! – "it may hurt you." Suck! Suck! Suck! "But that's OK because a woman's pain is good!"'

Her dog rushes up to her, bringing a massive smile to her face. She fluffs her fingers with delicate delight through his coat. Then he's off again, running along the beach. Aphrodite's happiness dies away.

204

'Look at me.' Which I do, intently. 'I'm a big girl. And proud of it. But back then . . .' She swallows, her features strained. This is hard for her to talk about. 'I was always what in my day they called "stout". I come from a very wealthy family with a tradition of hunting with guns and expecting their girl children to be wraith-like and super-thin. I got teased at school, called all kind of names by teachers—'

'Your teachers?'

She scoffs and laughs at my astonishment. 'You have no idea what teachers were like back then. Some were kind and others unbelievably cruel. As the years went on I grew into my body, which meant I got bigger. What you have to understand is that when I saw my doctor about my chronic pain I was already suffering with issues of insecurity about my body. I had terrible low self-esteem.'

I let her speak without interrupting. 'I went to see my doctor because I started having terrible pain in my pelvis and such headaches. Muscle and joint pain and I was so tired, so very tired. You know what Dr Dinosaur advised me? That all I needed was exercise and fresh air and my pain would magically disappear. For a year I followed what he told me to do. But the pain got worse. Some days I could hardly get out of bed.' Her voice croaks with emotion. 'I believed that if I didn't do something I was going to die.'

'And that's when you came across something advertising Vincent Fortune's services at Ocean Haven.'

'Actually, it was a young boy who gave me a leaflet near Tinfields Hospital.'

I stiffen. 'Do you mean Carol Shore's son, Jamie?'

'After I'd been at the house for a couple of weeks I saw him and realised who he was.'

'What was Fortune doing with Carol?'

'What I heard and was later confirmed by your mother was that Ocean Haven belonged to Carol. She had inherited when her husband died and I imagine that it naturally passed to her as a caretaker for when her son came of age.' She adds, 'Marcia was the only one who decided to do anything to help her.'

That sounds like my mother, giving both her hands to pull up someone who needed support, especially if they found themselves in danger. Yeah, my mother was, and will always be, a hero.

'How did Mummy help Carol and Jamie?'

'I'm not sure, because I left after a particularly nasty treatment. Then I heard your mother was dead. And Carol Shore.' She shakes her head sadly. 'I freely admit to being scared of Vincent Fortune. He was the kind of evil who would turn up on your doorstep in the middle of the night. So I walked away.'

'Why didn't you report Vincent Fortune to the police?'

'And say what?' She glares with exasperation. 'That I gave my consent to every last thing he did to me. To us. That I'd been sitting in a tree in an orange one-piece at night thinking I was ripening fruit? That I allowed myself to be electrocuted in an attempt to get my womb back because it had gone walkabout? It probably had the sense to go shopping on the high street.' I notice how she uses the rib-tickling power of dropping funny stuff into conversations to deflect from all that pent-up hurt I hear. I don't laugh.

'Vincent had a special gift for being able to read people. Do you know why he called me Buttercup?' She doesn't give me a chance to answer. 'Because he knew that it would make me feel what I'd wanted to be my whole life: small, dainty and ever so fragile, instead of the huge lumbering lump I felt like back then.'

A righteous sneer pulls her lips. 'But he got your mother so wrong. He called her Honeysuckle because he wanted her to feel like some posh lady who could afford to have afternoon tea every day, taking Marcia a million miles away from her so-called humdrum domestic existence of a mum. What he didn't figure out was how proud she was of her life.' A sadness comes over her. 'Your mother wasn't the only one who died. I don't mean like she did. A few died because they spent too long here getting bogus treatments when they should have been spending money on good doctors who cared. One left behind a daughter who I don't think ever got over what happened to her mum.'

I completely open up to her now. 'Did you know that my mother's name is on the ownership documents of the house?'

Aphrodite is surprised. 'No. But I do know she couldn't afford to pay the fee for Vincent's programme. She told me he made her sign a document attesting to the fact that he wasn't taking any money from her.' She rolls her eyes. 'Apparently he did it out of the goodness of his demonic heart.'

Finally, Aphrodite allows herself to stare up at Ocean Haven. It looks back down at us with an all-seeing eye. 'It took me years to be able to come back. That house is filled with ghosts who sometimes laugh, scream or are deadly silent. And through all of that I remember Marcia.' She turns back to me, her eyes blazing. 'Your mother had an aura of strength around her. By that I mean she was a strong woman. Don't you just hate that phrase, "strong women". Why would you assume that most women aren't strong? Once you start identifying some of us as "strong" it means the rest of us, the majority, are "weak".' She savours the next word. '"Women". The word doesn't need any attachments. It has strength enough to stand on its own.'

Standing, she hands me a business card. 'After I left Ocean Haven, it took me years to find the right medical practitioner who diagnosed me with lupus. I run an organisation for women who feel that the medical profession is turning a deaf ear to their pain. It's called "Believe Me".'

Lupus? I wonder if that was the illness that took Mummy. Or was the illness something called murder?

Aphrodite collects Eddie and tells me, 'Love to meet on the beach again. Next time let's do it with raspberry ripple ice creams.'

I'm not finished with her yet. 'They found the remains of a body up at Ocean Haven.' She freezes and averts her face from me. 'The cops think it's Vincent Fortune, whose real name was Robert Delbrook. They think he was gunned down.'

For a moment I think she's going to turn back to me. She doesn't. Eddie close beside her, she briskly walks off as if she can't get away from me quickly enough. Did she shoot Delbrook in his guise as Dr Vincent Fortune? Her family has a history of guns. As soon as I get to the house, I'll tell Craven what I found out and he can deep-dive into Aphrodite Jones's history.

Halfway back to the house a text pings on my smartphone from Craven:

Your mother was murdered.

CHAPTER 35

TWENTY-FIVE YEARS AGO

MARCIA

Marcia softly but urgently walked down the stairs after secretly meeting with Carol in her room. The conditions she had found the younger woman and her son living in in the attic both enraged her and broke her heart. There wasn't even a mattress on the old iron bed. Marcia had shoved back her feelings in order to decide with Carol what exactly needed to be in place for Carol and Jamie's escape from Ocean Haven to be a success. It was Monday today, which left only five more days before Vincent Fortune's business trip to the capital. When Marcia thought how she'd trusted Dr Vincent she felt like the stupidest person alive.

'*As long as your womb is useful, you as a woman are useful.*' What a load of old claptrap. Marcia was more than her womb. She wasn't just on this earth to give birth, there were so many other things she was here to do. She'd decided to go to the authorities about what Dr Vincent was doing at Ocean Haven once she'd rescued Carol and Jamie. Marcia had no idea whether he was committing a crime or not, but she wouldn't sleep right at night if she remained silent.

As she reached the reception area, Marcia heard a cry and groan coming from somewhere. She searched around. There it was again. It was coming from behind the door that appeared to lead to a basement or cellar. Marcia had already had one close call with Dr Vincent, she couldn't afford to have another. Still, it wasn't in her nature to turn her back on someone in distress.

She opened the cellar door and looked down the steps. It was dark down there. The handrail wobbled beneath Marcia's touch. There was another groan, sharper this time, which made her more determined than ever to go down and find out what was going on. The darkness swallowed her up. Marcia missed a step leaving her rocking one-footed in the air. The inkiness reared up threatening to snatch her up . . . Marcia managed to flatten her back against the wall. For a few seconds she drew in a few fortifying breaths and then proceeded back down. She reached the bottom. The brick-work was riddled with mildew, leaving a cat-pee stench clinging to the inside of Marcia's nose. A tiny shriek sounded. Marcia noticed a shotgun propped in a corner. This shook her up. Not only had she never seen a gun before, she didn't associate any weapon with Ocean Haven. She found a door and pushed it, revealing a room. It was long, claustrophobic, unwelcoming, with a frosted air pouring through the pores in the wall.

And in the middle of the room was a large old-style bath with Buttercup inside. Her friend was sobbing as she turned a knob. The water violently vibrated and Buttercup bit her lip to do her best not to call out.

Marcia rushed over. 'What the hell's going on?'

Buttercup looked terrible. Dark circles rimmed her eyes in a face that was stark and pale. 'This is my treatment. I've got to do it.' She turned the knob again and shrieked, her body arching.

Marcia's heart dropped as she guessed with dawning horror what was happening. 'Are you electrocuting yourself?'

Buttercup sobbed, her head falling back. 'Dr Vincent says the water has to be ice-cold for it to really help me. Today he told me to increase the current or my fat won't go away.'

Marcia trembled with such anger she wanted to scream. 'Don't touch it.'

Buttercup turned wild eyes on Marcia. 'I can't do this anymore. No. More.' Her face was mottled with anger as she scrambled out of the bath, water splashing on to the stone floor. She ran into the dank corridor before Marcia could get to her. And there stood Dr Vincent. Some of the other women looked on, shocked, from the staircase.

Dr Vincent was very calm. 'Buttercup, whatever the problem is let us talk together in my healing office.'

Sniffing, the veins in her neck prominent, she violently shook her head. 'No more. No more.'

He stretched his hand out, which triggered Buttercup into looking wildly about. She saw the shotgun and grabbed it.

Marcia gasped when she pointed it at Dr Vincent. 'You were meant to make me feel better. But the pain hasn't gone away. I'm still as fat as a cow. You told me that the electric would make it all go away.'

The strain now showed on his face. 'Everything has a time and a place.'

It was Marcia who said, 'Buttercup, please put the gun down.'

The other woman gazed at Marcia. 'I don't know whether to use it on him or me.' Her lips twisted. 'Yes, I do. On him.'

His face became ugly as he snarled, 'You better watch what you're saying, Buttercup.'

'Or what?' In that moment Marcia saw a fierceness in the younger woman she hadn't realised she possessed. '*You* better watch *your* back, creepy Dr Vincent, you never know when I might come back.'

She chucked the gun on the floor and, pushing by the other women, fled up the stairs. Whispering, the other women followed behind her.

Marcia was rocked by what she had witnessed. That shadow she had always sensed beneath Buttercup's funny-girl façade had surfaced. *That poor girl had been hurting for years. But then that's what Vincent Fortune did, lured women who were hurting.* Then again, this awful man was torturing Carol, so she shouldn't be shocked that he was getting Buttercup to electrocute herself. Marcia felt like a new woman who understood that there was nothing shameful about her body. And that men like Vincent Fortune took advantage of women like her, who lived with pain almost on a daily basis.

Dr Vincent didn't follow Buttercup. Instead, he turned to Marcia and took his time inspecting her face. 'I'm wondering if I'm always going to find you sneaking around our beautiful Haven.'

'I'm sorry.' She had to focus on Carol and Jamie, so she didn't flinch under his heated stare. 'I heard dreadful sounds of distress and being a mother I had to make sure that no one was hurt.'

He considered her face and then turned and went up the stairs.

Gulping, Marcia leaned a palm against the damp wall. How had she ever allowed herself to be duped by this charlatan? She'd love nothing better than to electrocute him. She had to get Carol and her son out of here as soon as possible.

As Marcia readied to leave, she observed Buttercup leaving in a cab and Dr Vincent securing the shotgun in the shack.

CHAPTER 36

Your mother was murdered. Your mother was murdered. I can't get Craven's killer words out of my head while I sit inside the coffee shop anxiously waiting for him. Murder? The enormity of it takes my breath away. How? Who? When? It was probably that house, Ocean Haven. I bet if I look deeper into its history it's been killing people for centuries.

Craven appears in the doorway. He looks like he's slept in his clothes, I notice as he heads to our usual spot in the coffee shop. I'm not one of those homely type of women, like Mummy was, who see it as part of my destiny to make sure men are neatly turned out, but, hell, Craven looks like he needs sorting out.

He sits and notices I've already got him a drink. 'Thanks for the latte. I didn't realise you noticed what my go-to poison was.'

I don't have time for pleasantries. 'How do you know Mummy was murdered?'

He brings his chair to my side of the table and pulls out a manila folder from his rucksack. All of a sudden I'm not sure I'm ready for this. I see me huddled with Salina and Karl, crying together at the hospital when Mummy died. No one ever told us what exactly it was that took her from us, including Dad.

Craven taps the top paper inside. 'I found her medical records.'

'But how?' I don't understand. 'You said they would've been destroyed after eight years.'

'Someone in her medical team thought your mother was being poisoned.'

I rock back in shock. Short spurts of air cut through my teeth. I can't even speak. Never in a million years had that occurred to me. 'Poisoned?'

'Because this concern was formally raised with a note left on her file that's probably why your mother's medical records were kept. To sum up this report, there were two different medical conclusions. One is that your mother was typical of many women who suddenly find their bodies react to the approach of middle age by developing constant pain.'

'That's absolute rubbish,' I seethe, my eyes on fire. 'The hospital dismissed her pain as a fairy tale with no happy-ever-after, Prince Charming ending.'

'Not everyone at the hospital held that belief.' He flicks through the papers and pulls one aside. 'This says that one of the staff who looked after her thought that she was being poisoned. That someone was doing her harm.'

I inspect what is written. Craven has done a good job of summing up what I read. I notice, 'It doesn't say who that person in her medical team was?'

'Unfortunately, it doesn't. The only name recorded is her consultant.' My face fills with hope. Craven bursts my bubble. 'He died six years ago. I did manage to talk to the guy who carried out the tests, who is now retired. But it wasn't him who reported the suspicions of poison.'

'Who else was on the medical team?'

'That's the thing, it doesn't record the names of any other staff who your mother came into contact with.'

Frustration makes me want to roll my hand into a fist and strike something – anything. 'Does that mean it's dead in the water?'

Craven considers my statement. 'I'll ask some of the old boys on the squad who were around back then. They may have a name.' His expression changes, becoming mournful. 'No one ever told me exactly what happened with Mum. There was an inquest into her death and the verdict was misadventure.' His features screw up. 'Mis. Adventure. They made it sound like she went on a trip one day that didn't go according to plan. Y'know, she forgot to put her sandwiches in her bag or her sunscreen. What a bloody mis-adventure.'

I press the tips of my fingers on to the top of his hand, which he probably doesn't realise is formed into a fist on the table. I don't say a thing, giving him the time he needs to shove all that pent-up, years-old fury back down.

Removing my fingers, I gently ask, 'Did you discover anything interesting about Aphrodite Jones?'

'Lady Aphrodite Jones, if you please.'

My mouth forms an 'O' of surprise. 'She told me her family were wealthy, but I didn't realise they were nobility.'

Craven thirstily knocks back his coffee. The wet glistens at the corner of his mouth. Yeah, I know, I shouldn't be noticing things like that. He tells me, 'Not only are they nobility, they are also the family that originally owned the tin mines, so they're a well-known name around here.'

'And guns?'

He puts his cup down; his eyes are animated. 'Forensics think it was a shotgun that was used to kill Delbrook.' I hear the blasts in my head and nervously swallow. 'Plenty of families around legally have guns. From what I can pick up, Aphrodite Jones isn't part of the hunting set. In fact, she's highly respected in the community for the work she does with women. Free of charge, apparently.'

My mind reruns my conversation with her on the beach. I see her frozen, barely breathing, when she hears that Dr Vincent's remains have been found. That he was shot to death. The innocent don't react like that, do they?

Then I remember. 'Aphrodite said she was introduced to Ocean Haven by a young boy near Tinfields General giving her a leaflet—'

'Let me guess. Young boy equals me,' he sourly butts in.

'Do you remember doing that?'

Leaning his head back, he noisily draws in air through his nose. He takes the time he needs before looking back at me. 'Dr Vincent would make me and some of the women go and hand out leaflets. I only did it a few times, because when Mum found out what was going on she kicked up a stink.' Craven pauses. 'What I don't understand is how a woman as wealthy as Lady Jones could get involved in a cult.'

'A cult?' My eyes widen with disbelief. 'I resent that. It was no cult. Don't you get it? The women there did not wear orange gowns as some type of uniform following a leader, they wore them pretending to be fruit because they genuinely believed it would help cure them. None of them were medically trained so why not believe a man when he tells you that if you have pain, the problem is your out-of-control womb. Calling it a cult is a huge disservice to the women who were let down by too many in the medical profession.'

Craven raises his hands. 'I surrender.' When they drop he sombrely adds, 'You're right. Have you got our makeshift investigation board?'

Our. I like that. I take out our squares of written evidence. I bring one to the centre of the table:

Marcia Lewis — Key figure in Haven ownership? How?

'Aphrodite confirmed my suspicions that Delbrook hoodwinked my mother into signing the documents. He dangled giving her treatment free and he needed her to confirm his fake generosity by signing some paperwork.'

'How could she have done?' Craven grinds out. 'Why didn't she take time to read what the hell she was signing.'

I fly to my mother's defence; I won't have anyone put her down, especially as she's not here to defend herself. 'Rich boy, why don't you come around my side of the table and see how the other half live. My parents were everyday people. My mum hardly had any spare cash and what she did have she usually spent on her kids.' The force of my heated words pushes me to lean over the table. 'Imagine this: she's sick, the medical profession don't want to know, but a man using the title of "doctor" is prepared to help her. For free. All she has to do is place her name and signature on some papers.'

'*We lived in a world that kept us in a perpetual state of shame.*' Aphrodite's haunting words come back to me and I wonder how much has really changed. Have I got the luck of the draw ending up with Steven Morris as a doctor or are the majority of doctors out there like him?

Our harsh breathing syncs across the table. Craven brushes his fingers through his spiky-topped hair. 'When I think of how that man swindled my mother out of our house I get so mad.'

I ease back. 'I get it. But we've got to leave the emotion outside the door. If we don't we'll both crumble and be no good for either of our mothers. They deserve the truth. Let that be what drives us through this.'

Craven says, 'Why would Delbrook have made your mother sign the ownership papers for Ocean Haven? She then owns it, not him.'

'Mummy didn't own Ocean Haven – she was a decoy.' I tell him what I found out about the ownership of the house.

'A decoy? How did he do it?'

'With great deception. He hoodwinked my mother and some-how manipulated her to sign those papers. His deception was put-ting a time limit on the life of the trust. Two years is up and the house is all his. It took me ages to unpick it all in the small print.'

'Do you think he was the one who was poisoning her?' Craven says aloud, the terrible question that's been forming in my mind. 'Slowly killing her to make sure she was dead when he claimed the house as his own?'

I want that to be the truth, that this despicable, greedy man who was manipulating my mother also murdered her. However, 'Mummy was already complaining about symptoms before she went to Dr Vincent. In fact that was the reason she got mixed up with him.'

Craven frowns. 'So someone else was poisoning her. Who would want to poison your mother?'

I don't reply because I'm trying to work through this question myself.

I continue with, 'I'll tell you what I am convinced of – that the remains are those of Delbrook because why did he never come forward to claim the house? And because he never did, that's why the ownership of a house that should be yours has become so complicated.'

He looks downcast. 'Me and Great Aunt Laura have been fight-ing for years to get it. Sometimes I just want to give up.'

'If you do that, Delbrook has won. Delbrook took advantage of so many women. But do you know what I realised after speaking to Aphrodite? He could only have peddled his frauds in a world where too many women were ignored and kept in ignorance about their bodies.'

I turn my attention back to our evidence and discard some of the old squares to edit and create new ones.

Carol, Marcia and Aphrodite — at Ocean Haven.

Carol murdered?

Marcia murdered. Poison.

Aphrodite familiar with guns.

I drag one of the new ones to centre stage in the middle of the table.

Who had the means and motive to poison Marcia Lewis?

CHAPTER 37

Twenty-Five years Ago

Marcia

Operation Freedom, that's what Marcia had decided to call her plan to liberate Carol and Jamie from the clutches of Vincent Fortune. She reminded herself of this fact as she walked into Tinfields railway station to carry out the next step of their escape. Saul worked at the train station, so Marcia wore a headscarf and hat, hoping that would help her maintain a low profile. The last thing she wanted was an encounter with her husband. She prayed hard that he was out in the field, as he liked to called it, which involved maintenance work, including repairing tracks. Sometimes he stayed late at night to supervise the transportation of dangerous chemical materials, some of which stayed in the station overnight. And on those days Salina often dropped off his packed lunch at the station.

Marcia briskly walked across Tinfields Station towards the ticket office. The station had an air of shabbiness but was also quaint. The ticket office was inside a pretty building that resembled a tiny red-brick house. It and the railway sign above the entrance dated back to the times when the town's tin mines were still active.

Marcia didn't know the man behind the counter by name, nevertheless she knew so much about him. He was Saul's manager, and her husband didn't have a good word to say about him. A self-righteous jobsworth was how Saul described him; his manager wanted everything done by the book with no cutting corners. Marcia had only ever met a few of Saul's co-workers by chance on the street when she'd been out and about with her husband in town; other than that he kept his work and family separate.

Marcia quietly asked, 'I'd like to purchase two one-way tickets to London for Saturday. An adult and a child.'

Saul's manager's brows hit his hairline in surprise. 'Saturday? There won't be any cheap ones left. If you'd bought one a month ago I could've got you a stunning deal.' His eyes lit up with relish at the prospect of the bargain he could have found.

'That doesn't matter. If you could find me the price.'

He shuffled closer to the glass that separated them. 'Now, what are you doing travelling on a one-way ticket? That's going to cost you a proper arm and a leg.' He squinted. 'What you getting a one-way ticket for anyway? I hope you're not moving out of this lovely town. I hear terrible stories about London. Full of people of low moral standing.'

Good grief! This man was sending her head into a spin. Suddenly she fully understood what Saul felt like having to work with him as his boss.

Marcia cut him off, her irritation showing. 'Please. If you can let me know about the ticket.'

Mumbling to himself he checked out the ticket.

Marcia and Carol had worked out that if she was going to escape she had to have a place to go, somewhere where she and her son would be safe. Finally, Carol had decided the ideal place would be her husband's Aunt Laura's, who lived in South London. Once there, Carol could work with the solicitors and police to get Vincent Fortune dealt with. And save Carol's house. Anger ballooned inside Marcia – that's what happened every time she thought about this awful situation. Sometimes she wanted to hold her head and cry.

Tickets secured, Marcia walked out of the ticket office and straight into Saul.

◆ ◆ ◆

'What are you doing here?'

Marcia flinched at the harshness of her husband's tone.

He escorted her, none too gently, to the sidings, where the station temporarily housed the trains that arrived with certain chemicals.

'I . . . I . . .' Marcia stammered to find an explanation. 'I had to buy a ticket, because the consultant has referred me to a specialist hospital in London.'

He glowered. 'How come you never told me that?'

'Because' – Marcia drew the word out – 'I needed to figure out what day I could go.'

Saul's lips twisted. Marcia felt him crowd her and saw his hand move towards his pocket. Oh hell, please not that. But she knew what was coming as his hand re-emerged with his pocket watch. 'One minute is all you've got to tell me the truth.'

Marcia stared at the watch and a fury spiralled up inside her so quick and hot she thought she was about to burst into flames. Vincent Fortune's face filled her mind, then it was replaced with Saul's. They seemed to be taking it in turns to taunt her. Marcia had had enough. With a tiny roar she yanked the watch out of the hand of the man she had vowed to love and obey sixteen years ago and threw it with victorious satisfaction on to the train track.

Saul's features turned to thunder and he raised his fist. He'd never raised a hand to her, ever.

Marcia reared forward, offering up herself. 'Go on, I dare you.' Her teeth were bared. 'You bring that bloody watch near me or my children one more time, I'm going to pack our bags and be gone.'

And with that, with pain shooting down her side, Marcia Lewis walked away from her husband. She felt his disbelieving eyes boring into her back, but she tilted her head high. His wife had been reborn.

◆ ◆ ◆

When she reached home Marcia found the kids watching telly in the sitting room, Gabby curled up on the settee with a book. They looked so happy, which left a faint smile on her face. If only her children could stay like that forever. Not wanting to disturb them, she headed upstairs and safely hid Carol and Jamie's get-away suitcase. The second part of her plan to help Carol and her son had been to buy them some clothing and toiletries, plus a small suitcase on wheels, because the last thing they wanted was for Vincent to catch Carol packing. Marcia was still tempted to go to the police station and report a crime. But what exactly would she tell them? What crime had really been committed? Marcia suspected that confronted by the cops, Vincent Fortune would easily wriggle out of it. A man who continued to con women again and again was bound to have a story or two ready to tell the police.

Marcia closed her eyes, drawing in long breaths of relief, her palms sinking into the softness of her bed. She hadn't been sure she would be able to do it all: get the ticket and then shop for clothing and toiletries. That meeting with Saul had been a bit too close for comfort. But she had done it.

'Mummy?' Salina – Marcia didn't need to see to know which daughter had spoken. 'Do you want me to do your face?'

Truthfully, the last thing Marcia needed was a makeover, but it was Salina's way of looking after her. Only her youngest daughter knew how to make her relax. Minutes later, Salina was rubbing moisturising cream across her face. She sank into the motion of the circular movement of her fingertips. Salina had such a delicate touch, she knew exactly the level of pressure to use. The beauty of butterfly wings fluttering and gliding against her skin, that's what it felt like. How had her daughter learned such gentleness in a home where the crashing noise of smashing things was the norm?

After her daughter had finished doing her face, Marcia drank a glass of Saul's refreshing homemade ginger beer.

Only two more days before Saturday. Before she clutched Carol's hand to escape.

CHAPTER 38

'I think you're being poisoned,' Dr Morris tells me, his expression very grave.

'Poisoned?' I stammer, not quite believing what he's told me. I give my head a quick shake.

'Or have been poisoned,' he quickly qualifies.

The warm blood drains from my skin, leaving me frozen and shaking. Dr Morris's mouth is still moving but I no longer hear what he's saying because there's a terrible roaring in my ears. My hands roll into shaking balls in my lap. Poisoned. Mummy was poisoned. Mummy died.

Somehow, I don't know how, I'm standing, slightly swaying. 'Am I going to die?' It's not the fear of it that makes me cover my mouth in shock, it's the horror of it. Of death. Since I came back to Tinfields, death has been stalking me. I feel the warmth of the doctor's arms come around me and lead me back to my chair. I don't recall him talking to his receptionist but he must have because she's somehow there, laying a cup of tea in front of me. I reach for it like a lifeline I remember seeing thrown to a fisherman in trouble as I stood with Dad on the beach looking out to sea. I wince at the sweetness of the tea, the steam against my lips.

God help me, am I going to die?

Steven Morris then brings his chair near me, careful to maintain a suitable professional distance. 'You've had a nasty shock, so please take your time.' Visibly he hesitates and then carefully chooses his words. 'If I'm right about what's happening here – and it's a big if – promise me you will be careful.'

'Careful? How?' I'm beginning to come out of my haze.

'From now on don't accept food or drink from anyone.' His palms cut over each other. 'No one. Understand?'

'Should I go to the police?'

He rubs the bridge of his nose. 'I need to carry out more tests to be completely sure—'

'What right do you have to tell me I'm being poisoned if you're not sure or haven't carried out all the adequate tests?' I'm annoyed now.

'I need to tell you something.' I've come to hate those words. 'I was your mother's doctor when she attended Tinfields hospital twenty-five years ago.'

'What did you say?' My mouth drops open in absolute confusion. Then it clenches tight in red-raw anger. 'You have no idea what you've done. If you had listened to Mummy, she might be alive today. She wouldn't have gone to that dreadful place. Probably never been poisoned—'

'Please.' He does his best to attempt to cut me off, but my words steamroller over his.

'Do you know how many years I have prayed to have a minute, just one minute, with the consultant who treated my mother as if she wasn't a breathing human being? You called her crazy—'

'I did not.'

My outrage grows. 'You were her doctor.'

'Not *that* doctor. I'm not the consultant Marcia Lewis saw. I was his medical student.'

'Student? What medical student?'

226

I let him speak. 'Marcia Lewis, your mother, came to see a consultant about her results and at the time he had a medical student. Me.' His face hardens. 'The way he dealt with your mother was wrong. Appalling. He didn't even introduce us. I'll never forget how he humiliated her, telling her that the cause of all her symptoms was her ovaries.'

I don't even have the words. Then it occurs to me. 'Were you the person in her medical team who wrote the note, document, I don't know what you call it, saying you suspected she was poisoned?'

He looks at me deeply. 'After the consultant discharged her with antidepressants, I couldn't get the symptoms your mother described out of my head. I tried to speak to her consultant but he accused me of making a fuss.'

'You should have kept on making a fuss.'

'I agree.' Guilt is written all over his face. 'There was no excuse. However, when I heard that your mother had passed away, I made it my business to make a written record of my suspicions and insist that they were left on your mother's record.'

He lets out a heavy sigh. 'It was the first time I ever saw how women can sometimes be treated by our medical profession.' Fairness makes him add, 'There are many doctors who care for patients and will spend the time to ensure they have the correct diagnosis and treatment.'

He continues, 'I have made it my life's work to ensure that all my patients receive the most outstanding care. In fact, I'm writing my PhD about women's experience in our health care system, co-authored with a female colleague. It was the gross treatment of your mother that pushed me on to that path.'

I imagine Mummy sick, scared, in a room with two men, one telling her she was more or less a timewaster and another who didn't feel free to express his opinion. Hell, I really hope things have changed or are changing.

227

I ask, 'Do you know which poison it was?'

'I wasn't able to analyse her blood. I think it may be arsenic. Not many people know that the tin mines also produced arsenic, so maybe whoever did this had the knowledge to extract it from an abandoned mine. I don't know.' He looks me in the eye. 'I suspect that it's the same poison that is being used on you.'

That leaves me breathless, my pulse pounding. 'Can you find out?'

Dr Morris picked up a notepad, his pen poised ready to write. 'I want you to tell me about what you do in a typical day . . .'

CHAPTER 39

I'm back on the beach, chin resting on my knees, my arms locked tight, way too tight around my raised legs. Ocean Haven is high above me, its eyes heavy on my back. The moving sea has a quietness about it, almost as if it's not there. I've been sitting here for hours, the light bleeding into the greying-black of night, trying to come to terms with what is happening to me. Sixth sense warns me that I don't need Dr Morris's results to tell me the truth of what I know: that I'm being poisoned. Someone is trying to kill me just as they killed Mummy. But is it the same person? Am I making a big assumption? Who could it be? My mind runs with too many faces and names: people who were part of this twenty-five years ago and who are also here now, and people who have appeared since. *People. People. People.* The dizzying jumble of it all leaves my head pounding. My hollow stomach rumbles because, following my doctor's advice to be careful, I haven't eaten or drunk anything. I'm so scared of what's going on here. Paranoid too. Who can I really trust? I reach for my phone to contact Craven, but then stop. Can I trust him? Remember, he's really Jamie.

My phone rings. What if it's Craven? I let it ring. It stops. The ring starts up again. Finally, I take it out. It's not Craven, it's a number I don't recognise.

Before I can speak a woman's panicked voice cracks, 'You've got to come to the hospital. Now. He needs you—'

'Slow down,' I interject, my legs falling flat, my spine stiffening. 'Who is this?'

'Jasmin.' *Jasmin. Jasmin.* I don't know anyone called that. *Jasmin.* 'You have to come. Karl . . .'

Jasmin. Karl's girlfriend. I'm on my feet. 'What's happened?'

What she says makes me run like I've never run before along the beach towards the path that leads to Ocean Haven and my car.

◆ ◆ ◆

I stumble to a halt when I see Jasmin in Tinfields General's Intensive Care Unit. Karl is dangerously ill. Gone is the supremely confident, tall, elegant blonde with the flawless skin I recall meeting at Karl's house in London. Now Jasmin sits slightly hunched, her face blotched with dried tears and emotional pain. In her shaking hand is a cup of weak tea, which is tipping back and forth. She puts it on the floor and climbs to her feet. Her arms waver by her sides as if unsure whether to embrace me. I make the decision, hugging her tight.

'Can I see him?' I ask once I've moved back from her.

With an exhausted shake of her head she points to a room. 'He's in there. They won't tell me what's wrong, won't let me in.'

I move towards the room and stare through the wired glass. Karl, my darling baby brother, lies unconscious, hooked up to a battery of monitors and drips. I choke up. I'm still not clear what happened. Jasmin was too distressed on the phone to tell me much. I'm so tired, so stressed that perhaps it's not surprising that sometimes, as I stare, I see Mummy lying, sick and still, in that bed instead of Karl. Then the person sick and still in the bed is me, then

Salina. Sometimes I imagine Salina is standing next to me. Then I realise to my shock that Salina really is standing next to me.

We stare at each other, both visibly choking with emotion, and fall into each other's arms. She holds on to me so tight, as if without my support she will fall apart.

'What have you found out?' she asks.

'His girlfriend says no one's telling her anything.'

Salina compresses her lips, then she says, 'We'll see about that.' She waves over the first doctor she sees. 'We need to know what's happening to our brother.'

The calm and friendly doctor explains, 'Your brother is in a coma. Our immediate concern was to make him stable. He's in a very serious condition and our priority remains to make him stable. I'm sorry . . .'

Rushing off, he leaves me and my sister to deal with this terrible news. Mummy sick, me and now Karl. I'm tempted to tell Salina about what Dr Morris told me, about what he thinks caused Mummy to die, but I don't because Salina looks devastated.

Weakly, tears shining in her eyes, she tells me, 'Karl managed to turn his life around, become someone Mum would be proud of. How can this be happening to him?'

I run my fingers gently up her arm. 'He'll be OK, you watch.'

'I'd better call Luke,' my sister says. 'He'll be so upset. He's only ever wanted the best for our brother.'

While she makes her call I look around for Jasmin and can't see her anywhere. It takes me a good few minutes to find her in the toilet. She's bent over, retching violently into the sink.

Alarmed, I rush over. 'Jasmin, you're obviously ill as well. I'm going to get a nurse, a doctor . . .'

She catches my arm, holding me back. 'I'm not ill, not like Karl. I'm pregnant.'

◆ ◆ ◆

'Does Karl know?' I gently ask.

I'm sitting with Jasmin on a bench outside the hospital entrance. She appears more composed as she finishes swiping away the last of her tears.

'Yes. He was so happy. He didn't have to tell me, I could see it glowing like hope in his eyes, that this was his chance to prove he could be the type of father he never had.'

I know that feeling too well. Every year for a decade my New Year's resolution was *Put me out of my misery if I turn into Saul Lewis.* How many of us waste years and years striving not to be our parents instead of focusing on trying to be our simple selves?

'Can you tell me what led up to Karl's collapse.'

She grips the soaked tissue and speaks. Her story is ragged, bitty. 'This evening at dinner in our hotel, Karl began to have problems with his fingers. He told me not to worry, that it was probably pins and needles. He tried massaging the pain away, but it wouldn't go.'

Jasmin pauses. This is so difficult for her. I don't intervene, allowing her the time she needs to start again. 'Then he got short of breath, really tired, cramps in his tummy, pain in his feet. It got so bad he left to get some fresh air. He insisted he was fine. He wouldn't let me go with him. When he didn't come back . . .'

Breathless, tired, painful stomach and feet. I go ice-cold. Those are the same symptoms I get. Mummy had. Oh my God! Is someone trying to poison my brother too?

Jasmin's eyes grow big with remembered horror, which matches the internal horror I hide from her. 'I found him slumped on a bench, holding on to it for dear life, shaking, gasping for breath, choking. Terrified. Hotel staff came to help and called an ambulance. The paramedics worked on him but he was getting steadily worse.'

Jasmin falls quiet. Then her voice is crushed as if it's been unplugged. 'It's my fault. I should have kept my mouth shut.'

But it's not her fault. It's mine. It's my fault that my brother might die. When I found Mummy's name on the deeds for Ocean Haven I should have left it alone. Why did I meddle, stir up the danger of the past? It's me who has pulled the joy of Karl becoming a father from right under him and instead what have I done? I've left him at death's door. I should get out of Tinfields and never look back. '*You ran out on me and Salina and left us.*' Karl's haunting accusation hits me hard. *That's what you do, Gabby Lewis, you run. And run. How many years have you been running? Twenty-five. If you'd kept on going Karl would be healthy, preparing for fatherhood.*

'This has got nothing to do with you, Jasmin,' I tell my brother's girlfriend. 'You've got nothing to blame yourself for.'

Jasmin shakes her head, her gaze burning bright. 'It's all my fault.' When I attempt to interrupt she raises a hand to stop me. 'You don't understand. I didn't want our baby to be born into the kind of anger I see eating up Karl. He wouldn't do it at first, but I begged him . . . and now this.'

Her words lift me out of my misery. Suddenly she has my full attention. 'What did you ask him to do?'

Jasmin says, 'Make the peace. Go and see his father.'

233

CHAPTER 40

TWENTY-FIVE YEARS AGO

MARCIA

'You appear distracted,' Vincent suggested to Marcia.

Marcia was stretched out on the couch in the calming room. Of all the rooms in the house, she had come to like this one the most. There was a peace here, a harmony between the neutral colours and the softness of its furnishings. Usually Marcia would be nice and relaxed, instead she was stretched as taut as a guitar string, the four walls creeping and creeping closer to her, pulling the oxygen from the room. How the hell could she be relaxed and chilled, knowing what she did about this evil man. What he was doing to Carol and her son. What he was doing in the shack.

It was Friday, her last session with him. Tomorrow she was going to help Carol escape in the night. The last thing on this earth Marcia had wanted to do was to have one of *his* treatments. To have to sit there and listen to him prattle his bogus hocus-pocus in her ear. At his statement, Marcia tensed up even more. Was it her imagination or did his tone sound careful like he was navigating broken glass? Did he know what she and Carol were planning to do? '*A wicked man goes about with crooked speech.*' That's what her pastor had preached about once.

'Distracted?' Her voice sounded panicked and high to her ears. In these types of situation Marcia had learned that it was best to go with the truth. Well, a type of truth that had nothing to do with the situation. 'It's my daughter Salina, she's really playing up. I suppose it's to be expected from a girl at the start of her teenage years.'

Salina *had* been playing up in the last few days, her moods swinging between her customary mischief-making and teenage-girl silence. She suspected this was due to her not being around as much for her daughter's makeover sessions, because Marcia was so engrossed in her plans to free Carol and Jamie. She hated the feeling of letting any of her children down, especially when it concerned encouraging their talents. Marcia vowed when all this was over she was taking Salina out for a special treat, maybe to the cosmetic counters of the new department store that had recently opened in the shopping centre. Yes, she liked that idea.

'Your daughter?' Vincent suddenly towered over her, peering down at her from above.

His body blocked out much of the sun from the room. Marcia hadn't heard him walking over to her. As he looked down at her, and with everything she now knew about him, there were things about his face she noticed. What she had once taken for the beginnings of a smile was a cruel twist. His eyes, bright and open, were those of someone checking and observing everything, a master manipulator at his trade. Vincent creeped her out.

He did not give her a chance to answer his statement. 'When you speak about your children, even when they are driving you up the wall, you always speak about them with such love. The love of a mother who will defend her child to the death.' The lines around his eyes deepened as he closely considered her. 'Something else is

235

making you . . . angry. You're not distracted, you're angry. I can feel it rolling off you in waves.'

I'm angry at you. You disgust me. Fill me with such rage at what you're doing. How can you do that to a young woman? You're a monster. Pure evil. And I'm going to make it my business to take you down. Of course she never said any of that.

'It's the pain,' she lied. 'It's come back with a vengeance. It was so bad.'

He said nothing, only continued to search her face. His gaze was penetrating, as if he could read her thoughts. Marcia held her breath, crippling fear rushing through her. She waited.

Vincent stepped back. 'I'm sad to hear that the pain has returned. But don't worry, it will not defeat us. Please, get up.'

Marcia headed for one of the armchairs, assuming that Vincent wanted to talk through the pain with her. She was stopped by his voice. 'We're going out.'

'What?' Surprise gripped her. She twisted back to him in a flash. 'Where? I thought you'd be busy getting ready for your business trip tomorrow.'

His response was to walk out of the room. Marcia hesitated and then quickly followed him. He led her outside. Across the driveway. Towards the shack.

Marcia battled to steady her breathing, her lungs burning with too much air. What was she going to do? She would not go in there with him. But if she didn't, all of Carol's plans would burn to ashes. She'd promised to help the young woman. She had a choice to make: either leave now or keep her promise. They got closer.

Leave now. Keep her promise.

Closer. And closer. Marcia's heart beat so violently against her chest surely the whole world could hear it. *He* could hear it. The last time she'd seen Carol rose like a nightmare in her mind. Carol crammed in that box. Misshapen, legs and arms twisted, pushing her head forward, like a balloon ready to pop. The horrifying image switched to Marcia in the box. Stuffed inside. Her limbs mangled and misshapen. Hot, horrible pain shooting through her body. The lid was shut, encasing her in suffocating darkness. Can't breathe. Can't breathe. Marcia's mind slammed back to the present. She must be disorientated, because someone was watching her. Weren't they? No one was. She felt eyes on her. She stumbled after Vincent. God forgive me, I can't do this. I've got to get away from here. I've got . . .

Vincent calmly strolled past the shack. And kept moving towards a path at the back. Knowing he wasn't taking her to the dreaded shack, Marcia steadied herself, following him. He took her to a clifftop high above the sea. Tentatively, Marcia joined him at the edge and glanced down. The waves below were strong, stretching and dragging, slapping high against the rocks with acrobatic flair and wheezing noisily as they retreated.

She half turned to him. 'What are we doing here?'

Vincent stepped back from the edge as he told her, 'Shut your eyes, Marcia.'

'What?' She scowled at him.

'Please.' His voice softened, gliding over her. 'Close the world out.' His words were a hush. 'The world that exists is you.'

The tone of his voice entranced Marcia, just as it had the first time she'd met him. It was silky, calm and ever so restful. Hypnotic. Caught in his mesmerising spell, she turned back to face the sea. The wind rippled across her face. The heat of his body was suddenly behind her.

'Inhale.' She did. 'Now exhale the pain away.'

The heat of him got stronger at her back. 'Use your breathing to grasp that pain and cast it out.'

His palm clasped her shoulder. 'It's not really there. It's all in your mind.'

His other hand cupped her other shoulder. 'That's it, Marcia. Let it all out.'

He leaned into her. 'Never forget, it's you who has the power over it, not the other way round.' He paused, his breath hot in her ear. 'It's strange that you should know about my business trip tomorrow.'

He moved, inching her body closer to the edge. The roar of the sea below rose up. Marcia's feet scratched against the earth.

'What?' Marcia couldn't move. She recalled how she'd mentioned it while they were in the calming room. Idiot!

'How did you know I was going away?'

She thought quick on her feet. 'I heard, I think, some of the women talking.'

'Did you?'

He pushed her closer. Her toes tipped over the edge. Marcia wobbled, swallowing the wet, salty wind. He knew. Knew what she and Carol had planned. She waited. Waited for him to push her over.

'Can you feel it leaving you?' His words disorientated her.

What did he mean? When she didn't answer, he told her, 'The pain. Can you feel it seeping away?'

Marcia realised that he believed her explanation about Saturday.

Something chilly and wet grazed the curve of Marcia's shoulder. She stiffened. She realised what it was, Dr Vincent was kissing her neck. His flesh was against her flesh. The sensation of it repelled her.

He whispered, 'Why don't you come with me on Saturday?'

Marcia was so shocked she didn't know how to respond. Or rather she had to hold back her initial reaction, which was to shove him and his nasty unwanted sexual advances away. But she was walking a tightrope here, and Carol and her son needed her – and them – to get to the end.

So, breathlessly she answered, 'I didn't know that you—'

'Found you attractive. All that delicious brown skin.' His tongue licked her neck. 'I've never slept with a black woman before.'

That got Marcia mad, really, really mad. He'd reduced her to a thing, not a human being, some *thing* he had to try out. Filthy was too good a word for him.

She told him the truth. 'I'm a married woman with children. I take my role as a wife and mother seriously.'

'Shame.' Abruptly he turned her to face him. He was so close. The edge was so close. If he let her go she'd go tumbling over.

'Dr Vincent,' she warned.

'What?' He wore a puzzled expression as if he hadn't kissed her moments earlier. His eyebrow shot up. 'My goodness.' Quickly he whipped her away from the edge. 'I didn't mean to frighten you. I thought you had read about this particular treatment in the brochure.'

Marcia scrambled slightly back from him. She had read the brochure he had given her inside out and was sure there was no mention of scaring someone silly on a clifftop. Or unwanted sexual advances.

Marcia shrugged off his words. 'I've got to go. *Saul and the kids* will be wondering where I've got to.'

As she hurried back to the house, Marcia again felt like someone was watching her. Nervously, her gaze searched ahead . . . No one there. She couldn't wait to get out of here. The next time she came here would be tomorrow night. To finally make sure that Carol and Jamie got away from this madman.

But the incident with Dr Vincent had unsettled her. What if he didn't go away tomorrow? What if when she came Dr Vincent was here waiting for her?

CHAPTER 41

'I knew you'd come back.' Dad's standing in his doorway, features smothered in the self-satisfied jeer of a man who has won a battle. 'After your behaviour last time, by rights I should slam the door in your face. But it's not in my nature to be cruel.'

He turns and moves steadily towards the living room. For once I don't hesitate, fury driving me inside. I have no idea if I close the door behind me or not. As soon as I enter the front room I know something isn't right. There's a body lying on the sofa screaming in pain. The body doesn't have enough hands to hold everywhere it hurts, so more hands appear to cover for them. A body with many hands is screaming at me. When the body turns its head to me, it's my mummy's face. She's contorted with pain and begging, 'Gabby, help me. Help me, baby. Don't let them take me away. They're trying to drag me into the abyss.'

Her painfully thin arms reach out to me. I rush forward and clasp her hand. But it's not her hand, it's air. I'm clasping nothing. I couldn't save her. Mummy's gone. Gone.

'Gabby! Gabby!' I hear my name being called as if from a distance. I know it's not Mummy's, it's too rough, too impatient. I realise it's Dad, his face up close and concerned. I'm trembling, with my back pressed against a wall. My legs feel so weak.

'Have you been drinking?' Dad inspects my face. 'You don't look right. You look a bit crazy actually.'

'I'm not crazy.' I push off the wall, making him step back. 'I've never been saner in my life.'

'You look like you could do with a doctor. You're obviously not well.'

'You're not calling a doctor. You're calling the police. You're a murderer. You murdered my mother and you tried to murder my brother. And me.'

He looks alarmed. 'What are you going on about? Murderer? Me?'

I inhale. 'Karl came to see you yesterday.'

'What of it?' is the sneering response.

'His girlfriend, Jasmin, was waiting for him in the car and she heard your voices becoming increasingly more heated. She told him to come to make peace with you.' I ignore his scoff. 'And he wanted you to know that he was going to be a father—'

At that, Dad laughs, head thrown wildly back. Then the laughter cuts off so abruptly it's as if it was never there at all. He levels cold eyes on me. 'A father? How can he be a father when he never understood how to be a child? What's he going to do, give his kid a knife so he can carve crap and then use it to eventually stab some poor soul to death?'

I won't react to his jibes. I know what he wants: to derail me, to ensure that he's the one in control of this. I. Won't. Let. Him. I carry on, 'Jasmin heard an increasingly violent argument in here that finished when Karl emerged, fists clenched, shaking with anger, hardly able to catch his breath.'

Dad rears forward. 'He never came here to make peace, he came to put me in my place.' He runs a scathing look over me. 'No one comes in here, my home, to put me in my place, especially not a child of mine. There's only one king of the castle in this kingdom and that's me.'

I press on. 'Do you know where Karl is?'

'Probably in whatever hell he's created for himself.'

'In hospital.' My voice rises, telling me I'm losing control. I ease it back. 'He's in a coma. You poisoned him when he came here.'

Dad's face has lost its colour. 'What? Poisoned him. You do need a doctor because you are losing your wits. There's a few nutters on your mother's side of the family.'

'I bet you gave him some of your homemade ginger beer when he came.'

He frowns. 'Of course. All you kids loved it.' His face falls. 'Now hold up—'

'And you left two bottles of it for me in the fridge, which I stupidly took.' I clench my teeth. 'I should've known better. I mean, when have you ever given us anything that didn't have a price tag with it? Every time I took a drink of the ginger beer I always ended up sick.'

I see myself guzzling it down in my former rented room, at Ocean Haven in my temporary bedroom. And each time after I was so sick.

'You murdered Mummy the same way. Did you find out she was going to Ocean Haven behind your back?'

'Ocean where?'

My finger stabs at him. 'If it wasn't for you poisoning her, she would have been in good health and never have had to go to that place. Never ended up in Robert Delbrook's clutches.'

Dad looks shocked. 'I'm going to get you help, daughter.'

He moves towards the door to get to the landline in the hallway, but he never makes it. My hand goes inside my bag where I find the half-empty bottle of ginger beer I kept at the house. I pull it back and throw it at him, unleashing all my pent-up anger. He manages to duck. The liquid splashes all over him.

I don't care that he looks like an old man, bent over, arm shielding his head, a relic from another age. 'I know how you did it. You stole the poison from the hazardous chemicals that came into Tinfields Station. You took enough that you could use it on Mummy all those years ago but kept some to use on me and Karl. Who was next? Salina?'

Dad regains his composure and unwinds to his full height. I haven't seen him appear this tall in years.

'Have you finished? Do you have evidence for these slanders? You work in the legal profession. You must know all about evidence and motives. Perhaps you can tell me why I wanted to slay my beloved wife?'

'Because you were screwing Jenny, her closest friend. Did Mummy find out? Is that why you got rid of her? Maybe you murdered Fred for the same reason.'

He pulls out his watch. My heart drops. Silence reigns while he waits for the big hand to reach the twelve. 'Two minutes, that's all the time I'm going to give you. So open those ears of yours and listen. I had no reason to kill my wife or the man who was the first person to welcome us to this neighbourhood. I admit my son has been a disappointment to me, but I have no wish to see him dead.' He steps closer to me. 'And as for you, daughter, of all of my children you are the one who has made me so proud. Who would've thought that I, who was barely a man when I came to England, and shared a room with two other men he'd never met before, would have a daughter who became a lawyer?'

I try to understand. 'Why did you treat us the way you did? Why do you have to control us with a watch?'

A text pings on my phone. I ignore it.

A faraway expression clouds his eyes. 'I grew up with my grandparents. Before school it was my job to feed the chickens. My grandfather would spit on the ground outside. I had to finish feeding the chickens before the hot sun dried that spit. If that spit dried before I got back he wouldn't beat me like you'd get in other families. No, what he'd do was smash up the little wooden toys I made. I was good with my hands. I always beat the clock. My grandfather told me, "Not wasting a minute of your life is what maketh the man."'

I've never heard Dad talk about his grandparents, never knew they brought him up. His story makes me so sad. Leaves me upset. All of a sudden I doubt my theory about him poisoning us. He's right, what motive would he have? But someone is poisoning me and Karl. Who? Unless Dad's lying.

'Time's up,' Dad announces, clutching his watch. 'I know I'm not an easy man, but I'm no killer. I would never poison my family.'

◆ ◆ ◆

As soon as I get in the car I check out the text I heard ping while I was with Dad. It's Jasmin. I'm overcome with emotion when I read her message:

Karl awake. Come quick.

◆ ◆ ◆

When I see my brother, tears prick and sting my eyes. That's the first time I've come close to crying since I left Mum and Dad's all those years ago. He's still got tubes and wires coming out of him, but there's more colour in his face and his eyes are open. His arm reaches out to me. I rush over and take his hand.

'What happened?'

He looks at the door as if to make sure we're alone. 'We need to speak.'

I listen and my hand tightens on his to the point of pain. At one point I ask him, 'When I asked you, why didn't you tell me you'd been to Ocean Haven more than once?'

'Because I still felt like I was betraying Mummy. Now I know different. Listen to me . . .'

What he tells me rocks my world.

CHAPTER 42

Twenty-Five Years Ago

Marcia

Sweat shone bright on Marcia's forehead as the pain tore through her in the hallway of her house. The pain had come back last night with a vengeance. The sip of Saul's ginger beer she'd had not that long ago was threatening to come back up. No! No! This couldn't be happening to her. Not now. Not when she had to get to the house to help Carol and Jamie. She had to get to them before Vincent came back. It felt like she'd been clock-watching all day, doing a countdown before the appointed time of eight tonight. The time was now approaching seven and she needed to be on her way.

Carol and Jamie.

If she didn't leave, God alone knew what that animal would do to them. Gathering her breath in short, awkward pants, Marcia reached out a trembling hand towards the rail to get her coat. Why was the rail moving? The coats all jumbled and jumping in the air? The wall slipping and sliding to the side? And the colour of the hallway was receding into shadow, getting darker and darker. The sweat on her face thickened and started to fall from her jawline.

Carol and Jamie.

'Mum, shall I put some make-up on you before you go out?'

That was Salina talking. Marcia knew that much. It was Salina who loved prettying her up with her paints and potions. Yesterday evening she'd let Salina do her face, which was Marcia's way of trying to give her child quality mother–daughter time, because she'd been thinking about Carol and Jamie so much. Now Marcia couldn't find her. Why couldn't she find her darling girl? The torment inside her grew, gripping and twisting the joints in her arms and the muscles in her belly. Her head pounded like someone was taking a hammer to it. She hurt so bad. So bad.

'Mum?' Alarm tore up Salina's voice. 'Mum? What's happening? Are you sick again?'

Marcia tried to respond, her jaw frantically moving, a muffled groan coming out instead of words.

She didn't hear the rush of Salina's footsteps on the stairs or her yelling, 'Gabby! Gabby! Something bad is wrong with Mummy.'

Carol and Jamie.

Those were the only two words Marcia heard, beating and battering inside her pounding head. She had to get to them. With all the force she could muster, Marcia lunged forward and managed to grab her coat. Her fingers clawed into the material for dear life as she sank into it, resting there for a while. Marcia knew she didn't have time to rest. *Just one minute, a few seconds, so I can feel the beating of my heart again.* She yanked the coat off the rail. She didn't have the strength to put it on. *I'll do that on the bus.* She was in such a delirious state, in such pain that her mind didn't add up that she should also get her purse.

'Mum?' It was Gabby this time. 'Mum, what's going on?'

Gabby was a haze to the side of her. Salina was crying somewhere. Why couldn't she find her favourite child?

'Mum.' Gabby rested her hand on Marcia, the feel of her touch sending shots of electric pain through Marcia, making her cry out.

'Call an ambulance.' That was Gabby again, taking charge like usual. 'Now.'

Carol and Jamie.

An ambulance? Marcia didn't have the time for one. She shook off her daughter's concerned hand and headed for the door. Her legs wobbled, she was so weak. Each step felt like she was heaving her feet through sticky mud. She managed to throw the front door back. The wind rippled over her in a wave of crazy patterns. She didn't hear the terrified shrieks and cries of her children, only the rough, noisy air gushing from her body. One step after another. One step after another. Agony ripped through the soles of both her feet. Marcia crumbled to her knees, her fingers desperately still trying to hang on to her coat.

'Mummy! Mummy!'

Where were those voices coming from? Who did they belong to? Why were they crying?

The pain crashed full force over her. Eyes wide, Marcia's mouth opened, bellowing a silent scream. What's going to happen to my children? Don't leave them with their father.

Then nothingness claimed her.

Saul Lewis couldn't contain his disbelief or anger. 'What do you mean, my wife hasn't been coming to the hospital for tests?'

He stood with his children in the corridor of the ward. He'd got the call at work from Gabby that Marcia had been rushed to the hospital. Saul would admit at first he was annoyed, tired of his wife and this make-believe world of pain she had created. Damn lazy, more like. That was what ailed her as far as he was concerned.

Trying to wriggle her way out of doing women's work, keeping his house tidy and his children clean, their bellies filled.

The doctor blinked at him, expression grave. 'Your wife's last appointment was several months ago, when she was signed off because the consultant could not find anything wrong with her.'

Gabby spoke in a daze. 'But Mummy was going to the hospital. She said so.'

The doctor's response was, 'Your wife is very sick, Mr Lewis.'

Saul threw his arms in the air. 'You just said that the hospital could find nothing wrong with her. Now you tell me she's really sick.'

Gabby spoke again, her voice so small. 'Can we see Mummy?'

The doctor glanced over at the confused children. 'For a very short time. Don't be alarmed at the wires you see or the machines. They are there to help her. And—'

He never finished because a nurse rushed over. 'You're needed. Now.'

There was something about the way her eyes darted to the children that told Gabby this concerned her mother. She flew behind the doctor and nurse, and as she suspected they ended up at the room where her mother was. Stunned, terror held her back in the doorway, watching as the medical team worked on her mother. Mummy wasn't moving, an arm hanging limp over the side of the bed. There was no sound of her breathing. No one noticed Gabby, the medical staff too busy frantically working on her mother. Her father and her brother and sister joined her. Arms went around her; whose they were she wasn't sure.

Then everything went silent. The doctor turned to them. He didn't have to say anything. Their mother was dead.

CHAPTER 43

A voicemail from my doctor's surgery has me pulling over. I'm kind of frightened to call them back, because someone is poisoning me and I can't figure out who. If it's Dad, how the hell is he doing it? With trepidation I call the surgery and the receptionist puts me through to Dr Morris. In my bones I know he has an answer to what's been happening to me.

'Doctor, what did the tests reveal? Am I definitely being poisoned?'

There are times in your life when you're listening to what someone says, but you don't really hear it. I have that now, just as I had with my brother less than an hour ago, where I know I can't be hearing what he's saying, because what he's conveying to me is so horrendous, so soul-destroying he must have me mixed up with another patient.

'What?' My voice trembles, I'm disorientated. Since leaving the hospital I've felt terrible.

He becomes concerned. 'Gabby? Are you following what I'm telling you?'

No. Never. Please let this be the part where I wake up and say, 'It was all a dream.' But I remember: dreams are for good people, nightmares for the rest of us.

My response is robotic. 'Yes. I've heard all that you say.'

'Get to the hospital. I'm going to call and report this to the police.'

I think that his last command is too late. I've been literally on my last legs since leaving Karl and Jasmin. My whole gut is in a ball of spasming fire. I open the car door and violently throw up in the gutter. Head hanging low, I greedily gulp oxygen as if it's running out. Go to the hospital. Go to the hospital. I can't. I can't.

I slump back in the car, freezing sweat clinging to my clothes. I wait. Wait for the sickness to pass like it always does. This is the longest it has ever taken. I can't wait any longer. I know what I have to do. Where I have to go.

◆ ◆ ◆

The blinds are down, curtains drawn, leaving the house bathed in a peculiar dark. It's clear that no one's at home. I clutch the door handle and hesitate. I don't want to do this. This is not a road I want to travel down. I don't have a choice. I have to do this. Inside I crush my emotions into a tiny ball and lock them away; the only way to do this is to be brutally clear-minded and focused.

I step out, manage to get part way across the road, when another figure emerges from a car. I slightly stumble, become off-balance. Then freeze. I squint, searching desperately through the thick evening light. I can't make out who it is because they are blended into the shadows. My pulse thunders, because there can only be one explanation: I've been caught. They knew I was coming. Were they waiting for me? Waiting to confront me in the street? Attack me? Drag me off to a place where no one would hear from me again?

Stop. It. Stay calm. You've got a pair of lungs on you and if they try any stupid stuff, use them.

251

The person gets closer, merging out of the dark. I widen my stance to remain grounded. Closer. Closer. I see who it is.

'I didn't ask for the cavalry to put in an appearance.'

Craven. I breathe easy.

'I think the question is what are you doing here without consulting with me? We're meant to be partners.'

I grab his sleeve as soon as he reaches me, to keep me steady. 'How did you even know I was here?'

'Dr Morris called me. He remembered that I brought you into the surgery after you collapsed in the street. His receptionist tracked me down at the station. I looked up this address.'

He's rocking on his heels ever so slightly as if he's thinking about embracing me. I slide the pads of my fingertips down his arm in a gesture of gratitude.

'Did the good doctor tell you what he suspected?'

'Suspected?' he spits. 'You know it's true.'

'Not until I find one hundred and ten per cent evidence I don't.'

Craven turns and walks towards the house. I catch up and in a rush say, 'What are you doing?'

He doesn't miss a stride. 'Together. We do this together. Or I'll call for assistance from my unit.'

I swear and walk with him. We reach the front door. He presses the bell, twice. No one comes. He takes off his jacket.

'What are you doing?'

He doesn't answer as he wraps the jacket around his fist and lower arm. 'Step back,' is all the warning I get before he punches his protected hand through a glass panel in the window. The jacket has muffled the sound of breaking glass scattering in the hallway near the door. I sway a bit with the sickness that has been biting me badly all day. My vision blurs, I shake my head until it clears. I want to lie down so badly and shut my eyes.

'Gabby?' Craven's alarm alerts me that I have actually closed my eyes. I'm leaning heavily against the door frame. I bend forward and dry heave horribly. Craven's arms are around me. 'That's it,' he says, 'I'm calling back-up.'

'No.' I wobble away from him until my back's resting against the wall. 'I've got to do this. Please.'

He's going to ignore me, I know he is . . . Mumbling that he needs his head seeing to, Craven sticks his arm through the glassless door panel, searching for the lock. He finds and opens it. Inside is dark, and as I reach for a light Craven cautions, 'No lights. The last thing we need is to alert someone we're here. Are we both agreed what we're looking for?'

'Any evidence of thallium.'

The poison that Dr Morris told me someone was trying to kill me with and it had certainly taken my mother's life. Before getting out of the car I'd looked it up online. Both me and Mummy displayed classic symptoms: nausea, tummy trouble, hair loss, tiredness. The poisoner had chosen well, because thallium is odourless, tasteless and almost colourless. It sends a shiver through me to think what I had been taking into my system.

We split up and search the house. It takes me a good thirty minutes before I enter a room that I've never been in before. It's done out like a studio with a desk, computer, state-of-the-art mic and home lighting. One wall looks like a multicoloured art installation with its rows and rows of different tones and shades of cosmetics – eye shadows, bronzes, blusher, face powder, mascara, lashes, even nail polish. And lipstick. On the opposite wall is a mini gallery of framed photos of Mummy and Salina.

Salina. I choke up thinking about my baby sister, thinking about what I don't want to face. I search the studio where she performs her Instagram streaming. I look and search and search. Then

I find something, but it's not the thallium I expect. What I find leaves me in stunned disbelief.

No! No! I can't comprehend what I've discovered. Craven is suddenly behind me, peering over my shoulder. 'What is it? You're not sick again?'

I pick up what I've found and sit with Craven at Salina's desk. It's a long, rectangular tin that age has worn at the edges. I open it and my worst suspicions are horrifyingly confirmed.

Craven again asks, 'What is it?'

I stare down at the old and very valuable coins. 'This was our neighbour Fred's coin collection. Twenty-five years ago he was murdered and the culprit was never found.'

'I know the case; many of the older officers talk about how shocking it was for the town. It's at the top of the tree of the cold cases they wish to solve before they retire.' His voice gentles. 'What does this mean, Fred's coins being here?'

I inhale a shattering breath. 'It means that Salina killed him all those years ago. People tried to blame Karl when he was a kid and all the time it was his sister. I don't understand why she did this.'

His questions remain soft. 'And how is this connected to Salina poisoning your mother and you? How did she do it?'

I pull out Mummy's lipstick that I found when I was going through her things. 'This lipstick was given to my mother by my sister. What not many people know is that was when Salina first started, she actually made her own make-up. I think one of her science teachers helped her. She was so creative at making cosmetics. She was fascinated by them.' I twist the tube of lipstick to face him so he has a clear view of the side of it. Where the writing is. 'She used the point of her school compass to crudely scratch in her now famous brand name.'

Salina.

'How did she poison you?'

'I've been using Mummy's lipstick. It made me feel closer to her.' I pull out another lipstick, the one that Salina gave me as a gift. Unlike when she was a child, her brand name, 'Salina' is written in professionally sleek lettering. 'Recently my sister gave this one to me as a gift to make me look more polished and cheer me up. I suspect that the poison in Mum's lipstick was probably weak after all these years – I don't know, I'm no expert. I suspect she put plenty of thallium in this newer one, which explains why I've been so sick. I think she's been trying to slowly kill me.'

'Why would she do that?'

'I don't know.' Quickly, I explain Dr Morris's connection to my mother. 'In order to try to pinpoint how I was being poisoned Dr Morris told me to carefully tell him what I did on a typical day, what clothes I wore, what I ate, what I drank. When I explained that I'd been using Mummy's lipstick he took a sample of it.' I take a breath. 'He called me back with the results today and confirmed that the lipstick had traces of thallium, even after all these years.'

'How would a thirteen-year-old girl all those years ago get her hands on thallium?' Craven's question is one I've asked myself over and over. I point to the books on the shelves. 'Those are all her books about make-up which she's been collecting since she was a young girl.'

He pulls me to my feet. 'Go to the hospital. Now. I'm going after Salina.'

I can't believe any of this. My sister, Salina? In an extreme state of traumatised shock, I tell myself, 'I can't believe she did this. She loved Mummy more than her own life. She would never murder Mummy. Never!'

CHAPTER 44

Twenty-Five Years Ago

Carol and Jamie

Half past eight. Carol knew that Marcia wasn't coming. What was she going to do? She couldn't get out of here without her trusted new friend. Marcia was the only person who would help her. The only one. She couldn't do it on her own. She couldn't physically leave the house without Marcia. Carol paced up and down, down and up inside the grim attic, her arms wrapped tight around her middle. Her gut twisted and heaved. She was going to be sick. She felt destroyed. Marcia was the only one who could literally lead her out of here.

She'd been arguing in the car with Dennis her husband when they had crashed. After he'd died, everything blacked out. From what they told her weeks later, she had collapsed and when she'd awakened, screaming without a pause, they'd had no choice but to transfer her to the psychiatric ward. Carol felt the scream whelming inside her again now.

Jamie wasn't the same anymore. He'd started changing after his father's death. He and Dennis had been so close. Then Dennis was gone. Jamie had been devastated. It didn't help that she'd crashed and burned as well; well, that was what she told herself. People said that she shouldn't blame herself, but Carol did. For all her days on this earth she would always feel that she'd abandoned her son in his time of greatest need.

Then Vincent Fortune had appeared in her life, a brimming light of hope in the darkness. Once he moved into Ocean Haven he'd started to change. She had tried to defy him, but he had soon shown her the consequences of her actions. Most nights she couldn't get to sleep without taking a few sleeping tabs. That night she'd downed the usual number, but for some reason she'd woken up. The room had been so chilly, the darkness pressing heavily on her. Something, a noise maybe, or a sixth sense that all wasn't right, had woken her. Jamie, that was her first thought. Her darling boy. Barefoot she had gone to her son's room and sucked in her breath, clinging tight to the door frame at the horror story she found. There, Vincent Fortune stood staring down at her sleeping son. There was no weapon in his hand, but he didn't need any. What petrified Carol was the expression he wore. It was evil incarnate, the lines etched across a face those of a madman about to do his worst. And those changeling eyes of his . . . that's where evil lurked the most. They brimmed with malice and hatred, changing the colour to a vivid green that shone like those belonging to a wild predator.

'What are you doing?' The words had quivered cold with fear on her lips.

Vincent had casually turned fully to her. And smiled. It was the same smile that had attracted her to him in the first place. Now she saw it for what it was: a stretching of the skin that was part of the tricks of the trade he used to manipulate people.

He told her, 'Children are so fragile. The simplest thing can sometimes break them apart.'

'Don't,' she pleaded, her nails digging into the wood of the door frame. 'Leave my son alone.'

His smile widened. 'My treatments are only trying to help you.'

Liar. Liar. The words never passed her lips. 'I don't want to do those treatments anymore. I hurt so bad after. The shack frightens me.'

The false smile dropped from his face. 'Don't you think you deserve to hurt after what you did to Dennis?' Carol's stomach tightened. 'All he did was get a job. To help his family. And what did you do as his wife? Did you support him? No. That wayward tongue of yours literally drove him to his grave.'

Carol had sagged, feeling utterly defeated, against the door. It was the truth. The truth. She had murdered Dennis as surely as if she had placed her hands around his throat and choked the life from him.

Vincent wouldn't shut up with the truth. 'Do you want Jamie involved in any of this?'

Horrified, Carol instantly shook her head.

'Come with me now.' He had walked over to her and stretched out his hand for her to take, which she did. 'Let me help you become the woman worthy to be Dennis's wife.'

That was the first night he had placed her inside the box. The day after he'd moved her and Jamie into the claustrophobic, freezing attic. After that she couldn't leave the house. The only way she made it to the shack was with Vincent literally marching her there. The worst feeling of all was that she had failed her son. Carol felt such shame and guilt, because how could she have allowed that terrible man into her son's life? Jamie had started answering questions with one-word answers, no matter how Carol tried to coax him to speak. He began withdrawing more and more into himself and there was nothing she could do about it. And now she'd lost what was rightfully his: his father's home. That's when she knew she had to get away from here. And someone had sent an angel called Marcia.

But Marcia wasn't coming. Carol was terrified, because she knew what she had to do. Somehow she had to get her and Jamie away from the house. Somehow she was going to have to take that dreaded step past the front door. She downed another pill for courage and then turned towards the pathetic bed and woke Jamie up. Confused, his darling face stared back at her. Despite his weight, she picked him up and wrapped him in her arms. They headed down flight after flight of stairs. At the main door Carol started breathing erratically. *I can't go outside. Can't go outside. It's too big out there, too much space. Something bad is waiting out there. Please . . .* Only when she felt her son's hands grip her own did Carol realise she'd put him down. His hand. *Take my hand*, that's what she'd told Marcia was the only way she could get her out of here, feeling the strength from the only person she trusted. However, there was another person she trusted – her precious son.

Carol let the strength from his hand in hers lead her outside. Then she lifted him back into her arms, held on to him tight, never letting him go, cocooning him closer. Carol didn't feel the savage wind lash her. She stared at the shack one final time. It looked bleak and shadowy in the night. Carol heard a noise. Panting she started running, looking over her shoulder. What if that sound meant Vincent was back? She picked up speed, checking the area, diving through the darkness. Forward and forward . . . Carol's feet tangled and she fell with her precious burden into the undergrowth and stinging nettles.

Jamie cried, 'I'm cold. I want to go home. Take me home.'

Carol scrambled to her feet and scooped her child back into the safety of her arms.

'Are you all right? You're not hurt? Don't worry, little one. We're going somewhere safe, very safe.'

They had to keep moving or Vincent would get them. She was too far gone with fear to recognise that it was the pills she'd taken that were making her paranoid. She was convinced that Vincent was behind her. Gaining on her. Nearly at her back.

'I'm cold. I want to go home. Take me home.' Carol didn't answer her son's cry. She didn't have time to. She held him tighter and kept moving. And moving. Her legs felt heavy like they were built of rocks.

'I'm scared. I want to go home,' Jamie whimpered.

She whispered, 'Hush little darling, everything is all right. Mummy's here now.'

Carol reached the edge of Cliff Heights. The light from the lighthouse crisscrossed over them. The sea crashed high against the rocks, its colour fathomless and angry. Its liquid splash left the jagged, jutting rocks so slippery, giving them life like they were about to move. She stepped slightly back to more stable ground. But her mind remained unstable. Terrible thoughts tumbled over and over again and again inside her head.

'You're not having my son,' she screeched into the wind.

Her beautiful son would be all right now. Safe with her forever. Carol clutched him tight. With a piercing scream she rushed forward and leapt over the edge.

CHAPTER 45

I enter Ocean Haven with no idea how I'm walking because the bottom of my world has gone. I haven't gone to the hospital; I've come back here. The emotional pain is worse than anything I've ever felt. Why? Why? Why? The walls of Ocean Haven feel heavy tonight as if they're conspiring against me. I shouldn't be here at all, I should be at the hospital like Craven told me to. But something drew me back here. I don't know what that something is. Maybe I'm hoping to see Mummy one last time. Hear her voice. See her smiling face. Suddenly this awareness of dread descends over me, thick and suffocating. I shouldn't have come here. I want to get out of here. Now. I rush into my makeshift bedroom on the ground floor, heart bouncing, and pull out my clothes—

'Gabby? What's the rush?'

I spin so fast I nearly topple sideways. Salina. Every muscle in me pulls tight. The shade of her face is a lifeless, bloodless brown, her cheeks are so sunken the imprint of her teeth is visible below her cheekbones. She wears no make-up. Something else is painted against her skin – vulnerability. It's stark and open with nowhere to hide. And lipstick. It's the same colour as Mummy's. A unique shade of red mixed with deep brown and a touch of purple. It's spread not on her lips but around them, thick and deep. I see what I should have always seen, my sister is a danger to so many people.

'Why did you kill her?' I ask in despair.

Please deny it. Please prove me wrong.

She considers me like I'm an insect she's going to tread on because I'm in her path. 'She was going to leave us. Mum was going to leave us.'

'What are you talking about?' I rack my brains trying to think. Think.

'I heard her and Dad arguing. She said she was fed up with the way he treated us and was going to pack her stuff, take us and go. He said she could go but yelled that she wasn't taking his children.' A wildness lights up her eyes. 'She was going to leave us with *him.*' We both know she's referring to our father.

My face contorts with confusion. 'But Mummy got better for a time. I remember her saying she wasn't in as much pain.'

'When I realised she wasn't going to leave I stopped doing it.' Her face suddenly beams with a brimming smile. 'Mummy was so beautiful when she was happy. The most beautiful woman in the world.' Her smile drops. 'Then I saw her with Fred. I saw Mummy kissing him.'

'But she did that all the time,' I cry out, devastated by her confession. 'Mummy was showing him gratitude for what he did for Karl. He was the kindest man, taking our baby brother under his wing.'

Salina won't have it. 'She was going to leave us for that fat git next door. She was going to run away. Abandon us.'

'She would never have done that.'

Salina's face turns belligerent as she steps closer. There's nowhere for me to run, she has me caught in a corner. In a matter-of-fact tone she explains, 'I waited for Fred to be alone, took the white-handled knife in their kitchen and pushed it into him. Again and again. And took his coin collection, so it looked like a burglary.'

The horror of what she admits consumes me. This is my baby sister, Salina. How could she have been so deceitful and cunning as a child? So cold.

She continues, her voice strong, 'I thought Mummy would understand after that, so I stopped putting the lipstick on her. I told her I wanted to see what her face looked like with make-up but minus the lipstick. Then she took up with that Dr Vincent in this very house.'

'How did you know that Mummy came here?'

Another step closer. 'Karl told me he came here with her a few times, so I followed her one day.' Her mouth turns violently down in disgust. 'And I saw him with his hands on her shoulders as they stood facing the sea. His hot stinking breath all over the side of her neck. And then he kissed her. Mummy had her bags packed ready to leave. I couldn't allow him to take Mum away.'

CHAPTER 46

Twenty-Five Years Ago

Robert Delbrook and Salina

Stupid, stupid bitch. Typical woman! Delbrook savagely cursed as he leaned heavily against the front door in the hallway of the house. He straightened his favourite green bow tie, then pulled out his concealed hip flask and knocked back an overgenerous slug of brandy. That idiot girl had only gone and topped herself, with the freaky mute kid in tow, which had brought the cops to his door. And it was *his* door, not hers, he'd seen to that. Marcia Lewis, what a thicko she was to sign papers she had never read. Mind you, these women were desperate for a cure for their pain. Unbeknownst to her she was the caretaker of his elaborate trust and then in a couple of years the prize would be his.

He'd come back from his visit to London to find that the cops were everywhere below the clifftop, down by the sea, and had cordoned off the place. He could've fled right away, but that would cast suspicion on him. Always play it calm. Always play it cool. That's what he'd learned after being struck off the medical register. He'd fallen so low he'd done a stint in prison. It was when he was banged up behind bars he'd learned about the ancient art of the con artist. And it was an art. The ability to charm and pull the wool over some fool's eyes and then fleece them was no easy thing. It took skill and patience and a deep understanding of human nature.

He'd been ready for when the cops came up to the house. His act all ready to rock 'n' roll. He played being shocked to the hilt:

Carol dead?

Her son critical?

How terrible.

Such a saintly girl.

Between me and you she was deeply troubled.

Of course you can see her room.

I'm so upset at the moment, can we rearrange another time for you to continue questioning me?

Was that a noise outside? Listening carefully, he placed the hip flask back in his pocket. It had better not be any of those gormless women coming back. He'd told everyone to go home, so that the house could observe a period of grieving for Carol and Jamie. There it was again, a more distinct sound this time, scuffing and creaking. Vincent headed for the window and looked out into the darkness, his lips compressing as another thought struck him. What if it was the coppers again? What if they hadn't believed his story and were now secretly back searching the property? Vincent knew his rights. He knew how to deal with the police. He strode with purpose to the front door. Setting his features to one of make-believe upset and grief, he pulled the door back and stepped outside. He glanced around; no one in sight.

Ten minutes later, he stood next to the entrance of the shack, having thoroughly checked outside where he had found no evidence of another living soul. The last place was this building. His lips twisted in revulsion; this building put the fear of God into him and that was saying something, because Vincent had seen the inside of some pretty scary places. Mind you, it had been a good place to store what he called his tools of the trade, especially in the cupboard. He opened up and was met with darkness. Of course no one was here, he chided himself, all the noise was the wildness of the coast at night. As he pivoted on his heel to leave, he was hit by a flash of light that blinded him. Instinctively, he raised his palm to shield his eyes so he could see.

His jaw dropped at what he saw. A girl, somewhere in her teenage years, held a torch, which was the source of light and a . . . he couldn't make out what she was holding.

'Who are you? What are you doing here?'

The girl, incredibly steady on her feet, no nerves in sight, inched closer to him. 'You're not having my mum.'

'Your mother?' Good grief, the whole area was full of nut jobs. There must be something in the gene pool around here. Vincent cast a stern stare over her. 'Young lady, you need to get off this property, because I will contact the police if I have to.'

The girl spat, 'I saw you with your hands on her shoulder, your stinking lips near her neck. You wanted to kiss her. My mum. You're trying to take her away from me.'

'Kissing your mother.' Vincent let out a humourless laugh. Then he knew exactly who it was who confronted him. 'You're Salina.' The widening of her eyes gave him his answer. 'Your mother loves you very much. She tells me how clever you are. The brightest of the bunch—'

'Liar,' Salina thundered with emotion, her voice banging against the walls. 'That's Gabby. She's the brains.'

'You're so wrong.' Vincent stepped naturally into a charm offensive, treating the girl like a targeted potential victim. 'Marcia told me how brilliant you are, especially with your hands. Drawing, painting, applying your mummy's make-up. Such a talented girl.'

Salina's face turned stony. 'You shouldn't have kissed her. She's mine, not yours. Now she's dead.'

Dead? Marcia Lewis was dead? That's when he noticed two things. The hole dug deep in a corner of the building. And the shotgun in her hand. His shotgun. His blood ran cold.

'Now look here . . .' He raised a protective hand. But it was too late. Those were the last words Robert Delbrook aka Vincent Fortune would ever speak. The shotgun clicked back. The blast that caught him in his belly, picked him off his feet and blew him with force on to the wooden wall. An expression of stunned disbelief twisting his features, the life already draining out of him from the enormous shotgun wound in his middle, he crashed to the dirty floor. He was dead before Salina reached him.

It took Salina Lewis a solid minute to drag his body across the shack. Then half an hour to shovel the dirt over him. The last thing she did before placing the box and broken table on top of the earth was to spit on his grave.

267

CHAPTER 47

'You murdered Robert Delbrook. Dr Vincent.' I'm in a daze of disbelief. I can barely take in what Salina is telling me.

Another reality dawns on me. 'That's the reason you got so mad with Luke on the day Robert Delbrook's body was found here.' Yes, it's coming back to me. 'You told him to make sure the builders didn't disturb the outbuilding on the pretext of wanting to build a sauna. But that wasn't true. You knew if they dug it up they would discover the remains of the man you shot to death. But the builders made a mistake, got confused and dug up the ground.' More and more is starting to fall into place. 'It was you, wasn't it, who sent the anonymous letter to the solicitor claiming that Delbrook had been seen years later? Was that your way of discouraging any other potential buyers of Ocean Haven?'

Salina snarls, 'He should never have touched her. She was ours not his.'

I plead with her. 'Why did you murder Mum? Why did you poison her?'

My baby sister gets cross. 'It wasn't really poisoning her. I just wanted her to understand that I was the only person who would be able to take care of her. Then she would have to stay with us. I put a little bit on her lipstick. Not a lot, just enough to make her realise that I was the only one who could make her better.'

In my mind's eye I see the many instances of girl-Salina looking after Mum when she was ill, and all the time she had caused the sickness. I see her carefully painting our mother's mouth with lipstick. Lethal lipstick.

Furtively, I still consider how to get out of here. 'How did you get the poison?'

She glares at me. 'So, clever Gabby never figured it out.' Another step. 'When I took Dad his packed lunches at the railway station, I saw the trains with the dangerous chemical skull-and-crossbones sign. No one paid any attention to a teenage girl.' She catches my eye. 'The first book about make-up I ever got from the library was about the poisonous history of cosmetics. Did you know that European women through the ages used lead to give their faces an ultra-white complexion?'

Her face falls. 'When I saw the suitcase I knew she was leaving us for good.'

'What suitcase?'

Salina's voice rises. 'The suitcase she packed to run away in the night.'

'What are you talking about . . .' My voice skids to a halt as a truth hits me. 'I think the suitcase was filled with things she packed to help some people in this house escape. She was trying to help a mother and her young son get away from here.'

Salina shakes her head. 'I didn't mean to kill her, but when I saw the suitcase I knew that the lipstick wasn't going to be enough. Thallium is also absorbed through the skin, so I made Mum a face powder. It was only meant to stop her coming back to Delbrook. But I used too much . . .' Her eyes shine with tears. 'I never meant to kill Mummy, I swear.'

'All those times you told me to stop looking into Ocean Haven, to let Mummy rest in peace. The time you wanted me to move into your house. And Karl' – I cry our brother's name – 'he came to see you after he visited Dad. I'd assumed Dad had poisoned him – and me – with his ginger beer. But Karl told me he visited you after seeing Dad. Did you make him a special drink? You poisoned him too.'

'He said he was going to tell you the truth. I had to stop him.'

I've had enough. 'You stupid, stupid murderer. Our mother gave you everything and you murdered her. You—'

She sprays something in my face. Crying out, I cover it. Oddly, there's no pain. My gaze flashes dangerously at her. 'Salina, what have you done?'

She waves a see-through perfume bottle at me. 'Just something I made. Eau de Thallium.'

The room starts moving, or is it me? My surroundings begin to blur. Fade. I try to get out, but my legs won't work. The sharpest pain seizes me with such force I collapse to my knees.

I try pleading with her. 'Stop this. Stop. Please . . .' My voice comes slower and slower until I can't hear myself anymore. 'Ple . . .'

Darkness smothers me.

◆ ◆ ◆

My eyes feel sticky as they weakly flutter open. I'm lying in my bed at Ocean Haven. My limbs are like lead. The room's tilting to the side. What's going on? I remember – Salina. I need to get out of here. My lifeless fingers reach for the edge of the cover. Someone appears by the bed. Craven. His face is murky. His mouth's moving, but there's a fog in my brain, so I can't hear him. He leans down to me. I rear back in the bed at what I see behind him.

Salina.

She's holding something in her hand. I try to warn him. *Craven, turn around. Now. Please. Turn. Around. Why can't you hear me?* He twists, sensing danger. Salina's almost on him, smiling like she's lost her mind. She lashes out with the wood, hitting him on the head. Craven goes down. Leaning over him, Salina sprays him with her deadly perfume.

No! No! No! Appalling grief chokes me.

I slip back into a world of nothing.

◆ ◆ ◆

I wake up to the sound of whistling above me. It's Salina, merry and happy, with her wide assortment of make-up brushes. I can only see out of one eye because she's applying eyeshadow to one of my lids. My sister has lost her mind.

'There.' She beams, her lipstick looking ghoulish, and leans back looking at her handiwork. 'That's how you should look.' Her chilled lips kiss my cheek. I feel the sticky imprint of Mummy's-colour lipstick they leave behind. 'I made my own version of Mummy's lipstick, non-toxic of course. I'll look after you. Always.'

Out of the corner of my eye, I despairingly see Craven still unconscious on the floor. Or is he dead? I rail at my sister. *Murderer. Murderer. Murderer.* My lips don't move. This time I pretend to fall unconscious. I hear my sister shuffling around. Then silence. Immediately I open my eyes and notice that outside it must be night-time. I test my legs. They aren't back to normal, but they feel lighter. I have to get out of here, get help for Craven. I manage to get out of bed and rush as quick as possible towards the door.

'Gabby, where are you going?'

Her furious voice makes me run even faster. Her voice, laced with unearthly menace, chases me out of the front door. Salina will follow. She has to. On the coast road below, a car is heading our way in the darkness. I flee down the gravel path to flag it down, slipping and sliding on my shaking feet. I run into the road, desperately waving one arm, using the other to shield my eyes from the full beam of the car's headlamps. The driver violently swerves at the same time as hitting his horn for what seems like for ever. He misses me by inches before his red lights disappear as he accelerates up the road. There is no more traffic on the road and the only sound is that of the waves falling on the beach.

When I look up to Ocean Haven it's to see Salina standing in the doorway flanked by its two white columns that look like those you see on graves in cemeteries. The yellow light from the hall behind has turned her into a silhouette with no features. A figure of darkness like an angel of death in a medieval tableau that hangs in a cathedral. She doesn't move nor does she speak. But I know she's coming for me. She has to.

Down the road is Tinfields town centre, a few miles away. I could run or hope to flag down a more helpful driver. But it only takes me a few moments to realise that won't work, nor will the road in the other direction. Salina will find me soon enough and hunt me down. She's fitter, stronger and more athletic than me, she always has been. And she hasn't been poisoned. Only upwards offers any hope, towards Cliff Heights, where there are woods, bracken and heather to hide in. She won't find me up in the undergrowth there and I can sit things out till daylight. But then there's Craven. He's probably already dead, but if not, he'll certainly be dead by daybreak. He needs help now. In the distance, overlooking Cliff Heights, is Tinfields lighthouse. Its beam slowly revolves around the coast. They have keepers, don't they? But even if they don't, it's Craven's only chance.

Crouching low, I skirt the walls of Ocean Haven, peeping over them to see what's happening. The doorway is still filled with yellow light.

But the angel of death has gone.

I avoid the path that leads up to the Heights. It will be too easy for Salina to catch me there. Instead, I plunge into the undergrowth.

There's so much noise, I might as well be banging a drum: yelps when thorns scratch my arms or the trailing bushes trip me up, the crunch of bracken under my feet or dry twigs exploded by my footsteps. There are so many obstacles in my way, I feel like I'm moving in slow motion. The path becomes the only way forward. I struggle over to it and begin to run, the soft clump of my steps on the sand and grass. Every few moments, I stop, look around and listen. I know she's nearby. I can smell evil. I can hear evil. I can feel evil. I know she's nearby.

The beam from the lighthouse illuminates a sign: an ancient red one, flaking with rust. 'Danger. Cliff Edge. Tinfields District Council.' Panting with fear and exhaustion, I fall to my knees and grip the pole it's attached to as if it might protect me. When I look around, I can see nothing and hear nothing. I grip the pole more tightly. I'm literally scared stiff, too frightened to move. My fingers couldn't be prised from this pole with pliers. Salina's going to find me. She was always cleverer than me, always smarter, and my flight is just a game to her. She's going to kill me.

How long am I here, frozen to this pole? Long enough for the beam from the lighthouse to come back round again, throwing light down on to the path over which I fled. It briefly throws shadows over what looks like a tree trunk, black and solid. Only when the features of a face briefly flicker do I realise that it's actually my sister, standing by the path, her hands clasping what looks like a long baseball bat. She's wearing a black coat and a black hat as camouflage as she chases me. She thinks of everything. My sister must have been there waiting ever since I grabbed the pole, however long that's been. In the last of the light, our eyes meet before it goes dark again.

What's in her eyes? There's nothing in them at all.

I yank my arms to free my frozen fingers but they won't come loose. A sing-song voice, like that of a little girl, comes up the path floating on the night. 'Now, where's my big sister gone? Is she here?' A whoosh followed by a terrific blow hitting a tree, shaking the undergrowth beneath me. 'Or is she here?' Another blow, even more violent than the previous one. 'No, she's not there. Perhaps she's over there, clinging on to that sign.' Her voice rises to a squeal of delight. 'Yes! There she is. She's over there!'

Only as this shadow approaches me, swinging her bat, do my fingers finally spring free. I scramble into the undergrowth, but it's only a few paces before I tumble again. When I look up, Salina is standing over me, the bat resting on her shoulder. As the beam from the lighthouse swings around again, she wipes her face with the sleeve of her coat. The light catches her face full on this time. Her beautiful features are contorted with a smile of hatred, her lipstick smeared over her cheeks like a malevolent clown, her mascara dripping down her face like teardrops and her lush hair sticking to her forehead like cobwebs in a witch's cave.

'Why do you need to do this, Salina?'

I don't know what she hears, but it must be another question. 'Don't try and deconstruct me, sis. Don't try and work me out, you haven't got the chops for it!'

She raises both hands above her head with the bat tightly gripped in them and brings it down on my prone body. I cry out as my fingers grab a handful of thorns and I pull myself out from under the blow. My hands thrash around, where they find a stick of their own. When I spring to my feet, I'm shocked to my core when I lash out wildly in the darkness with my makeshift weapon and it catches my sister full on the side of the head. My arm judders with the recoil from the blow, while my sister goes over with a groan. Then I'm disgusted when I hear myself say, 'I'm sorry, Salina, are you all right?'

She doesn't answer, but she's struggling to her feet.

274

It doesn't occur to me to hit her again. I'm choking on fear, adrenaline and a refusal to believe this is really happening to my sister and me. The stick gets thrown away and my feet carry me back to the path and onwards and upwards into the clearing, which I first visited to see where Carol Shore fell to her death. There's a new sign installed here. I lean on it for a few moments, gasping for breath. There's not much left inside me now. This is nearly over. Why do I read the sign? What am I doing? The sign reads: 'Warning! These Cliffs Are Dangerous. Stay Well Back From The Edge.' Underneath, the message is repeated in French and German. Another sign has two matchstick people looking over a cliff edge with a red line through it. Next to that is yet another sign which asks the question: 'What Is Coastal Erosion?'

The path up to the lighthouse is only a few hundred yards. I struggle on, but my legs give way again and again. Salina is right behind me. She loses her black hat as she runs wide to cut off my route to the building, before turning towards me. She runs, howling like a banshee, and her fingers clasp themselves around my throat like iron clips. We tumble to the ground and roll over, but her grip only tightens. We're face to face for a final time as the beam of light comes round again. Her face is barely human now, contorted and pulled out of shape, all the colours of the make-up that she's painted on it seeming to merge into one hideous mask. And behind her eyes, there is nothing. Nothing at all.

My head is bloated with blood as I'm strangled, my tongue is forced through my lips and my vision begins to fade and die. My feeble arms and hands have no force and Salina doesn't even notice my attempts to push her off. In these last moments, her clenched hands slowly loosen and my lungs seize the chance to breathe air. My body ripples with agonising pain as life begins to flow through it again. Salina looks up and around furtively, as if she fears she's being watched. Her hands come off my neck and she wipes them on her coat, before climbing to her feet, taking a few steps and then using them to seize me by the ankles to be dragged towards the cliff edge. My legs only shiver slightly when I try to kick free.

It's a few dozen yards before she drops my ankles a short distance from the cliff edge. Salina peers over at the beach below. She's looking around again as if worried about witnesses, but that can't be so. She spends a long time looking at the beach below, long enough for me to recover a little. If I pushed her hard now with both my feet, she's probably close enough to go over. But I won't. The moment passes and Salina turns, grabs my legs again, facing me with her back to the edge, and drags me the final few feet. As she lets my feet drop, there's a steady whooshing sound as the sand and earth begin to give way. Salina starts sinking in front of my eyes. Beneath me, I can feel the earth creasing. She grabs my legs again to steady herself. The whoosh and the creasing pause for a few moments before beginning again.

I'm thrown to one side as the ground under me begins to disintegrate. Salina lets go of my legs and begins desperately clawing at the cliffs with her fingers. As sand and earth fly around, I can see less and less of her body as she disappears until only her hands and wrists are visible. A cry like a wounded animal pierces the air. 'Gabby! Help me!'

The cliff is still falling in bits and pieces around us, but I summon enough energy to crawl to the edge. Salina's hands are grasping crumbling material and one foot is perched precariously on an outcrop she's using to steady herself. Her face is turned upwards. But it's no longer the masked face of the monster with nothing in her eyes who's just tried to kill me. It's my little sister's face with her little sister's pleading eyes, full of life. 'Gabby! Help me!'

While I stretch out my hand, she reaches out hers and they nearly touch for a moment. But before they do, she begins to slide away down the cliff, slowly at first, then with gathering speed in a cloud of sand until she falls away from the cliff into the air and plunges on to the beach below. A gentle wave of the incoming tide slowly creeps up the beach and washes over her body. She's gone for a moment as the wave hesitates before slowly going back down the beach. My sister's wet and cleansed body lies still where it fell.

Something touches me. Flinching, I twist around. It's Craven. He's alive. He draws me into his arms. We collapse to our knees, holding each other tight.

CHAPTER 48

I'm so exhausted, I have no idea how I manage to lift my legs out of the car. I stand in front of the house that was my childhood home.

When Dad opens the door I tell him, right there on his doorstep, 'Salina is dead.'

Initially he wears the shock of a parent who has lost a child, then he recovers with the usual disdainful twist of his mouth. 'That's what happens to bad seeds, they wither and die. Even when you try to water them they suck you dry like a bloodsucker.'

If I ever doubted I hate this man, his despicable words put me straight. 'She murdered Mum.'

'What?' His question is hoarse with disbelief.

'And you could have saved her.'

'I don't know what you're talking about.'

I get in his face with my fury. 'Karl told me that you knew that Salina killed Fred. The day after Fred was murdered he heard you talking to Salina about the knife she used—'

He sneers. 'Can you imagine how people would have pointed at me every time I showed myself in the street. The shame. Of course I got rid of the knife for her. Working on the railways there's a million and one places where things will never see the light of day again.'

'But that didn't stop you from telling the police that the culprit might be your own son. How could you do that to Karl? He was the baby of our family, the one out of all of us you should have been looking out for.'

His eyes blaze. 'That boy was trouble from the time he was pulled from the womb and put into my arms. At least Salina kept your mum happy with all that make-up crap.'

Happy? I can barely speak with the anger like a fire burning through my tongue. 'That's how she killed Mum. With her make-up. She laced it with poison. And do you know why she did it?'

Dad keeps his mouth stubbornly tight so I carry on, 'Because she was terrified Mummy would leave and then we'd be all alone with you. And Salina was right. When I think of what you did to her and Karl after I left.'

He tries to speak, but I won't let him. I've had enough of the evil that drips from his mouth.

A calmness settles over me. 'It's taken me years to figure out that when you would violently smash our keepsakes, our precious things, what you were really trying to do was to break us mentally. I'll never forget the day you punched our family portrait in the dining room.' A stray tear falls and stains my frozen cheek. 'I never understood how you could do that to us. We are your flesh and blood, your children. Mummy was the woman who did everything in her power for you, your wife. Why did you hate us so much? Salina might have poisoned me and Karl. And Mummy, darling, beautiful Mummy. But it was you who really poisoned this family.'

I walk out of that house and I will never go back or see my dad again.

CHAPTER 49

A YEAR LATER

Ocean Haven and its grounds are filled with the laughter of children. Its ground floor overspills with people eating and drinking and admiring the grandeur of the house. Ocean Haven has been restored to its former glory.

'Isn't she beautiful?' I admire the gorgeous baby who is the focus of everyone's attention.

Her parents, Jasmin and Karl, smile back. It's little Flora's christening and family and friends have come from far and near to celebrate.

Karl bounces his bundle of joy in his arms. 'She's the best of us all.'

The sides of his and Jasmin's heads touch in a loving gesture. To see my brother so alive and fulfilled and surrounded by love was something that I never thought I would see. *Mummy, I wish you were here. You would be so proud.*

'Gotcha.' My hand is caught by a playful Jamie Craven, who tugs me off towards the trees. They are empty. The ravens disappeared after Salina's death. I sometimes wonder if they were watching over me? Craven stands beside me as we look up at Ocean

Haven and at all the festivities. Once the story of Robert Delbrook's fraud and the terrible fallout of it was revealed, Luke had given the house and deeds to Carol Shore's son. My heart aches when I think of my brother-in-law, who was devastated and shattered by what Salina had done. Luke sold up and left the area, but I make it my business to phone and visit him; he will always be a member of this family.

Craven says, 'Do you think it's going OK?' He's nervous because today was the big one, the one where he allowed guests to visit for the first time.

I squeeze his hand, noting he hasn't let go of mine. 'The house is starting to grow its beauty back.'

And it is. The aura of darkness that had surrounded it has faded to allow the light to shine through. It stands strong and proud on the hill.

We have an arrangement where I live upstairs and he resides on the ground floor. For three days of the week we meet for dinner in the restored dining room, and for the remainder of the time we give each other space. Admittedly that space has been growing less and less as the weeks go by.

Craven stretches his hand out to mine. 'Coming in?'

I sense that taking his hand will be a major line I cross.

I take his hand.

AUTHORS' NOTE

This book is dedicated both to all the women who have received an unequal service when it comes to having their health concerns taken seriously and to the tireless, devoted and skilled medical professionals who put our welfare at the heart of their hard work. If *Believe Me* has piqued your interest in finding out more about the history of health care and the treatment of women, we would recommend you read *Unwell Women: A Journey Through Medicine and Myth in a Man-Made World* by Elinor Cleghorn. The range of research is both incredible and outstanding.

ACKNOWLEDGEMENTS

We couldn't have written *Believe Me* without the amazing support and expertise of our phenomenal editor, Victoria Oundjian. She is simply one of the best in the business. And, from our hearts to yours Victoria, thanks a million for all the personal support you continue to provide during what has been a momentous time in our lives. Bless you! A mighty thanks to editor Ian Pindar for loving the book and shedding a brighter light on Gabby's journey. Your encouraging comments made us smile. Thank you thank you to our Amazon Publishing family for all their support and for just being there. Huge hugs and love coming your way.

ABOUT THE AUTHORS

Her Majesty, Queen Elizabeth II appointed Dreda an MBE in her New Year's Honours' List, 2020.

She scooped the CWA's John Creasey Dagger (New Blood) Award for best first-time crime novel in 2005, the first time a Black British author has received this honour.

Ryan and Dreda write across the crime and mystery genre – psychological thrillers, gritty gangland crime and fast-paced action books.

Spare Room, their first psychological thriller, was a #1 UK and US Amazon Bestseller. Dreda is a passionate campaigner and speaker on social issues and the arts. She has appeared on television, including *Celebrity Pointless, Celebrity Eggheads, Alan Carr's Adventures with Agatha Christie, BBC Breakfast, Sunday Morning Live, Newsnight, The Review Show* and *Front Row Late* on BBC2.

Ryan and Dreda performed a specially commissioned monologue for the ground-breaking Sky Arts' *Art 50* on Sky TV.

Dreda is one of twelve international bestselling women writers who have written a reimagined Miss Marple short story for the thrilling new anthology, *Marple*.

Dreda has been a guest on many radio shows and presented BBC Radio 4's flagship books programme, *Open Book*. She has written in a number of leading newspapers including the *Guardian* and was thrilled to be named one of Britain's 50 Remarkable Women by Lady Geek in association with Nokia. She is a trustee of the Royal Literary Fund and an ambassador for The Reading Agency.

Some of their books are currently in development as TV and film adaptations.

Dreda's parents are from the beautiful Caribbean island of Grenada. Her name, Dreda, is Irish and pronounced with a long vowel ee sound in the middle.

Follow the Authors on Amazon

If you enjoyed this book, follow Dreda Say Mitchell and Ryan Carter on Amazon to be notified when the authors release a new book!

To do this, please follow these instructions:

Desktop:

1) Search for the authors' names on Amazon or in the Amazon App.
2) Click on the authors' names to arrive on their Amazon page.
3) Click the 'Follow' button.

Mobile and Tablet:

1) Search for the authors' names on Amazon or in the Amazon App.
2) Click on one of their books.
3) Click on the authors' names to arrive on their Amazon page.

4) Click the 'Follow' button.

Kindle eReader and Kindle App:
If you enjoyed this book on a Kindle eReader or in the Kindle App, you will find the authors' 'Follow' button after the last page.